SHADOWS IN

THE MIST

BOOKS BY JERI WESTERSON

Crispin Guest Medieval Noir Mystery Series

*Veil of Lies**

*Serpent in the Thorns**

*The Demon's Parchment**

*Troubled Bones**

*Blood Lance**

*Shadow of the Alchemist**

The Silence of Stones

A Maiden Weeping

Season of Blood

The Deepest Grave

Cup of Blood, a prequel to *Veil of Lies*

Booke of the Hidden Series

Booke of the Hidden

Deadly Rising

*Shadows in the Mist**

*Deadly Rising**

Historical Fiction

Though Heaven Fall

Roses in the Tempest

Native Spirit, writing as Anne Castell

*available as a JABberwocky ebook

SHADOWS IN
THE MIST

BOOK THREE IN
THE BOOKE OF THE HIDDEN SERIES

JERI WESTERSON

Published by JABberwocky Literary Agency, Inc.

Though he is a shadowy presence, my husband Craig is all goodness and light. This is for you Craig, you devil, you.

CHAPTER ONE

ONE WALL. One dumb wall in my seventeenth-century house in this dumb small town… No, that wasn't fair. The *town* wasn't dumb. I actually still liked the little town of Moody Bog, Maine. As picturesque as they came. White church steeple and village green. Check. Quaint little houses on sleepy streets. Check. A pumpkin on every porch with beautiful fall colors in the surrounding woods. Double check. And friendly people…for the most part. If you don't count the demons. What's not to like?

Except for that dumb wall that I broke into one night in my shop and found the Booke of the Hidden inside. I was the last person to guess that creatures and demons—stuff I never knew existed—would all pour out of there. Because of me. Because of that damned Booke that I opened.

And now my ex, Jeff, was a werewolf. Because of me and that Booke. WereJeff, I guess. What else was I going to call him? If it weren't for my coven of local Wiccans—Doc, Seraphina, Nick, and Jolene—I'd be a dead tea shop owner five times over.

And even now, there they were, standing by me. Helping me. Sometimes with spells, sometimes with just a hug. But there was no time for hugs with demons and evil gods on the loose. Was this really my life now?

Someone had summoned the demon Andras to kill me. A winged guy with a strange skin-tight hide suit. I was pretty sure I knew who summoned him. Our own Mayflower queen, Ruth Russell. Anti-Wiccan, anti-Kylie. Or it could have been the biker gang run by Sheriff Ed's brother…

"Shit!" I suddenly remembered Ed outside.

Andras had knocked WereJeff out, and Nick and the other Wiccans had carried him inside my shop. Doc was ministering to him. But Ed hadn't known such things were real in Moody Bog until he'd seen Andras and WereJeff in a battle royale.

Surprise.

I stuck my head out of the doorway of my shop again. Sheriff Ed was still standing on my gravel parking lot. At least he'd holstered his gun. One of those big white feathers from Andras' wings was in his hand. He examined it as if it were something amazing. I guessed it was.

When he raised his face to mine, it was all written there in his eyes.

"You'd better come in, Ed. I don't think it's safe out there."

He stood a moment more before he slowly began to approach the doorway and cross the threshold.

He pulled up short again when he saw Jeff. The blond werewolf was breathing oddly, lying prone on my settee surrounded by my friendly neighborhood coven.

"Kylie," he rasped, "what the hell's going on?"

Seraphina, our middle-aged boho witch, took a step toward him to offer her gentle explanations. I headed her off and dragged him into the kitchen, where he didn't have to look at Jeff, and sat him down at my farm table. He deserved to hear it from me. "It's kind of a long story."

He didn't look good. He looked like he was going to faint…or throw up.

"Do you want some brandy or something?"

"Bourbon. Do you have bourbon?"

"Yeah." I rushed to the kitchen cupboard that doubled as a bar and took down the untouched bourbon bottle that I had for guests. I didn't indulge. But I was starting to rethink that.

I poured a short glass and handed it over. I expected him to knock it back, but he sipped it instead. Good old Ed. Practical even in a panic situation.

His mic squawked. Deputy George was responding to his call. "Sheriff! I'm on my way."

Ed must have sussed out my face, because he pulled the mic toward him. "No. It's okay, George. We're...we're okay. False alarm."

There was a pause before his crackly voice came back on. "Sheriff, are you sure?"

"Yeah. Just a...a deer. I've got it. Bradbury out." His hand fell to his lap again, and his attention was on me.

"So...so when I bought this place pretty much sight unseen," I began. And then once I started, I couldn't stop. Like a roller coaster. I was talking faster and faster. "I knew it was old. From the seventeen hundreds. Which was good. I mean, it wasn't exactly sight unseen. I'd seen pictures on the internet. It looked perfect for my herb and tea shop. Living quarters above." I pointed to my ceiling. "I was fixing it up the week before I opened, and I tore down this crooked shelf, and when I did, I accidentally made this giant hole in the wall. And then there was this bricked wall inside that. Which seemed odd, you know. So, on a whim, I took a sledgehammer to it."

His eyes tracked me. "On a whim," he parroted vaguely.

"Yeah, on a whim. And a little Chardonnay. Inside the wall was..."

I heard it whoosh toward me. Ducking just in time, Ed was nearly struck by the Booke of the Hidden soaring through the doorway. It stopped mid-air, hovering just before me. I gently grasped it and laid it on the table. It seemed to become more active the longer I dealt with it, as if it were fully awakening.

To Ed's credit, he didn't so much as flinch. Well...maybe he flinched a tiny bit.

"This. This was inside. This damned Booke. And then I opened it to take a look, like anyone would, right? But all the pages were blank." I unlocked the latch, opened the cover, and showed him. Except for the ones I had written on with my own blood, all the parchmenty pages were empty. "But it was more than that. By opening it, I sort of opened a gateway, and all sorts of crazy things came out of it…and continue to come out of it."

His voice was gravelly. "Things like…that guy with wings?"

"No, actually, he was a demon. Someone else summoned him. He's an assassin. To kill me."

"An assassin demon?"

"Yeah. But…the thing that killed Karl Waters and that bicyclist…that was a succubus."

He shook his head. "I don't even know what that is."

"It doesn't matter. It's dead."

"What about…those missing women? Was that a…a succubus too?"

"No. That was a kelpie. Um…it's also dead. Or…just gone, I guess. Back into the Booke, or wherever it is they come from."

"I don't understand."

I walked away from the table, pacing across the floor from table to sink and back again. Ed's gaze followed me like his life depended on it.

"See, *I* have to put things right. *I'm* the one who opened the Booke. Only *I* can stop these things."

"Kylie…are you saying that…all this time…"

"Yeah, I'm sorry. I didn't want you to know. I just wanted you to think I was a normal person, especially on our…our dates."

He looked down at his hands fidgeting with the feather on the worn, wood table. "All this was going on at the same time?"

"I'm sorry."

"No." He shook his head. "This has to be a mass illusion. Drugs. Hallucinogens. This isn't real." He stared at the feather again, twisting it in his fingers. The black blood spatter on it looked real enough. I could see him trying to work it out in his head: the reality of the fantastic in his fingers.

Maybe it was a good thing Ed finally knew. Maybe he could help. But not if he went nuts on me. So I raised my hand, waiting for it. Sure enough, in seconds the chthonic crossbow screamed through the house and slapped into my open palm.

Ed jolted from his chair, knocking it over.

"It's not a hallucination," I told him. I gently laid the crossbow on the table between us. "I got this from Erasmus. He's…he's the demon of the Booke." A sharp pang stabbed my heart when I spoke his name. After all, Erasmus was still out there. And his time had run out.

"I *knew* something was up with that guy," he growled.

His jealousy suddenly made me angry. "So demons you believe in."

He ran his hand over his face before crouching to right the chair. The feather that had fallen from his hand fluttered to the floor.

Ed staggered toward the sink and leaned over it. Maybe he *was* going to get sick this time.

He was quiet for a long moment, before speaking in a soft and even tone. "If I hadn't seen Karl and the bicyclist for myself, I might have had a hard time believing you. But as it is…" He turned his head. His eyes were haunted. It was a familiar expression—the same one I saw every time *I* looked in the mirror these days. "So that's why you're friends with Doc's coven."

"Doc fixed the hole in my plaster, and then he mentioned the Wiccans. I needed help. They've been helpful."

Did I dare tell him about his brother? Doug had already been a handful to Ed, getting into trouble with his biker gang. Was Ed ready to hear that his own brother was a practitioner of black magic?

"So you do…spells and stuff?"

He was looking pretty forlorn. I wondered if I shouldn't have hugged him first thing. "No. I don't do magic. I just opened the Booke and it all started. I don't know how to do anything but run a tea shop. This is all new to me too."

He glanced toward the living room. "That guy is a werewolf?"

"Yeah. My old boyfriend."

"Was he…always a werewolf?"

"No. A werewolf came out of the Booke and bit him."

He shook his head slowly, breathing in and out.

I wrung my hands. "At this point, I'm not sure whether or not to…to tell you about Doug."

There was color back in his face when he whipped around. "What *about* Doug? Does he have something to do with all this?"

I sat and clasped my fingers together on the table. The Booke and the crossbow sat before me. I was aware of both of them like a throbbing heartbeat. I couldn't *not* be aware. "He and his gang dabble in the dark side of Wicca. They summoned a god, Baphomet. And he's loose out there too. We don't know what'll happen."

I didn't think Ed could take much more. He looked to be on the edge of what was left of his sanity.

He stumbled to the table and landed back in his chair. "This has to be a dream. A nightmare."

"I wish it were."

A howl from the other room startled us both. I leapt to my feet and ran to the doorway.

Jeff stirred. His fur was falling off in chunks. Already his face was beginning to draw back to normal, until only his ears were still long and pointed. But even those were receding. He opened his eyes and looked at me. They were wolf eyes at first but soon morphed into human eyes.

Our teen Wiccan Jolene tossed the crocheted throw over him just in time as all the fur fell off, leaving a naked Jeff. I was at his side in an instant. "Jeff?"

"Yeah," he gasped. "Yeah, I'm back."

"Are you okay?"

"I guess." He sat up and realized the throw was covering him. "Whoa. Am I ever gonna get used to that?"

Then he looked up and spotted Ed.

"Uh…how do we explain…?"

"Already done." I swiveled to face Ed. "Are you buying all this? I don't think there's much time to dwell on it."

He hitched his utility belt, physically *and*, I supposed, meta-phorically. Then he straightened his Smokey Bear hat. "Yeah. Got it."

He didn't. Wouldn't, for a while. But he was getting there.

There was a knock at the door. My heart gave a lurch. *Erasmus!* I was up and running for it before I could think and threw it open.

Stupid Shabiri. With her stupid face and her stupid catsuit and her stupid English accent.

"What the hell do *you* want?" I snapped.

"*So* not friendly," she said, lounging against the doorjamb. Her hair had a green streak running through it. She gave a lazy perusal of the room and my Wiccans standing protectively in front of Jeff.

"Did you not hear me the last time we met? When you sent my grandpa back to the Land of the Dead? I said I'd kill you."

"I don't see a crossbow."

It thumped into my upraised hand from the other room. She straightened, a worried look on her face. "I thought that was broken."

"You thought wrong. Oh, and look." It had armed itself. "Looks like that special arrow that Erasmus made just for you."

"Made?" She took a step back, staring at the bolt.

"Yeah." I took a step toward her, aiming. "He did a really weird thing. He took the bolt and jammed it in his eye. Said it was now tipped with a poisonous venom that could kill you."

Her eyes widened.

No, bitch, I wasn't bluffing.

"Who the hell is this?" Ed stomped forward. "Put the weapon down, Kylie."

"Yes," said Shabiri, suddenly intrigued. She looked Ed up and down like he was a juicy T-bone. "Put the weapon down, Kylie. And tell me about this gorgeous hunk of human."

Ed twitched. I guess being called human—by someone who clearly was not—gave him pause.

"He's the law around these parts," I said and winced at how it sounded like dialogue from a bad western.

"The law?" She slinked into the room but only so far. My coven had surrounded us so it wasn't likely she was getting much farther into my shop. Not without a face full of salt first. But she was reaching only for Ed. He flinched away from her touch. "Not like any constable *I* can remember. Tell me your name?"

"You first," said Ed.

She smiled. "I'm sure Kylie will tell you all about—"

"Her name is Shabiri and your brother summoned her. She's not on our side."

"Oh, *that's* why you look so familiar," she cooed. "You're dear Doug's brother. My, my."

"Jesus Christ," he muttered. "I can't believe Doug would do this. I can't believe he *can*."

"There's so much, I'll wager, you couldn't believe dear Dougie capable of doing." She tried to touch him again but he stepped back, reaching for his gun. She frowned down at his hand. "Dear me. Manners, I'm afraid, are lacking in your family." She glanced once more around the room—raising her eyes at Jeff squirming to cover himself and at the rest of the Wiccans sneering at her—and moved backward outside to my gravel parking lot. "Looks like a party I have no interest in attending. I merely heard Erasmus was gone and I just wanted to offer my services."

I stuck the butt of the crossbow into my shoulder and aimed it at her. "What have you heard? From whom?"

"The Netherworld rumor mill. Erasmus was trying to be all mysterious and got caught up in…*things*. Rumor had it that the Powers That Be…" She snapped her fingers.

I winced.

"And so I merely thought—"

"You've got two seconds to get out."

She didn't take two. She vanished immediately. I swung back into my shop. My Wiccans trailed after me, but I waved them off, tossing the crossbow to the chair. It had disarmed when Shabiri disappeared.

8

Ed didn't seem to know what to do now, but I didn't have anything left in me to try to comfort him. I had problems of my own. Doc and Seraphina were speaking gently to him as I left him so I could pace around until I couldn't stand it. Then I went outside to pace around my backyard instead, somehow thinking Erasmus would make an appearance, that I would run into him. I must have been at it for hours, ruminating over what Shabiri said. Had the Powers That Be killed him? Had *we* killed him with our spell?

I was chilled to the bone when I finally came through my back door again. I trudged through the kitchen and into the warm main room where the Wiccans sat around, looking forlorn. Maybe someone had explained Erasmus' situation to Ed, or maybe they hadn't. Either way, it didn't matter. Erasmus had failed. He wasn't coming back. He was dead. I knew it. They knew it.

Even though I crouched before the fireplace, I was cold inside. Colder than I had ever felt before. He was just a demon, and once I'd fulfilled my purpose, he would get his reward. He would eat my soul. That was what he was created for. Yet he had promised—and for some reason I believed him—that he wouldn't, and no one knew what *that* would do to him.

Stupidly, I had allowed him to mean far more to me than he should have. I dared not name the feeling, but I was empty. I didn't even care that his mission had been for naught. What difference would it make anyway? Ever since the Booke came into my life, I felt a clock ticking that *my* time would soon be up. This was only a brief delay. An interval.

I wanted to cry, but the tears didn't come. I think I had been wrung dry by all that had happened recently.

The clock chimed. It was hours past the time Erasmus had to return before the Wiccan's spell killed him.

I rose with difficulty. "I think we should call it a night," I said.

"Kylie…" Doc was by my side first. Of course, he was. I think he knew how I felt. Oh, they all knew that Erasmus and I had been intimate. Well, they knew about the first time, not the second.

Ed didn't know at all.

"Is there really any point in still hanging around, Doc?"

He didn't seem to know what to say to that, so he wisely kept quiet. I could tell Seraphina longed to comfort me with an embrace, but Doc seemed to be holding her back. Our Goth lite Wiccan Nick put a comforting arm around Jolene.

As if reacting to some silent signal, they broke rank and began gathering their things. It meant we'd have to figure out how to fight a god on our own without Erasmus' help. Baphomet was still out there, and no one knew what kind of havoc he intended to wreak. I knew we could do it. At least we could try. But it would have been easier with—

Tap, tap, tap.

We all jumped. A raven was pecking at the window. We stared at it, horrified, as it began to peck again more persistently.

I looked to Doc. "What…what *is* that?"

He shook his head. "I don't know."

I tugged my coat over my chest. I couldn't seem to warm up. "I'm . . . I'm going to go see."

Nick grabbed my arm. "Are you crazy? You don't know what or who that is. It could be Shabiri in disguise."

I wasn't getting a Shabiri vibe from the sleek, black bird. I didn't quite know how to convey that, so I just gently dislodged his hand and crossed the room toward the window. It hopped away as I approached. I turned the lock and pushed up the sash. A cold blast of air gusted in, flaring the curtains. I stared at the raven standing on my porch, glaring its beady eye before it spread its wings and zoomed toward me. With a cry, I ducked, and it swept in over my head. I whipped around to look at it, expecting it to transform into someone. Maybe Shabiri after all. But it merely circled Doc before it reared back, shot forward, and hit the wall with such force that I felt the room shake. It spattered in a gore of feathers and black blood…until the feathers fell away and the black ooze dripped down my wall, forming into something like letters.

I heard the sound of a camera shutter. Jolene had taken a picture with her tablet, before lowering it with a look of awe on her face. No doubt she would analyze it. The letters clearly weren't English. Elvish, for all I knew.

"What the *hell* was that?" cried Nick.

I cautiously approached and looked over the weird dripping script. "A message, I guess. But from whom?"

Doc scratched his white-haired head. "As soon as we decipher it—that is, Jolene and I—we can tell you."

"Why do you need it deciphered?" asked Jeff, struggling to keep the crocheted throw around him.

"Because, Jeff," I said, exhausted to my marrow, "we don't speak splatter."

"*I* can read it," he said.

Slowly, everyone turned toward him. He caught the movement and glared back. "Can't you?"

"No, Jeff. We can't. It's in some weird language."

"It isn't. I can read it."

I was about to let him have it when Doc intervened. "Now hold on, Kylie. Jeff, are you telling us you can read that message?"

"Why is everyone freaking out? It's English."

"It's a demon language, far as I can tell," said Jolene.

"Curious," said Seraphina. She crossed her arms over her chest, the bangles on her wrists clinking softly.

Doc nodded slowly. "If it's a demon language then I suppose it makes sense that Jeff can now read it. He's part, well, creature. Almost a demon. Or at least of the same realm."

"Great," said Jeff. "That's just great."

"So what does it say?" asked Jolene.

Jeff squinted at the splatter slowly dripping into long lines of black. "It says, 'I should have died hours ago but I'm still holding on. I'm coming back to you.'"

"Erasmus," I whispered. I walked up to the wall and touched the ichor when it suddenly vanished, black feathers and all. I whipped around. "Where is he?"

"I can't believe it," said Doc incredulously. "How could he possibly have survived?"

"He did." My heart felt three sizes larger, and it was beating madly. "He's out there. We've got to go look for him."

"Kylie, it could be a trick. Shabiri could have sent it to lure you out there."

"I've got to take the chance. I'll find him." I stomped toward the door when a hand closed on my arm and pulled me back.

Ed looked down on me. "There's something you're not telling me."

I shook him off. "I don't have time for this. Erasmus is in trouble." I buttoned up my coat and threw open the door. My face was blasted with cold.

I could hear the others behind me. Some of them were calling me back, but I heard Nick swear as he hurried along the gravel, muttering and struggling into his jacket. "Whichever way you go, I'll go the opposite," he said. "Cover more territory."

"Thanks, Nick. I'm going towards the woods."

"Then I'll head up the other way over the hill. I hope I don't get killed." He tossed the words out like a joke, but there was an underlying current of gallows humor. After all, he *could* get killed. So could I. Not only were Andras and Baphomet out there, but the Booke could have released another creature to catch us completely off guard.

I stumbled over the bracken. Taking out my phone, I switched on the flashlight. The light shone over the woods, bringing out new shadows, transforming every mound of dead leaves and gnarled root into something sinister. I didn't care anymore if other things out there could hear me coming. It didn't matter. "Erasmus!" I called. "Erasmus!"

The trees grew denser, their dark trunks rising in straight lines in front of me, an endless march into the deepening mist. "Erasmus!" In the distance, I think I heard Nick call out his name, too. It gave me hope. No one else liked the demon or trusted him.

But for Nick to do this for me… I choked back my tears and cleared my throat. "Erasmus!"

Wait. Was that a groan?

I listened, cocking my head and straining my ears. Standing perfectly still, I waited to hear it again. It could have been my imagination, or just hope playing on my feelings. I almost called out again when I thought I heard that soft sound once more. I moved carefully in the direction of the noise and stopped when I clearly heard it.

I ran, the light from my phone jostling up and down. The moaning came louder, until I knew I was close by. I moved the phone's light slowly in a circle. There! Not a clump of leaves. Someone was on the ground. I rushed to him and fell to my knees.

"Erasmus!"

He moaned again, then out of his mouth in a rusty voice came, "Kylie?"

"I can't believe it." I gently turned him over…and gasped. A fist-sized hole on his chest was oozing black blood. "Oh my God!"

"It's nothing."

"Erasmus, there's a *hole* in you!"

"You *are* wont to state the obvious," he grunted. "Yes, there is a hole, but it will heal."

"But what about…what about the melted coin? Doc was supposed to get it out of you."

"I believe that was taken care of. Do you not see this *enormous hole in my chest?*" He coughed, then winced in pain.

"But how did you—?"

"We have to go, Kylie. Now."

I was about to ask when I heard it. Twigs snapping, brush moving. A sluggish step, followed by many more. And then the sounds of voices, speaking in a guttural tongue, coming toward us.

CHAPTER TWO

"YOU CAME OUT into the darkness without your crossbow?" Even in pain, his English-accented voice was accusatory.

I grunted as I heaved him to his feet. "You're yelling at me *now*?"

"Foolish mortal," he muttered. I got under his arm and moved with him, but it was clear we weren't going to outrun whatever was coming toward us. And now there was a familiar smell on the wind, one that reminded me of the succubus. The smell of death.

"Another succubus?"

"No. They are the ones who ripped out my chest. And a good thing, too. That coin was killing me."

"They? What are *they*?"

We couldn't move fast enough. Out of the mist, I could see shambling figures approaching. "Oh, shit. Erasmus, you have to *move*!"

"Leave me. *Run*, Kylie."

"I won't leave you."

He tried to shake me off but seemed too weak and slumped against me. "They don't want me. They want *you*."

My grip on him tightened. "I'm not leaving you."

"Dammit, why can't you listen to me?"

"Because you're a liar."

SHADOWS IN THE MIST

The figures in the mist drew closer. As they shambled forward, I was beginning to make out some of their details. "What the actual hell?" Some were bent over, as if heavy weights were on their shoulders. As they drew closer, I realized—to my horror—that it was because they had lost an arm…or an ear…or the side of their torso. They wore long tunics with bits of armor buckled to their chests, and chain mail hanging almost to their knees. Some wore dented helmets covering their heads like pointed caps, with parts that came down and covered their noses. They were carrying axes, round broken wooden shields, and short swords, the blades of some snapped off. A few had beards and ratty braids hanging from the sides of their temples.

But their faces… I could smell them as they approached. That sweet, overpowering smell of rotting flesh. Some of their faces were little better than skulls. What flesh remained was drawn taut over cheekbones and sunken around eye sockets. They smiled from ghastly mouths with no lips. And some were missing limbs. No…not missing. They were still hanging by stretching lengths of tendons, dragging those limbs along the ground. Skin and muscle hung from some of their faces and necks, where I could see right through to their spines. They were walking corpses. I was in the middle of *Knight of the Living Dead*.

"Are you *kidding* me?" I gasped. "Are these freakin' *zombies?*"

"The Draugr. You would know them as Vikings."

"*Viking* zombies? Because *regular* zombies aren't bad *enough?*"

"Can you move faster?"

"*I* can't, because *you* can't."

"They tore into me before realizing I was a demon. It was lucky for me, for when they tore through my flesh, they also expelled the coin and ended the spell. Though I don't know how I lasted this long once the spell expired."

I heaved him along. A new urgency gave me the strength, but I could tell it wasn't going to be enough. "What happened when they realized you were a demon?"

"They left me alone. They knew they cannot consume me. You, on the other hand, are fresh meat."

"Crap." I urged him faster.

"So it is best you leave me. I will be fine. I will heal. But you are in danger."

I looked up into the tangled shadows of branches. "Why isn't the crossbow coming?"

"Because you have nothing that can readily kill a Draugr."

"But if they're from the Booke…"

"They aren't from the book."

"*What?*"

"Kylie, there is no time to argue. You must go."

"I won't leave you."

"Beelze's tail! I tell you I am not in danger. *You* are!"

That stench was getting stronger, and one of the fellows with a rusty but still mean-looking axe was lumbering closer. He slid his jaw back and forth with a horrible clicking sound. Something icky was oozing from his rotten-toothed grimace. I debated whether to cover my nose or not. "Are you *sure* they won't hurt you?"

"They would have eaten me already."

Now you know how it feels, Mr. Soul-Eater, I wanted to say. But now was definitely not the time. I had only seconds to decide when I tripped over a damned root. Erasmus fell one way and I fell the other down a shallow ravine. I rolled through the leaves and stopped when I hit a boulder.

"Ow." Rubbing my head, I looked up. I saw sky…before rotting Viking heads poked into my view.

"Crap!" The axe whistled toward me as I rolled out of the way. Then it came down again in the direction I was rolling, so I went the other way and sure enough, it came down over there too.

Trapped. On my back was a real bad place to be. One of them lunged toward me, and this time my reaction seemed to have nothing to do with the absent crossbow. I somehow sprang to my feet with a sort of cartwheel. Before I could think about how I'd pulled that off, I shot straight up into the air and grabbed onto a tree branch just as the Draugr advanced on me, dumbly looking around the place I used to be.

Still shocked that I had managed these ninja moves, I hung on the branch, looking down at milling zombies waving their rusty weapons around below me. I was about fifteen feet up. There was no way—even with all the adrenaline in the world—I could have leapt that high on my own. It had to have something to do with the Booke. Chosen Host skills.

Of course, I was still fifteen feet up. What was I going to do now?

I looked around. Surrounded by pine trees. No convenient Tarzan vines. Somehow, I was either going to have to climb higher or drop. I didn't love the idea of dropping, considering the zombies below. But my grip was slipping. Bark was not the best thing to hang from. For one, it hurts. And two...did I really need a two?

I decided to go on instinct. Instinct had gotten me out of trouble in the past, so I let the Chosen Host powers do their thing. But unfortunately, their "thing" was—

"Oh, no!"

—dropping down on the Vikings.

Three of them had gathered below me. I fell like a rock, smashing them down into the leaf duff. Their rotted bones crunched and their flesh squelched as all three doubled under me.

I scrambled free, vowing to throw my boots away after this.

But when I looked up, more Draugr were approaching from over the hill.

"Running," I muttered breathlessly. "Running's a good option." My feet hit the ground as I pelted out of there, hoping that Erasmus hadn't lied to me. Praying that he'd be all right.

I ran hard down into the ravine, through the steep "V" in the terrain. I heard armor clanking behind me and risked looking back. "Ho-ly shit." They could run! I amped up my speed, but I knew that running through such a narrow space was strategically bad. I had to get out. I ran as fast as I could up the angled sides of the ravine. When I reached the top, I stopped and looked back. Bad idea. At least ten of them were converging out of the woods. They opened their boney jaws as one and howled an inhuman sound. Waving their weapons, they started for me again.

I was running out of ideas. I could sprint back to my shop, but then what? Would I just be trapped? And what about everyone else in the village? Was I leading them back to more innocent people? Or were they just after me like the incubus had been? Because if they didn't emerge from the Booke, then I had a pretty good notion where they *did* come from.

"Doug, you son of a bitch," I rasped. My new ninja skills made me grab for a big branch that I was sure I wouldn't be able to lift…but looky there. I could!

I gripped it hard and spun around. The closest Viking got a face-full of bark and soared backwards. One of his arms fell off as he flipped over. No time to think about that as I was already lunging at another one. His booted feet went up in the air, and he was down and out. Another one came at me, swinging his sword. I held up the branch to block the blow, the blade getting stuck in the wood. While he was trying to pull it free, I flung him, branch and all, toward a tree. He smacked into it with a sort of splat.

But now I'd lost my branch, and the other seven were still coming toward me. I had no weapon. I desperately searched for anything, a rock, a branch, a hefty squirrel—*anything*!

That horrible rotting smell was far too close to me, and when I whipped my head around, a zombie Viking was right there in my personal space. I screamed…and then his head exploded.

Wait, what?

The body fell at my feet, exploded brains all over me, and there was Ed, still aiming his smoking gun with both hands and feet apart. He lowered the gun only slightly. "Kylie, what the hell are these?"

"Um…zombie Vikings."

"What?"

"Ed, look out!"

I pointed behind him, and he spun, firing. Right in the head again. That seemed to do the trick, but the ones I had smacked with my tree branch were getting up.

"We've got to go get Erasmus," I told him, grabbing his arm.

"We've got to get out of here."

"*With* Erasmus."

"I really *hate* that guy," he muttered, but he ran with me anyway.

Erasmus was propped against a tree, eyes closed, looking seriously injured. Or dead. No, he couldn't be dead.

"Erasmus!" I cried, landing on my knees by his side.

His eyes snapped open and he glared. "What are you—" But then he caught sight of Ed. "What is he—"

"He knows." I grabbed him by the arm and dragged him to his feet.

Erasmus leaned into me. "What do you mean 'he knows'?"

"He *knows*. Everything."

"Even about…me?"

"Yeah, I know you're a demon," said Ed, roughly taking Erasmus' other arm. "Like that's a big surprise."

"I see." He narrowed his eyes at Ed but didn't fight as we pulled him to his feet. With two of us, we were able to make better speed.

We threaded through the woods at a good trot. The moonlight blazed a path for us. I looked back over my shoulder. The Draugr still followed, but they seemed to be slowing down, falling back. It wasn't the moon after all that brightened our path, but the morning sky, filling the spaces between the trees with a rose-hued glow.

We kept running, dragging Erasmus, who tried to keep up, until we got to the shopfront. As we pushed through the door, the Wiccans, who had been sitting around the fireplace, stood up.

Nick was back, and he helped me get Erasmus to a chair. Under the electric light, I could see how bad his chest was…or rather, how bad it used to be. The hole had closed up. His shirt was still covered in the black gore of his blood, but already his face looked better.

"Holy crow," whispered Doc. "How'd he survive our spell?"

"We've got bigger problems." I looked back at Ed, bolting the door and peering out the windows. "There are Draugr out there."

Jolene stepped toward me, wide-eyed. "Are you serious?"

Nick squinted at her. "What's a Draugr? Do I want to know?"

"You don't," I said at the same time that Jolene recited, "They're undead warriors. Zombie Vikings."

"No way," he said breathlessly.

"Way," I said. "And Erasmus says they aren't from the Booke."

Jeff, fully recovered and fully dressed in a T-shirt, jeans, but no shoes, stood over me as I knelt by Erasmus. Was it my imagination or was Jeff…buffing out a bit? "Kylie, are you serious? Undead Vikings?"

"I'm really not in the mood to make that up. I saw them. I fought them."

"Whoa," he said, sinking onto the arm of a chair.

"Mr. Dark," said Doc, standing at the back of Erasmus' chair and leaning in. "Are you certain they aren't from the book?"

"I am intimately entwined with the book," he growled. "I know what came from it and what did not with complete certainty."

I rose. "It was Doug and company. They must have summoned them."

"But why?" asked Seraphina, approaching Erasmus.

"I don't know," I said. "But I guess that's our next move—discover why and stop them."

She worried at her bracelets. "But what about Andras? And Baphomet?"

Erasmus looked up. "Did you say Andras? He's here?"

I nodded. "All wings and threats. He's after me."

He turned away, eyes searching unseeable depths. I didn't like his expression.

I rubbed my temple. "One thing at a time. We're going to have to prioritize."

"We're not going to do anything for now," said Doc. "We're going to go back to our respective homes and get some sleep. We're all exhausted."

"I don't think Kylie should be alone," interjected Nick.

"She's not alone," said Erasmus and Ed at the same time.

That was just great. I looked from Ed to Erasmus as they turned their glares on each other. I don't know who was growling the loudest.

"Okay," I said, standing between them. "Ed, you go home. I'll take care of Erasmus."

The demon stood unsteadily, his black blood all over my wingback. "I don't need taking care of."

"Yeah, you look just peachy."

"I'm healing. In another hour, I will be back to normal."

"I'm not leaving until he does," said Ed, crossing his arms over his chest.

I wanted to kill them both. "No, Ed. I said go home."

He stared at me incredulously while Erasmus, smug as could be, raised an imperious brow.

"But Kylie—" said Ed.

"Do you mind? I've got this. And everyone else, go home. We'll strategize later this afternoon when we've all had a chance to rest."

Nick glanced toward the windows. "But what about the… the zombies?"

"They disappear at daybreak," said Jolene, hugging her Hello Kitty witch bag.

We all made our way to the windows and slid the curtains aside. No zombies. Just shadows being cast by a steadily rising sun.

Someone yawned, which started the rest of us off.

"Go home, everyone," I said more gently. "We'll meet up later."

They were tired, I could tell, but they were still reluctant to leave. I made shooing motions toward the door, and, one by one, they filed out. Nick cautiously peered into the nearby woods.

Ed stood at the door, a frown on his face. "I don't think I should leave you alone with that guy."

"You know very well who 'that guy' is. And what."

"Which is why I don't feel comfortable leaving you alone with him."

"Look, Ed, I know all this is a lot to take in. But I'll be fine. I need Erasmus. He's the only one who really knows what to do about the Booke."

Bracing himself against the wingback, Erasmus stood straight, raising his chin in defiance. Ed huffed deeply, then leaned toward me, eyes fixed on Erasmus, and kissed me.

"Call me," he said gruffly when he pulled back. With a long, pointed look at Erasmus, he turned toward the door and finally left.

Pissing match averted, I locked the door after him.

"Proud of yourself?" I said.

Erasmus smiled slowly. "Immensely." He stumbled and made his way back to the chair.

"You're not all right yet."

"Maybe some of that brandy you have would help?"

I shook my head and went to the kitchen to get it.

* * *

I STAYED UP a little while to drink with Erasmus and make sure he was okay, but he told me to go to bed when my head drooped to my chest for the second time.

I slept deeply and didn't remember dreaming, which was probably a blessing. When I awoke, it was around two in the afternoon.

The time shocked me. I scrambled out of bed and stumbled downstairs with bed hair and bleary eyes. "Gotta open the shop!" I got down near the bottom of the steps to see Erasmus stuff a teapot into a brown bag with handles and shove it at a customer. "Do come again," he said with a smarmy smile.

The elderly woman tittered like a coquette, taking the bag and fluttering her lashes at Erasmus the whole way to the door.

I rubbed the last bit of sleep from my face. "What was that?"

He startled with the guiltiest look on his face. "You...you were asleep."

"And *you* opened my shop?"

He gestured toward the parking lot. "There were customers. And you claim to need this place of business for your upkeep."

I stepped down the last stair, gripping the banister. "I do. I just didn't imagine...you...you as a shopkeeper."

"I am no such thing. I merely showed my gratitude to you by helping you with a few little purchases."

"How did you figure out the register?"

"The what?"

"That," I said, pointing to it on the counter.

He shrugged. "I didn't. They simply paid me in your currency." He dug into his pocket and pulled out a wad of bills.

I stumbled toward him. "How much did you sell?"

He waved vaguely. "A few teapots and other assorted nonsense. The whole point of this shop is beyond me."

"But..." I took the bundle. Good grief, what did he charge people? "Erasmus, there is no way people bought this much merchandise."

He postured. "Are you accusing me of lying?"

"No, but..."

"Then take the money and be grateful."

"I...I am, but...there's no coins or anything. How—"

"They just gave it to me, gladly. They told me to 'keep the change,' whatever that means."

I bit my lip. "Did you do some sort of hocus pocus on them? Some sort of demon hoodoo?"

"I haven't the least idea what you're talking about." He rubbed at his nose, which didn't seem to help. Just in time, he pulled out a handkerchief and sneezed into it. "Damned tea," he muttered, wiping his nose.

He was allergic to tea. It was ridiculously endearing.

"Thank you for minding the store. I really appreciate it. It was very thoughtful of you."

Was he blushing? "Well…" He opened and closed one of my herb drawers absently—the herb called "chase devil" as it happens. "It seemed the least I could do."

I laid a hand gently on his arm.

He looked down at my hand and then slowly at me.

"So…what did you learn in the Netherworld? We still need a way to subdue a god."

"I know. But I'm afraid I learned very little. There might be something, though. I will likely have to explain it to the child."

"You mean Jolene."

"There must be some sort of rule on the minimum age of your Wiccans."

I crossed my arms. "Are you *concerned* for her?"

"Of course not! Her young age could be a liability to us."

"Oh, of course. I see."

"Stop looking at me like that. Have *you* passed a mirror of late?"

I grabbed my hair. "No, why?" And then I remembered I hadn't even brushed my teeth. I clamped my hand over my mouth and ran upstairs to take a shower. As long as Erasmus could run the shop, I knew I had time to get ready. Even with whatever spell he was casting on my customers.

When I got out of the shower and padded into the bedroom, I found a steaming mug of coffee on my bedside table. I stared at it for a good long while before I sank onto the bed. That Erasmus. He was pulling out all the stops. Could it be…he was *glad* to see me again? He did send that note, after all. That weirdly disturbing note in the form of an exploded crow, but still…

I smiled as I came downstairs, this time with my hair neatly brushed, wearing a cashmere sweater and jeans and carrying the mug in my hand. Erasmus was escorting another customer to the door. It was odd, him in his black leather duster jacket tending my business. He hardly looked like a proper clerk for a tea shop, but this was Moody Bog. Maybe it was more normal that I had originally thought.

"Hey," I said as casually as I could while sweet thoughts about him swirled around my head.

He glanced my way, did a double take, and then tried to look as if he hadn't by straightening his jacket. "'Hey'?" he mocked. "Is this truly an appropriate greeting?"

"It is in this century."

"There is a lot lacking in this century."

"Okay, enough. We've got to talk about these Draugr." I settled on a bar stool behind the counter and cupped my mug to warm my hands. "By the way," I said, lifting the mug and offering him a heartfelt smile. "Thanks for this."

"It wasn't hard to figure out your coffee contraption," he said smugly. "I've watched you often enough. A child could do it."

"Even a demon child," I said into the cup.

"What was that?"

I looked up, blinking innocently. "Nothing. What about these Vikings?"

"They are the risen corpses of Viking warriors."

"Yeah, I figured that out all by myself." I rolled my eyes. "So what is their deal? Do they eat brains?"

"Brains? If they did, there would be mighty slim pickings around here."

"Oh, ha ha."

He folded his arms and shook his head. "Where do you get these notions? They don't bother with eating brains. They have enormous strength and literally crush their enemies to death, drinking their blood. They walk to protect their hoard of gold, rising at sunset and disappearing again at sunrise."

"So what do they want with us? We don't have any Viking gold."

"Are you certain? As I said, they didn't come from the book. Who else do you know who might have designs on a gold hoard?"

"Doug. And Shabiri probably helped him."

"Yes, and no doubt she left out the little tidbit about the Draugr walking the night in search of it, killing as they go."

"You mean the Ordo would also be in danger?" Our least favorite biker gang called themselves the Order of the Right Hand of the Devil—the *Ordo Dextarae Diaboli*, or just Ordo for short. They were short a few brain cells, that was for sure. They dabbled where they shouldn't have, like summoning Baphomet and allowing him access to this plane of existence. I don't mind sharing our plane with friendly spirits, but since we were currently using it, a baddie who wanted to destroy us was not welcome.

Andras, the demon assassin, was another story though. Who summoned him? I had my doubts that the Ordo were capable.

"Everyone is in danger," Erasmus was saying.

"Right. Then what's our priority? Andras, Baphomet, Draugr?"

"You're forgetting that something has yet to come from the book."

"Believe me, I haven't forgotten the stupid Booke of the Hidden."

As I said it, the Booke popped into the space between us, like a middle finger to my disdain. I would have thrown it through my front window if Erasmus hadn't held my wrist. Instead, I put it down on the counter and opened it. I had only filled three pages. That was how I contained the creatures who'd escaped and put them back where they belong; I wrote about them in the Booke, usually after I shot them with the chthonic crossbow. But there were *so* many pages left to go.

"Erasmus, we have to destroy this Booke," I said for the umpteenth time, worrying at the demon-faced amulet hanging from my neck. It was the only clear way to stop the destruction and death. And to protect future generations of Chosen Hosts from getting caught in its curse. "Any ideas?"

"As I have said before, it cannot be done."

"But there must be a god or being in charge in the Netherworld who could stand up to the Powers That Be."

He seemed uncomfortable, squirming. "Of course, there is."

"Well…who then?"

His gaze settled on mine. "Satan," he whispered.

"Wait. *The* Satan?"

"No, *Fred* Satan. Of course, *the* Satan!"

"Wow." I slumped on my stool. "I just didn't imagine…I mean, it never occurred to me that…Really?"

"Yes," he hissed.

"Is there…is there any way we could, well, *talk* to him? Maybe reason with him?"

He snapped to his feet. "Are you *insane*? No, we cannot *talk* to Him."

"Oh, come on, Erasmus. You're a demon. Are you saying you're afraid of him?"

"Yes! I'm terrified." And he suddenly looked it. Anything that could put that look on his face… "I don't want Him aware of me. At all."

It dawned on me again that once the Booke goes, so does he. As Guardian of the Booke, he'd be out of a job. And in the Netherworld, that meant a quick trip to non-existence. Was *I* ready for that? Judging by my reaction to his long absence when I thought he was dead, the answer was a decided "no."

"Oh, okay, forget it. I'm sorry I mentioned it."

"Never mention it again."

"Okay!" I sipped my coffee and noticed that it was growing cold. "Erasmus, you were missing for something like eight hours past the time you were supposed to return. How…how did you survive all that time? You weren't lying there with a hole in your chest for eight hours, were you?"

His angry expression—maybe I should say his *usual* expression—morphed into one of puzzlement. "I don't know. Maybe your Wiccans did the spell wrong."

"Maybe. And by the way, your pal Shabiri was here."

That old scowl was back. "What did *she* want?"

"She'd heard on the Netherworld grapevine that something had happened to you and offered her services as Booke Guardian."

"She *what?*"

"Hey, don't kill the messenger. I just want to know how she knew. I thought the whole point of that stupid spell was to keep you incognito down there."

"It was supposed to. It *did* work…" He mulled it over, slowly rising. "I felt it. I moved about with impunity. No one and nothing detected me. I ventured to places I would have been instantly killed. It *did* work."

His eyes met mine. Something else was going on, and neither of us liked the implications. Was it the Big Guy, the Head Honcho? Satan? Was he aware of Erasmus despite our precautions?

"You can't go back."

"Don't be a fool. If summoned, I must."

"But they'll…they'll…"

"They might. They might not."

"Erasmus…"

He sighed, looking away. "We both have our roles to play."

We certainly did. He cast a glance toward the Booke. Mine had been a whirlwind. His was centuries old.

I took a deep breath and tried not to think about it. "Then…priorities?"

He pushed away from the counter, suddenly on edge. "Discuss it with your Wiccans. I have places to be."

"Wait—Erasmus!" I put the mug down and scrambled after him. He stopped abruptly, and I stumbled into him. When he turned, we were toe to toe, his dark eyes so close to mine.

His previously tight muscles seemed to soften. The intensity of his gaze did as well.

"I'm glad you're back." I swallowed. "Safe and sound."

Even his shirt had repaired itself. Either that or he had an endless supply of black shirts somewhere in his demon closet.

"I'm…glad to be back," he said quietly. "Safe and sound."

We breathed at each other intensely for long seconds. I swore he was leaning into me when the damned bell above the door jingled.

Sheriff Ed postured in the doorway. "Am I interrupting something?"

Erasmus hissed at him, like *Bride of Frankenstein* hissing. A stark reminder that he wasn't human. Erasmus took several strides toward Ed, peeled back his lips in a smiling grimace with too many pointed teeth, and vanished into a wisp of smoke.

As tough as Ed was trying to be, the expression on his face gave him away. Horrified. Maybe he had half-believed it in the dark of night, but this was daytime.

He looked at me. "You're having a relationship with that guy?"

"Um, well…yeah. Sort of."

He breathed harshly through his teeth. "You could have told me."

"I never said we were exclusive."

"It was implied."

"Really? When?"

"Well…" He stalked into the room and looked around. "*I* thought we were," he barked. "I thought *I* was your boyfriend. You said so yourself."

"Okay. You're right. It seemed like we were going in that direction. But…" Had I strung Ed along? I suddenly felt like a monster. Most of the time I was just trying to convince myself *not* to have a relationship with Erasmus.

How's that working out for you, Kylie?

"For God's sake, Kylie. He's a demon."

"I know!"

Ed fell against a post, hands dangling. "You've had more time to process this than I have," he said quietly.

I nodded. "I know that, too. But Ed, I don't have time for you to process it. I need your help."

"I…I feel like we need to evacuate the town."

"But what would you tell everyone?"

He swiped his hat off his head and griped it in whitening fingers. "I don't know."

I wish he could. It would make things easier. But I couldn't help but feel that the creatures would just move toward the next place. Hansen Mills, probably. And with the ley lines—invisible lines of power—running through there, who knew what could happen? It made me realize how much more there was to tell Ed; about my grandfather's ghost, about the Founders and Ruth Russell, and so many other things.

"I'm kind of worried about this Andras guy."

He straightened, trying to be all business. "So there's a demon after you."

"Yeah."

"Sent by whom? Doug?"

"Maybe. With Shabiri's help."

"And Shabiri is also a demon."

"Yup. I'd be careful. I think she's taken a shine to you."

"Well, if we're not exclusive, maybe I should—"

I slammed him up against the wall. The force of it surprised both of us. Chosen Host skills again. "This isn't a joke. Don't get mixed up in this."

"But it's okay for you?"

"Dammit, Ed. This has nothing to do with…" I stepped back and took a breath. "Look, *I'm* stuck in this. *I* have no choice. And yeah, I shouldn't have gotten involved with Erasmus, but I did. It doesn't mean you should endanger yourself. Shabiri does not have your best interests at heart."

"And Erasmus Dark has yours?"

"Yes. Yes, I think he does."

He stared at me incredulously for a few seconds before shaking his head. "If it helps you sleep at night," he muttered.

"I sleep very well, thanks!"

This was not how I'd hoped this would go. I rubbed my face vigorously to calm myself and looked up at him. "I need your help. If I'm going to survive this—and I really have no expectations as the days go on—you have got to get over this."

He took a step closer. "Kylie," he said softly. "I care about you. I mean, I really care. I…I hoped that you might care for me. I thought we had something going."

I softened too. "We do." I got close to him and rested my hands on his chest. "I know that you called yourself my boyfriend."

"And you took your time answering that. Now I see why."

Did he mean Erasmus or everything else?

"I'll help you regardless," he continued, "but where does this leave us?"

He must have seen the look in my eye, because he closed his. "I'm sorry. I guess you've got more on your mind right now."

I drew away, making space between us. "I do. That's really great of you. Thanks for understanding."

He seemed to gird himself. "How can I help?"

Now that I finally had his help, I didn't know what to do with it. "Well…" I laughed. He must have thought I'd lost it at last. "I don't really know. Be on the lookout, I guess. And help us out when we have to go out on calls."

"Calls?"

"Yeah. Sometimes we have to hunt the creatures. And sometimes we've got to stop Doug from whatever it is he's doing—"

"Him, I can take."

"Okay, just hold on." I had to physically restrain Ed because it looked like he intended to go out and get Doug right now. "No one does anything on their own. We all work together. We get as much information as we can, and we work as a team. Got it?"

He paused before a smile formed on his lips. "And you're in charge."

"Yeah." I poked him in the chest. "You got a problem with that?"

"No, ma'am," he said, his smile broadening.

I couldn't help but smile back. "I see. Are you…turned on by a lady with a crossbow?"

"Well, I'm not turned off." He appeared to think about it for another second. "And maybe just a little turned on, too."

I got closer again. "This is so wrong."

He slid his arm around my waist. "It is, kind of." He was leaning in and I was reaching up.

The bell above the door jangled again.

Nick stood in the doorway, somewhat abashed by what he was seeing. "The door was open…"

I stepped past Ed. "Come on in, Nick."

"You did say to come this afternoon."

"I did. I guess the others will be here soon."

"What about…" Nick gave Ed a sidelong glance. *Mister Dark*, he mouthed, as he stepped into my shop.

"He's not here."

"But we need him!"

Ed slapped his hat against his thigh. "Boy, I'm really tired of people saying that about *that guy.*"

"He's not 'that guy,'" I told him. "He's a demon. One intimately connected with the Booke. And we *do* need him. So get over it."

"It's the 'intimately connected' that I…" He ran his hand through his hair and smacked his hat against his thigh again. "Okay. Got it."

I wanted to tell him that I understood why he felt that way. That I was sorry things were panning out as they were. But you know what? I just didn't have the energy. And if he liked me, he'd figure that out for himself.

The roar of an engine permeating through my tightly shut windows made us all look. Speak of the devil… Well, not Erasmus this time. But Doug.

He and his gang rolled slowly down Lyndon Road, giving us all an unhurried perusal. Ed took three strides to the door and threw it open, standing on the porch like he was challenging all comers. I slid in beside him to watch the spectacle. I had seen their bikes before—all Harleys and all in pretty fine shape. But it looked like they had all gotten new rides and tricked them out too. There was Doug on a black Softail, with chrome-laced wheels and whitewall tires, full-skirted metal fenders, chromed triple headlamps—the works. Trying to get alongside him was Charise Walker, her red hair caught up in a long braid, ring in her nose and scar on her face. Sneering at me, of course. Bob Willis, a farm boy with floppy blond hair, kept his eye on Charise, who only had eyes for Doug. And in the rear position was Dean Fitch, a big bruiser of a guy with an upside-down pentagram tattooed on the side of his skinhead. And who could forget their matching black leather jackets? Each jacket had Goat Guy—Baphomet—emblazoned in all his glory in an upside-down pentagram on the back. The words *Ordo Dexterae Diaboli*, written in flames, curved around Baphy's face.

Doug smiled. I don't know why I never saw it before, but he was the spitting image of Ed, except with a full dark beard cropped close to his face. He gave me a little salute. Charise gave me a little salute, too, but it wasn't the polite kind. Doug gunned his chromed engine, which must have been the signal, because they all suddenly peeled out and disappeared into Moody Bog. Marge Todd from Moody Bog Market had been walking along the street and suddenly had to jump out of the way.

"Damn him," sneered Ed.

"Pretty expensive rides they were on," I said, hoping to redirect Ed's ire.

It did the trick. He stopped scowling and moved back into the warmth of the shop. "Yeah. Where'd *he* get the money for that? My folks never would have leant any to him."

"They all had fancy bikes," I said. "Any banks been robbed lately?"

It was a joke, but Ed took it seriously. He got on his shoulder mic. "George, check the sheet to see if there've been any sort of burglaries in the area. Check Hansen Mills, too."

"No robberies," said Deputy George, "but a few break-ins, and some vandalism has been reported out in the willie-whacks. Some pretty strange things been coming in."

"Strange things…like what?"

"You know those folks down there, sheriff. They think everything's out to get them."

"Just what is it they think, deputy?"

"It's crazy. If it's anything, it's folks dressing up early for Halloween. Are you ready for this? They said *Vikings*. And *skeletons*. There's a little too much boozing going on there, if you ask me. We should check the area for illegal stills or meth labs."

Ed gave me a significant look. "Got it, George. Thanks. Keep checking."

"Will do, sheriff. Miller out."

I flopped into one of my wing chairs. The Draugr. So far, it sounded like they hadn't hurt anyone. At least most people seemed to be staying indoors when the sun set, since it was colder than you-know-what.

Nick kept pushing the curtain aside to search up and down the street. Fortunately, it wasn't dark yet, though the fall sunlight was slanting awfully low through the trees. A golden trail shone along the street for the rolling leaves to follow.

"When are the others coming?" he asked nervously.

I glanced at the clock. Jolene would be coming soon. It was her after-school job. And Seraphina would swan in whenever she liked, with Doc not too far behind. "Pretty soon."

"Do you want me to make some tea or something?" said Nick.

"You don't have to."

"Hey, barista extraordinaire here. I can do both coffee *and* tea if it is so desired."

I smiled at him. He bowed and headed toward the kitchen. If he stayed busy, he'd be less nervous. But after hearing a lot of clanking and clattering coming from the kitchen, I decided to help him out.

"I got this," he said when I pushed open the door.

"I'll help."

We began working in concert. I prepared tea—a spicy ginger breakfast blend because I could really use the wake-up—while Nick made the coffee. He kept stealing glances at me until I finally faced him. "What? It looks like you want to ask me something."

"Well…I was wondering. Since the sheriff knows now, I'm wondering if I could…you know, tell George."

I sighed. "I know you and Deputy George have a thing, but do we really need more people to know about all this?"

"The more creatures get out of the book, the more it's going to get noticed. I don't know how long the sheriff can divert people's attention."

"Hmm. Maybe that *is* a good role for him."

"S'cuse me." He waved his hand in front of my face. "We're talking about me right now."

I touched his arm. "He means a lot to you, huh?"

He busied himself with the grounds in the filter. "I'm into him, yeah. Even as stodgy as he is. It's kind of…cute."

"It's the mustache."

He laughed. "What?"

"I sort of have a nickname for him. Deputy Mustache."

"Oh God!" he howled. "Don't *ever* say that in front of him. He is alarmingly proud of that thing. I think it needs its own zip code."

We shared a laugh before Ed poked his head in. "What are you two laughing over?"

"Nothing." I pushed him toward the door. "Here. Make yourself useful and take this tray out there." I thrust a tray with cups, a sugar bowl, and creamer at him. He grabbed it awkwardly and went through the door, looking back at me.

"He's a much better choice," said Nick, using his eyebrows to gesture toward Ed.

"We're not discussing this."

"Oh? So you can impugn my secret boyfriend's mustache, but I can't tell you that Ed's a better deal than a demon?"

Clutching the teapot, I shoved the door open with my rear end. "Yup."

It wasn't long before the rest of the coven showed up, with

Jeff trailing in too. He sat sullenly far from everyone else. I felt bad that he was, well, depressed. Once everyone had a cup of something in their hands, I sidled over toward him.

"Jeff."

"Kylie." He wouldn't meet my eyes.

"What's wrong?"

"Oh, you mean besides being a freakin' werewolf?" he hissed.

"I'm sorry, Jeff. I can't even imagine how difficult this must be…"

"No, you can't. And you know what else is hard? Standing around, watching you juggle two guys when you were once mine… And knowing that *I* screwed it all up."

I had nothing to say to that. I was crouching by his chair, looking at his blond hair. When he wolfed out, his entire body was covered with that same silky blond. Surfer wolf.

"I don't know what to say."

"You don't have to say anything."

"Jeff…"

"Your coven wants you." He shrugged toward Doc, who was clearing his throat to get my attention. I left Jeff there. He had a lot to work through.

I went to the door to flip the OPEN sign over to CLOSED when I noticed a little girl standing in the middle of the road. She was looking down toward the village.

Even though there wasn't likely to be much traffic at this hour of the afternoon, standing in the road probably wasn't a good idea. I unlocked the door, opened it, and stuck my head out. "Little girl! Hey, honey! Come out of the street."

She didn't look at me.

I stepped out to my gravel parking lot. "Hey! Little girl! Come away from there." I searched around and didn't see any adults nearby. And the sun was going down. That meant that the Draugr would be out soon. I race-walked toward her and leaned over to touch her arm. "Honey, let's get you to the shop and see if we can call your parents."

She turned her head toward me then. Her eyes, round and clear blue, looked me over. She was maybe six or seven, wearing a plaid dress with red tights. Too young to be out on the street at twilight.

I smiled, trying to look friendly and nonthreatening. "I have tea. And maybe I can scrounge up a cookie while we phone your folks. Shall we do that?"

She looked up at me placidly. And then she opened her mouth and screeched an unearthly sound.

I stumbled back.

Her teeth were covered in blood and her eyes suddenly glowed yellow. And then she fell forward, got down on all fours, and bounded away.

CHAPTER THREE

"DID YOU SEE that?" cried Nick from the doorway. Everyone had gathered when they saw me go outside. All their faces were white and stark. I was willing to bet they hadn't seen anything like that before either.

I turned my attention back to the creature quickly disappearing into the rising mist. My instinct was to scream, but I started fiercely trembling instead.

Ed was at my side. "What the hell was that?"

I shook my head. Couldn't speak. Would scream if I tried. But something else took over—those damned Chosen Host skills—making me take off and run after her.

She was far ahead, and I wasn't gaining on her, even going full pelt as I was. While her strange gait—butt in the air, running on hands and feet—was freaking me out, I had to keep her in my sights. Something told me to raise my arm; the familiar whistling sound of the crossbow coming toward me gave me a smidgen of confidence. When it slapped into my hand, I clutched it hard. I glanced quickly at the bolt in the flight groove and knew I'd never seen it before.

She was still galloping down the street when she made a sudden turn at the church. She ran past it and toward the dark gates of the cemetery. *Don't go in, don't go in,* I chanted in my head. But when had anything gone my way lately?

She leapt right over the closed gate. I slowed, my boots slapping the wet pavement as I came up to a halt in front of the gate and clutched the cold metal bars in my hand.

Nick and then Ed came up on either side of me, breathing hard. "What the hell *was* that?" Ed asked again.

"Call me crazy," I said, "but I'm betting that wasn't really a little girl."

"But I know her," said Ed. "And...Jesus." He loosened his tie and his collar. "A few days ago— It's Lexy Johnson."

Nick snapped his head toward Ed. "Lexy Johnson? You mean...the little girl who...who..."

Ed nodded. He stepped up to the gate and peered through, scanning the tombstones and monuments.

"She what?" I asked Nick, then Ed. "She what?"

Nick finally answered. "She died. She fell off the roof of her house three days ago. Her funeral was yesterday."

"She wasn't a ghost." I checked the crossbow. It wouldn't need to shoot a ghost. This bolt was designed to kill something from the Booke. "But she's dead. And she's not a Viking."

"Wait," said Nick. "You mean she's a zombie?"

"I don't know. Hey," I turned, looking back down the street. "Where's the rest of the coven?"

Nick's eyes were wide, scanning our surroundings. He licked his lips. "Ed told Jeff to stay and tell the others when they arrived." Nick couldn't seem to help himself from looking behind him again. "I left before I realized what I was doing."

"For what it's worth, I'm glad you're here." I girded myself, securing the loaded crossbow in my hands. "I'm going in."

Ed's hand wrapped around my arm and squeezed. "Kylie, no."

"Ed." I lifted the crossbow to show him. "I've got *this,* and it armed itself. That means I'm up."

"You're serious about this? Jesus. Let me do it. Hand *me* the crossbow."

I snatched it back. "Don't you get it? This is *my* mission. It's mine."

"But…" He didn't know how to argue it.

I could see the pain on his face, and I wanted more than anything to kiss it away from him.

"Then have my back," I said gently.

I saw the change in him immediately. He straightened and had his gun in his hand so fast it seemed a blur.

Nick raised his trembling hand. "Uh…third banana, here. Without a weapon, I'd like to remind you all."

"You don't have to come, Nick."

He looked behind him one more time to the darkening street, filling with mist. "Well, I'm not going back there alone."

No more talk. I pushed against the gate, which opened with a good, old-fashioned horror movie whine. I stepped up the walkway and looked around. "Ed, do you know where her…her grave is?"

"Yeah. Up this way."

It was the perfect cliché cemetery. There was a kneeling, weeping angel to my right and a vine-covered crypt up ahead to the left. Did they deliberately design these places to look extra scary?

"I am sooo creeped out right now," said Nick.

"Me, too," I said, yet my feet kept moving.

Ed led the way up onto the grass. We walked between tombstones as the light was falling and fog was rising, sending fingers of mist hovering over the lawn. I hadn't even had time to grab my jacket. I wish the crossbow could have picked it up on its way out.

I held the crossbow at my shoulder and aimed it forward but kept looking all around. We came to a rise and walked upward. Ed stopped, and I came up behind him.

"What is it?"

He was shaking his head at something ahead of us. "What. The. Hell."

I had a feeling he'd be saying that a lot in the near future. When I came around him, I saw it too. The grave had been opened, with dirt sprayed all over as if it had been dug up by some enormous dog. The coffin had been dragged up out of the grave. A child's coffin. It was white with a sort of lace pattern— something dainty for a little girl. And it was spattered with blood.

The lid had been torn open, hanging on one remaining hinge. I didn't want to look. I was about to chicken out and make Ed go…when my hands tightened over the smooth ebony and silver contours of the crossbow, feeling its organic lines and sensuous curves. It reminded me that it was my job to look, to investigate, and to kill whatever it was that had possessed that innocent child.

Ed was surprised when he saw I was right beside him. "Kylie, you need to step back."

"Ed, what I need to do is go forward."

"Sweetheart, there's blood all over that."

I stopped. "You…called me 'sweetheart.'"

He blinked. "Yeah."

I slowly blew out a breath. I liked the feeling I got from his words a little too much, but I had to shove that aside. "I have to see what happened."

"Are you sure?"

"I'm sure I'm *not* going over there," said Nick, his voice quavering.

I barely acknowledged him. This might be the worst thing I'd ever had to do. No, my mother's funeral was the worst thing I'd ever had to do. But this was a close second.

We got to the opened hole. I could now see streaks of claw marks on the coffin and more dug into the edge of the grave— and I could smell something too. It was the scent of death, but more than that. It was what I smelled when I was at the murder scene of Dan Parker, the old Congregational Church's caretaker. He'd been murdered—sacrificed, so the Wiccans believed. And we hadn't a clue as to who had done it. That was another thing we'd have to discuss with Ed.

We slowly rounded the other side of the open coffin, and I got my first glimpse of the contents. "Oh, God."

She was there. But…parts of her were missing. And a big chunk was cut out of her abdomen. Wait. Not cut.

I stepped closer.

Bitten. Chewed. Eaten.

I turned away and threw up all over someone's grandmother's tombstone. I sank down and leaned on the stone when I was empty.

Nick winced and squirmed somewhere behind me. "Jesus, Kylie. I'll pay you anything not to tell me."

Ed's hands were on my shoulders, a comforting presence. "You should go. I've got to call this in."

"No, wait. I have to—"

"You don't have to do anything else."

I put a trembling hand to my forehead. "Is it her?"

He turned and grimaced as he looked it over. "Down to the same plaid dress and red tights."

"So…something got her just as we caught up to the grave?"

"That doesn't seem likely." Ever the detective, Ed's eyes constantly roved around the scene as he spoke, searching. "I don't…I don't think she left her coffin."

I ran my sleeve over my sweaty forehead. Sweat and freezing cold. What a great combination. "What do you mean?"

"I'm looking at her shoes, her hands. She wasn't running on mud and gravel. She's clean…as far as that goes. And…you know. The rest of her…her face—mouth and eyes. Still sewn shut. It wasn't her."

"Then…what was it we saw?"

"I don't know. That's the Wiccan's department, isn't it?"

I looked down at the crossbow. It had disarmed.

"Go, Kylie," he said. "Take Nick with you."

I lifted the crossbow weakly. "But maybe I should…"

"You should go back to the shop."

"I'm not leaving you alone." I spit the bile from my mouth and unsteadily raised the crossbow.

There was an endearing twinkle in his eye. "Then wait here while I call it in."

He spoke into his shoulder mic and got Deputy George, while we waited. It wasn't long till we spotted the flashing lights of his police Jeep rambling up the drive. He got out and stared at Nick. Deputy George didn't often acknowledge him in public, but Nick gave him a bro-style chin raise in greeting.

"Jeezum rice!" cried George when he saw what Ed was staring at. I slipped away toward Nick.

"Hey!" George called after me. "Where do you think you're going? Put down the weapon." He reached for the flap snapped down over his holster, but Ed covered his hand.

"She can go," he said.

"But Sheriff…"

"She and Nick can go."

Deputy George squared on Nick, mustache and all. "Ni— uh, Mr. Riley? What are you…what are you doing here?"

Nick gave me a desperate look, but it was Ed who saved the day. "They followed some animal into the cemetery and called me."

"An animal? What kind of animal?"

"They don't know." Ed gestured for me to go.

I swung the crossbow down, trying to hide it by carrying it next to my thigh with one hand, and took Nick's arm with the other. We hurried down to the cemetery gate. Nick looked back, but the deputy never glanced his way. Once we got to the street, we ran.

Nick tried to slow me down. "What's the hurry?"

"The Draugr."

"Shit!" He then grabbed *my* arm, and we sprinted back to the shop. When we got to the porch, I scanned the woods.

"Fog is thick around here," I said.

"I've never seen it like this."

"Really?"

"I mean, sometimes it comes up from the coast when a storm's coming—the ocean's only over that ridge and down the road—but this is wicked thick."

"Do you suppose it comes with—" Was something moving out there? "Let's get inside. Maybe Jolene—"

"Yeah. We've got a lot to ask that girl." He held me back as I grabbed for the door latch. "Do you think George and Ed will be okay?"

"They're both armed, and they've got a car. And good old-fashioned bullets seem to do the trick with those zombie guys…at least for a while."

"I know I said we should tell George, but maybe it isn't a good idea. He already hates that I'm into the occult."

"What if he knew it was real?"

"He's an every-Sunday churchgoer. He already thinks it's real, and that I'll go to Hell for being involved in it."

"But can't you tell him you're one of the good guys?"

"I don't think he thinks there *are* good guys involved with this."

"Yeah. When I saw him at the Chamber of Commerce get-together at the church, he seemed part of the Ruth Russell crowd."

Nick sighed. "He's Mister Conservative all right. Why do you think he's closeted?"

"Well, Mission One is to convince him that you *are* one of the good guys."

"Isn't Mission One to get rid of the Draugr?"

"It's one of the many missions. There's a whole list. Haven't you noticed?"

When I pulled open the door, Doc was suddenly in front of us. "What happened? Where's Sheriff Ed?"

Seraphina grabbed me and looked me over. "Good goddess, that was terrible. Jeff said—"

I pushed past her and went straight to Jolene. "Ed's fine. We're all okay. And that was no little girl. Ed said that it was someone called Lexy Johnson and that she died a few days ago. We followed her…it…whatever…to the cemetery, and when we got to her grave, it was all dug up, the coffin was hauled up and opened, and she was partially…well, eaten. At least, that's what it looked like. But the sheriff said that she didn't appear to have left her coffin. So…what was it?"

Jolene didn't even need to grab her tablet. "That sounds like a ghoul. They hang around graveyards, mostly prey on children, and eat the dead. Then they take on the form of the ones they recently…um, ate."

"So it wasn't Lexy."

"No. It was the ghoul just taking on her form."

"I'm pretty sure it came out of the Booke. The crossbow armed itself with a bolt I've never seen before."

"You are correct," said Erasmus Dark, appearing out of nowhere.

We all started.

I shook the crossbow at him. "Stop *doing* that!"

He looked at me with just the merest of smiles. "Doing what?"

Ignoring him seemed the most sensible thing to do. "Okay," I said, pacing with the crossbow. I felt better holding it. "We've got a ghoul from the Booke, the Draugr from…who knows where, Andras out hunting me, and Baphomet. Have I left anything out?"

"The pentagram you saw at the church," said Seraphina.

"And the gruesome death of Dan Parker," said Doc.

I nodded. That was…a lot. "Help me out here." I continued pacing in front of my fireplace. "What should we do first? I'm feeling a little overwhelmed. Like I need to delegate."

"That's exactly what you *should* do, Kylie," said Doc. "I think you need to concentrate on the ghoul since you're the only one who can get rid of it."

"Okay. Good idea."

"And Mr. Dark," he continued, "needs to stay close to you in order to keep an eye out for Andras. He could pounce at any time and, well, they're both demons, so…"

Erasmus flashed a smile full of extra teeth. "Yes." He drew the sound out till it was almost a hiss. A feeling that wasn't entirely unpleasant rippled up my spine in response.

I nodded. "Then how about Jolene and Seraphina research the Draugr—"

"And I can hunt them down," said Jeff, with a distinctly wolfy growling voice. The way he now seemed to linger in the shadows made me forget he was there.

Doc was momentarily distracted by the change in Jeff's voice. After all, Jeff's ears were also getting pointy. "Uh…yes, Mr. Chase. That seems like a good idea. You might even be immune from them." He glanced at Nick. "And Nick and I will investigate the pentagram."

"What about Dan?" said Nick.

"Well, now that Sheriff Ed is…one of us, he can investigate it with new eyes and, hopefully, with new suspects in mind."

Good. This was good. Breaking it down into bite-sized chunks was easier. Except that "bite-sized chunks" made me think of poor Lexy, making me queasy all over again. I set the crossbow beside me as I sank into a chair. "All right. Jolene, the ghoul. Will it be looking for another body? And if it isn't, how can I find it?"

"It likes hanging out in graveyards, and since we only have the one in town, that should make it easier, I guess."

"Yeah. You're right. Then…I should go back tonight?"

"Are you up to it?" asked Nick.

"Yes, she is," said Erasmus.

Nick got in close to him, which was pretty brave considering how the demon mostly just scared him. "Is she allowed to speak for herself?"

"She is sitting right here," I reminded them. "And yes." I picked up the crossbow and rose. "I'm up to it."

Nick folded his arms, clearly at his wit's end with Erasmus. "Kylie, you don't have to go."

"Yeah, I kind of do. Check out the pentagram thing." I saluted with the crossbow, grabbed my coat this time, and went outside.

I shoved the crossbow into Erasmus' hands while I slipped on the heavy jacket.

"So now your *lover* knows about all this," he commented matter-of-factly.

I zipped up my jacket and snatched the crossbow back, then

dug out the beast-faced amulet from under my shirt and thrust it at him. He narrowed his eyes and scowled. "See this? You and me. This is our relationship. And the Booke. That's it."

The scowl deepened.

I stuffed his amulet back into my jacket and adjusted the collar before turning toward the street. Tendrils of mist curled around the silver-barked tree trunks of the woods across the way. With a steadying breath, I stepped onto the wet pavement.

"I sent you a message," he said. "Did you receive it?"

My heart lurched. That raven splatter, the message just for me, saying he was coming back...*to me*. His words were meant to cause that reaction. I gave him the satisfaction of turning toward him. "Yes. How...how did you manage to do it? I mean...that was weird magic, right? Weren't you mortally injured from the spell?"

His scowl turned to puzzlement. "I don't know how I managed it."

"Could have at least sent it in English."

"I was a little distracted at the time...with unimaginable pain."

He knew that would do it.

I stepped toward him. "I'm sorry. I'm sorry for all of it. In the end, it seemed like a waste of time and it could have killed you. I don't want you dead."

He gave me one of those heart-meltingly intense looks. I almost...*almost* leaned into him.

"Come on," I said instead, marching up the road.

CHAPTER FOUR

I KEPT AN eye out for the Draugr, looking over my shoulder about every five seconds. Erasmus sighed with impatience. "We don't have to walk, you know."

"Oh. I forgot about your particular mode of transportation. Do you want to…?"

He stepped forward. Without another word, he took my arm and stood with his face inches from mine. We locked eyes, and the sudden dark cold of teleportation took my breath away. When I blinked and looked past his shoulder, we were in the cemetery again.

But he hadn't let me go or stood back. He was still looking at me as if he wanted something. And I knew what that was. Why was it that when I was with Erasmus I wanted him, and when I was with Ed I wanted *him*? Could you juggle two men? Only if they agreed to it, I supposed.

"Erasmus…" I pleaded.

His fingers slowly uncurled from around my arms, and then his warmth was gone.

The sheriff and deputy were still there. I could see the flashing lights from Deputy George's Jeep as well as a few more cars. Maybe the coroner and some techs. We'd have to avoid them.

"I wonder if any other corpses are newly buried here. Maybe Dan Parker. But where would he be?"

"I can smell them, you know."

"Charming. Any more unique talents I should know about?"

A smirk lifted one corner of his mouth. "I daresay, you know some of them already."

"Erasmus."

"Sorry," he said without apology. He looked more animal than human as he raised his face and sniffed the air. And worse, he seemed to be enjoying it. Enjoying sniffing out a corpse. It was just one of many reminders that he wasn't human and that I shouldn't ever really let my guard down around him.

He pointed. "That way."

I followed him up a rise and under some wide-spreading oak boughs. I'm sure the cemetery was lovely during the day, all green lawns and shady trees. But at night it was dark, foggy, shadowed, and downright creepy.

I could hear vague voices of the techs and coroner on the wind, which made it hard to listen to other things, like Viking zombies and a ghoul. Whatever a ghoul sounded like.

Erasmus moved steadily ahead but stopped at the top of another rise. I came up beside him and followed his gaze. Something small and wiry was digging furiously at a grave. It reminded me a lot of Gollum from the *Lord of the Rings* stories. Only this was much worse.

Erasmus made sure we were upwind as we carefully approached. The ghoul was more than boney—effectively a skeleton with skin stretched over it, wearing only rags. It had wisps of hair that looked green in the moonlight. Its mouth was set in a grimace that revealed long, human-like teeth, like a skull would have. And it kept on snapping its jaws in irritation. Its eyes bulged out too, or at least looked that way staring out of deep, bruised sockets. It was digging hard, tossing dirt everywhere. Like a meth addict trying to get its next fix.

The crossbow was armed. I stopped and stood firmly on the uneven ground to get my balance. I raised the weapon to my shoulder, taking careful aim.

Just as I was about to pull the trigger, it looked up, alarmed. It's ping-pong ball-sized eyes focused on me as it drew back its thin lips and hissed, a skull grimace in full.

I pulled the trigger, but it was too late. The ghoul had already moved. The bolt pinged off a tombstone and disappeared in the shadows. I didn't worry since I knew it would magically appear back in the crossbow in an eye blink.

The ghoul fell forward and started running on all fours as it had done when it was disguised as Lexy.

I plunged down the hill, giving chase. Erasmus was beside me but soon pulled away, gaining on the ghoul with supernatural speed. He reached an arm out and nabbed the little creep. They tumbled on the turf, smacking against a tall, moss-covered obelisk.

I slowed as I came up to them. Erasmus was wrestling with it, trying to hold it still. "Any time, Kylie," he grunted.

"Oh." I swung the crossbow up, armed of course, and took aim. The thing was pretty pathetic-looking. It was whining and snapping its jaws and waving its thin skeleton arms. Its hair and skin tone *were* green, pale and sickly.

"Kylie!" Erasmus reminded me as he continued to struggle with it.

"Okay, okay." I took aim again. It just seemed unsavory to shoot it point-blank like that. My finger tapped above the trigger. It fed on corpses. Not nice, but not dangerous either. Just icky. But…I guess Jolene said it preyed on children, and I wasn't sure if that meant live children or only dead ones. Not that either was good…

"Dammit, Kylie!"

The crossbow had sagged in my grasp as I argued with myself, but I raised it again. I was about to squeeze the trigger with the full intention of dispatching the ghoul, when I was suddenly knocked aside.

I tumbled and rolled, losing the weapon even as a sharp pain wracked my shoulder. I caught a glimpse of a shadow swooping down and lots of white feathers.

Erasmus growled and crouched like an animal, glaring up into the sky. The ghoul saw his chance and ran, disappearing into the veiling fog.

I felt stupid. I should have just shot it. I would have to eventually anyway. But now my shoulder was screaming in pain, and Andras was circling me.

He hovered lower, wingbeats blasting me with cold air and throwing my hair back. "You see, Kylie Strange," he said from above me, "I can get to you anytime I like."

I pointed an accusing finger at him. "You're an asshole!"

He seemed taken aback by that. "A very crude era," he scoffed, raising his owl-like face like an aristocrat to a peasant.

Screw this guy. I lifted my hand, and when the crossbow slapped into it, I aimed and fired.

The bolt hit him square in the chest. His wingbeats faltered, and he slipped from the sky, landing hard on the lawn in front of me. Erasmus was on him instantly.

The growling and snarling sounded like a terrible dog-fight. White feathers scattered. The crossbow re-armed with another kind of bolt. I didn't hesitate. I aimed carefully and fired again.

It hit his neck and he cried out, throwing his head back. He squared on me again, his eyes becoming wide, glowing red embers. He snarled his sharp teeth at me as I fired again.

Andras stumbled back, releasing Erasmus. Erasmus jolted to his feet, barking, fingers curled into claws, nails grown to talons. He was a fierce beast, not the Erasmus I knew at all.

Andras' wings drooped behind him. He reached for the bolts at his chest, neck, side. Black blood oozed from the wounds. He was only weakened. I knew they wouldn't kill him.

He tugged at the bolts even as he clumsily unfurled his wings and slowly beat them to lift himself into the air. Erasmus lunged, but Andras kicked out with his taloned feet. Black gore spattered off his skin with each flap of his enormous wings.

He was so angry he could only spit and snarl at me. Maybe it wasn't the best course of action, getting the assassin sent just for you really angry. But darn it, he pissed me off!

He rose brokenly into the sky and soon zoomed from view.

Panting, Erasmus was back to normal. And he was smiling. "Well done, Kylie. He's afraid of you now. He thought he had an average simpering human to dispatch. But you are far from average." I had never been showered with so many compliments from him. He turned to me with bright eyes and a very human smile before he grabbed me.

The kiss was one of pride, but it morphed pretty quickly into lust and maybe something deeper. I grabbed a good handful of his hair and held him in place, taking what *I* wanted too. And how I wanted.

His hands slid around me, fingers kneading, slipping here and there, grasping handfuls of my bottom and bringing my hips in full contact with his. Oh yes, he clearly wanted me, too.

"Erasmus," I breathed into his voracious lips.

"Kylie," he purred, mistaking the reason why I whispered his name.

"No, Erasmus…" I didn't want to stop. I really didn't. But I pushed him back, pushed hard at his chest. "Erasmus…no."

His burning eyes simmered. "No…as in 'no'?" He still held me but with more space between us now, not every inch of us touching.

"The time and place is just not…" I slid my gaze toward the flashing police lights in the distance, the tombs and gravestones. Somewhere in the cemetery, a ghoul was looking for lunch. At least, I hoped it was in the cemetery. What if it was out there looking for some new kid to munch on? Yeah, I screwed that up. I wouldn't make the same mistake twice.

Erasmus looked toward the flashing lights too and seemed to read the rest of my thoughts. He licked the kiss from his lips and let me go. His expression had cooled. There was even a little bit of blame in his eyes, which I felt keenly. Why hadn't I been stronger? Why did I always have this reaction whenever he was around?

"I'm sorry." I couldn't help but say it.

He ignored me. "Would you pursue Andras or the ghoul?"

"Um…ghoul."

Without another word or glance, he leapt forward and started running through the cemetery. It took me half a second to wake up and realize what he was doing, and then I was running too.

I saw a figure in silhouette up ahead near one of the crypts. I slowed and lifted the crossbow, taking a bead down the flight groove. When I got just a little closer, something felt wrong. For one, the crossbow hadn't armed itself. And for another…it just wasn't right.

The figure rose and turned toward me. A light gust of wind ruffled the shading trees. Moonlight peeked between the leaves just enough to illuminate that face.

"Ms. Strange?"

I whipped the crossbow behind my back. "Ruth? What… what are you doing here?"

CHAPTER FIVE

RUTH RUSSELL, MOODY Bog's own socialite, Founder descendent, and keeper of all things genteel and *noblesse oblige*, glared at me. Her pruney mouth frowned into a deep scowl. She was dressed as she always was—a conservative sweater/skirt combination, with a jacket thrown over in deference to the weather. A glint of jewelry peeked through the jacket.

"What am *I* doing here?" She merely glanced at the crypt. I looked, too. It said *RUSSELL* across the top in chiseled uppercase letters. Oh. Her husband. She had just placed some flowers in the oversized urn next to the crypt's locked gate. "What are *you* doing here?" she asked me in an accusatory tone.

"Me? Well, I…"

"Kylie!" called Erasmus from somewhere behind us. "It's over here."

"I-it is?"

"Yes," he said coming into view. "Your grandfather's grave."

I looked at him with such gratitude that he turned and stepped aside, slightly embarrassed. I could see the blush of his cheek, despite the falling light.

"Listen, Ruth, maybe you should get back to your car. Night's falling and…you just never know."

"*You're* here."

"But I've got Erasmus."

She looked his way and narrowed her eyes. "So you do." She knelt and picked up something—like a little pouch—before closing it up and stuffing it in her purse. But she was still staring at me, studying me. "For a moment, I thought I saw you... carrying something."

I kept the crossbow pressed to my back and skirted around toward Erasmus, sliding my feet to keep my back away from her prying eyes. "Flowers," I lied.

"Cemetery's almost closed. As you say, night is falling." She didn't make a move to leave the crypt. Just kept glaring at me.

"Well. I gotta go. I hope to see you some time. At the shop."

"I sincerely doubt that."

"I don't know. I think we may have a lot to talk about. Mutual ancestors and...such." I kept shuffling away from her.

"That isn't very likely, now is it?"

"I'm inviting you, Ruth. I think we really should talk."

She adjusted her purse's strap over her forearm and lifted her head. "Have a good evening. Be careful out here. The sheriff seems to have discovered some sort of trouble." She didn't so much as glance his way. But she dismissed me with a flick of her head and made her way toward the road that wound throughout the cemetery. Her car was parked there in the shadows.

I hurried through the hedges to meet up with Erasmus. "Thanks for that. That was quick thinking."

"Except that I truly *did* find your grandfather's grave." He gestured away from the path.

Curious now, I followed him. In a quiet spot near a tree, two tombstones stood side by side. I took out my phone and shined the flashlight on them. One said Josephine Hampton Strange and the other Robert Stephen Strange. My grandparents.

I glanced around. A secluded spot. Maybe that's what Grandpa wanted. Away from the hustle and bustle of crypts like Ruth's husband's. But I also realized that no one likely visited their graves. Ever. A spell had been cast on my grandpa's house to make everyone forget he ever existed, that the *Stranges* ever existed in Moody Bog. Even the local historians had conveniently left them out of the history of the town's Founders. I hadn't known—or hadn't remembered—that I'd spent my summers here as a child. But now that magic was fading. And that, too, was my fault. It seemed the more you mentioned the forgotten history to people, the more they remembered it. And maybe it wasn't such a good thing for people to know about me and my ancestors.

"Grandpa, I wish you could appear and give me a little help."

"I'm certain if he were to appear, his spirit would most likely be attached to his house."

We'd met his spirit, but then he'd gotten on the wrong side of Shabiri and she had sent him away. I hoped there was a way to get him back. That is, if he wanted to come back.

He'd given us a message right before he was forced to leave. *Village in danger. Door is opening.* I hadn't liked the sound of that.

"I'm glad you found this, Erasmus. It's good to know it's here."

"You needn't worry. No ghoul will disturb their graves. They've been too long dead." Harsh words but still reassuring. I had begun to worry about that. I didn't like the idea that my grandpa or grandma would suddenly appear on the streets to threaten me or anyone else.

"Also, it wouldn't go amiss to take some dirt from his grave. It can be useful for incantations."

"What? That's like desecration. I'm not going to do that!"

"Well, that's what that Russell woman was doing."

"Are you kidding me?"

"I don't 'kid.' I saw her. She had the pouch on the ground. She picked it up and put it in her purse."

"She did?" I looked back, but she was long gone.

"I suggest you do the same."

I didn't bother asking any more questions. I didn't have a convenient grave dirt pouch like Ruth, so I used one of the gloves in my pocket to scoop up some of the softened dirt from atop his grave. "Sorry, Grandpa," I whispered. When the glove looked more like a disembodied hand, I folded the top and put it back in my jacket.

"Is it worth pursuing the ghoul or have we lost it?"

He sniffed around and squinted into the dense fog. "It's gone. You'd be better off getting a good night's sleep."

It was probably just as well. The emotional ups and downs had been more exhausting than the running. Erasmus teleported me back to the shop, and we walked in together. Doc was pacing and explaining something to Nick, who was typing into his laptop. They both looked up when we came in.

"Well?" said Doc.

I shook my head. "It got away. And it was trying to eat Dan Parker."

"Good God."

"And Andras made another visit, too." I rubbed my sore shoulder and sank into one of the wing chairs, dropping the crossbow beside me. "Where are Seraphina and Jolene?"

"I sent Seraphina to take Jolene home. But Jolene left this note for you." He handed me a piece of paper.

Draugr can't be summoned.

"Huh. So…does that mean the Ordo *didn't* bring them?"

"It doesn't sound possible."

"And they aren't from the Booke. Then…where *did* they come from?" Someone thrust a hot mug of tea at me. "Thank y—"

Erasmus was trying to look cool and relaxed while also trying not to sneeze.

"Did *you* make this?"

"Yes."

I looked into the mug. He had tossed perhaps a handful of loose tea into a mug of hot water. It would be mud and full of tea leaves. I drank a gulp of it anyway, trying to surreptitiously chew the tea leaves so that Erasmus wouldn't see. Boy, was he trying hard. "Thank you, Erasmus," I choked.

He shrugged and turned away, examining a tea cozy as if it were the Holy Grail.

When I looked up at Doc, he was giving me a very withering look. I sipped the mud tea nonchalantly, before finally setting it down. "And I also ran into Ruth Russell in the cemetery."

"This late?"

"Yeah. She was collecting grave dirt from her family mausoleum."

Nick sprang from his chair. "What?"

I reached into my pocket and pulled out the glove, laying it carefully on the side table. "And I got some of my own. From my grandfather's grave. Erasmus thought it might be useful."

Nick picked it up delicately between two fingers and made a face. "This is a little gross."

"But can it be used for spells and stuff?"

"Yeah," he said. "Pretty powerful ones. And you say Ruth-Stick-Up-Her-Butt-Russell was doing it too?"

"Now, Nick," admonished Doc.

"Sorry, but it's true. If she was doing that, then she knows just a little more about Wicca than she's willing to admit."

"That's what I was thinking. Looks like I'm going to have to grill my dear cousin on what she might know."

Doc rubbed his chin. "Kylie, I wouldn't go doing that just yet. We don't know what Ruth might be up to. It could very well have been *her* who put that pentagram in the church."

"Or ritually murdered Dan Parker," said Nick with a little too much relish.

I was surprised when Doc didn't deny it. "We'll just have to see," was all he said.

Crap. Who knew little ole Moody Bog would turn out to be such a D&D session?

I sighed and pulled out my phone. I didn't know if Ed was done with the crime scene, but I supposed I'd have to tell him about Dan Parker's grave, too.

"Kylie," he said in a clipped voice.

SHADOWS IN THE MIST

"Hi, Ed. Um…I was just at the cemetery—"

"Just now?"

"Yeah. We went back looking for the…the thing, the ghoul. Looks like it goes for any recent burial, so you might want to take a look at Dan Parker's grave too."

"Damn."

"Yeah. And speaking of which, his murder. It was no ordinary murder. Someone did it for a ritual. You might want to readjust your investigation accordingly."

"You mean like my brother?"

"Maybe."

He sighed over the line. "Looks like I have to readjust a lot of things."

"I'm really sorry."

"Look, Kylie. Maybe…" His voice got quieter. I could picture him walking farther from the techs and putting his hand over the phone. "Maybe we've been moving too fast, you and I. Maybe we should take a break. Just till it all blows over."

I was momentarily speechless. A tightness suddenly clutched at my chest. "I see," I finally managed.

"It's been a lot to take in."

"You don't have to explain."

"I feel like I do."

"You don't."

"I mean that Erasmus guy…"

"Is that really what this is about?"

He paused. I could hear him breathing. "I don't know. Maybe. I'm not as modern as I thought I was. I'm not much interested in sharing my girlfriend."

"Why does it have to be so…so…"

"For me, it just does." He sighed. "I need to think about things."

I gripped the phone hard. "Fine. When you have more info, give us a call." I clicked it off, cutting off his, "Kylie."

Not entirely unexpected. But it still hurt. Like Jeff-running-around-with-other-women hurt. But maybe I was doing the same thing. I somehow felt that I'd failed Ed and myself. It made me want to kick something. Or shoot something with my crossbow.

It was Nick who asked, "Is he coming over now?"

"Sounds like he's too busy." I clutched the phone, turning it face down on my thigh.

"Kylie has dealt with enough tonight. It's best you all go home."

All three of us looked at Erasmus with surprise. He stood in the kitchen doorway with the harsh light behind him. His duster clung to his legs, and his expression was grim—as usual.

"Mr. Dark," said Doc. "Do you plan on staying here?"

"I'm guarding the book."

"Kylie doesn't need you to guard the book."

He stepped into the shop's main room and stood over me. "I'm also guarding her."

After a long, tense moment…Doc patted Nick on the shoulder. "All right, then. Good night, you two."

Nick's head was ready to spin off as it wrenched between Erasmus and Doc. "You're not just going to leave him here, are you?"

"That's what I'm doing. Let's go, Nick."

"Doc!"

"Nick," I said. "Good night. I'll be fine."

Nick threw his hands up and stalked out the door that Doc was holding open. I could hear the crunch of gravel as they both got into their respective cars. Soon, two sets of headlights were sweeping over my windows and then disappearing down Lyndon Road.

Everything suddenly fell quiet.

A low growl sounded—one that wasn't coming from Erasmus. I spun, ready to grab anything I could use as a weapon.

Jeff rose out of the shadows in the corner. "I guess everyone forgot again about old werewolf Jeff."

I took a calming breath. "Doc should have—"

"Doc's got a lot on his mind," he said, walking past me with tensed muscles. He stood in front of Erasmus. "I've got your number, dude."

"My number?"

"Yeah. I see the moves. I get what you're doing. From a guy's point of view and a…a creature's. I speak demon now, apparently."

Erasmus narrowed his eyes and raised his chin slightly. "Whatever are you talking about?"

Jeff forked his fingers and jabbed from near his own eyes to point them toward Erasmus. "I'm watching you," he growled.

"Jeff," I said. "Don't wolf out."

"Not wolfing. Just…watching."

He kept his eyes on Erasmus even as he tugged the front door open. *Watching*, he mouthed, nodding. He slipped through the door onto the wet street. His clothes suddenly shed from him as he morphed into a blond wolf; arms shortening, ears pointing, snout elongating. He fell forward onto his paws and glared back at me through the window, eyes glowing yellow. He threw back his head and howled, a long lonely sound, before giving one last nod and taking off up the street, loping toward my grandpa's. I watched him until the tip of his tail disappeared from view.

CHAPTER SIX

I CLOSED THE curtains and turned. Erasmus and I were finally alone.

He strode to the door and threw the bolt. He'd certainly seen me do it enough times. Which was why he checked outside and drew the curtains on the other windows as well. Then he moved to stand before the fireplace, watching the flames.

"Don't pay any attention to Jeff," I said, even as I felt sorry for my ex. His new life couldn't be any easier than mine.

"I have no intention of paying him the least bit of attention."

The fire crackled and the beams of the house settled. The wind kicked up a bit outside, tossing leaves against the walls, but it was otherwise still in the room, and quiet.

"This is cozy," I said finally. My ears still prickled, listening for the dragging of feet and clanking of armor from our new zombie friends.

"It's nothing of the kind. I'm here protecting you. You should…you should go off to bed."

"And what will you do?"

His eyes were too shadowed to discern any intent. "Stay here…and guard."

Even though I was hurt that Ed was giving us "a break" when we'd only just started, it was hard to blame him when I couldn't help but give Erasmus smoldering looks.

I swallowed. Ed wanted a break. Fair enough. "You don't have to stay down here."

"I promise I will not disturb you."

"But you do. You know you do."

"I…don't know what you…"

Looking at him steadily, I walked forward and took his hand. It was warm and dry. "Come upstairs."

"What about…your constable?"

"I think *that* is something we both don't have to worry about for now."

He took a deep breath and expelled it. "You want me." It was a growl. It seemed a bit triumphant.

"I thought that would be obvious."

He let me lead him up the stairs by the hand and to my room.

I could tell he was looking around for any dangers first before he turned to me. "I will protect you," he whispered.

I smiled my wickedest smile. "But who's going to protect *you?*"

He frowned at first, and then his lips changed to a lop-sided grin. "I see."

"You will."

He reached for me, but I got to him first, peeling that ever-present duster over his shoulders. He sloughed it off, and it slid down his arms, pooling on the floor.

Was I doing this? My last date with Ed was barely cold, barely a memory. His breaking it off had hurt, no matter how temporary or permanent. Yet I still wasn't stopping.

"What is it about you?" I said, shaking my head and unbuttoning his shirt.

He watched me do it before lifting his eyes. "I assure you, I am applying no 'demon hoodoo,' as you put it."

"Are you sure?" I slid his open shirt down over his arms, which bulged with clenching muscles. I couldn't help but touch

63

them, easing my fingers over their contours. The shirt fell away, and there was that toned torso again, furred at the chest. A line of dark hair traced the pattern of the tattoo that speared down the center of his frame, a tattoo that marked him as an Eater of Souls. Chosen Host souls. *My* soul.

I dug my fingers into the dark hair and touched the tattoo. It must have been sensitive, because he grabbed my hand and gently redirected it. Then he cupped my face and brought me closer to kiss.

His lips were soft but hot, and his mouth tasted like embers. It might sound strange, but it was soothing and warm and sweet-tasting. Like hot spices. Like nothing of this earth.

He held my face and kissed me deeply, turning his head slightly to taste a different part of my mouth, my lips. I ran my hands down his neck, down his arms, under his ribcage. I could feel his heat and smelled the smoke. He was smoldering again. When I felt my own clothes fall away, I realized that he had reduced them to ash. Dusky pieces drifted to the floor at my feet.

"I liked that sweater," I whispered against his lips.

"I'll find you another." His hands moved past my jaw and tangled in my hair, lifting it from my neck and grasping it in his fingers. Using it to steady my head and hold my mouth where he wanted me. I pressed against him since there was nothing between us. His own trousers seemed to have burned away as well and I could feel his hardness digging into my thigh.

"Are you certain," he said between kisses, "that *you* are not using human 'hoodoo' on *me*?"

"I'm not magic."

"The hell you aren't." His mouth stopped all conversation, working over my lips with deep intent. He pulled me downward and I was surprised when we hit the bed. He didn't bother throwing back the comforter. He moved over me, arms encircling my bare skin, and lips moving over my neck.

This, my mind said. *This.* I don't really know what it meant, only that I didn't need to think, didn't want to. I suddenly grabbed *his* hair and yanked his head toward me. I looked him in the eye before I pulled his neck down to *my* mouth, took his skin between *my* teeth, and bit down.

When I drew back, he had a weird look on his face that then turned dreamy. I pushed at him hard. Startled by my aggression, he seemed puzzled when he suddenly found himself beneath me. He tried to rise but I shoved him back down. He tried to rise a second time until I got on top of him and…settled in.

His mouth fell open and his eyes rolled back. But it wasn't long till he got the hang of it, and those kneading hands found my hips before sliding up to my breasts. I threw my head back, letting him touch me, letting him look at me. His face, usually so guarded and so stiff, was finally open and full of abandon. He seemed to thrill to his new-found freedom, and his hands fell to my waist and clutched tighter, enjoying *us* together, raising his hips into me.

With both of us writhing, I didn't think it would last long. His urgent movements matched my own. One hand tightened on my hip, the other snaked between us. I felt him surge within me, my own arousal rising to meet his, especially with what his hands were doing. He growled, breathing harshly through clenched teeth when he reached his peak. I reached mine a little after, eyes closing as I let it wash over me in trembling waves… with the scent of smoke in the room. I chuckled a little at the thought at how *literally* smokin' hot we were.

Pressing a hand to his chest to steady myself, I swept my damp hair out of my eyes.

He was looking at me with some surprise.

"What's the matter?" I took in my fill of his handsome features sheened with sweat. "No woman has ever taken charge of you before?"

He shook his head slightly, and I grinned. Rolling off of his chest, I lay beside him, letting the sweat cool on my skin. "Welcome to the twenty-first century."

"It's certainly an interesting century, I'll admit."

The room was cold, and I nudged him to move so that I could get under the covers. He complied sluggishly and after a moment of hesitation got under them with me. He had turned his head to look at me—perhaps to see if he needed permission—and didn't seem to have any intention of turning away. "I would have thought that you and your constable..."

"Do you really want to talk about Ed right now?" I'd pushed Ed from my mind completely. I might have felt a twinge of guilt about him, but it quickly disappeared. We still weren't exclusive. Especially with a break.

"Hmm. I find that I don't."

Facing him on the pillow, I could run my hands through his chest hair. This time, he made no move to stop me, even when I brushed against that damned tattoo. I studied his features in the strands of moonlight that wisped through the curtains. It seemed like he was looking at me for cues as to what to do next. Maybe Mr. Demon Lover wasn't as experienced as he let on.

"You've been alive a long time, haven't you?"

"As I have said before." His voice was deep and resonant, eyes lidded. "Eons and eons."

"And you've been with...human women."

He raised an inquiring brow. "Not as many as your imagination is concluding." He pressed a finger delicately to my forehead. "I can see it in your eyes."

I pushed the finger away. "You had me believe—"

"You are easy to bait."

"Oh, thanks."

"It seems that in earlier centuries, both men and women were too afraid and cautious of demons. There were only a few encounters with each of your species."

"*Men* and women?"

"Of course."

I mulled that over. My hand stopped stroking. "They were afraid of you. Too afraid to—" I gestured stupidly.

"I have encountered many different belief systems. It is only this century where they seem…scattered."

"*I* don't have a belief system."

He nodded. "My point. And that, too, is intriguing."

I turned to lay on my back. "To tell you the truth, I just don't know what to believe." A sudden thought made me shift uncomfortably. "If there's a Hell, is there also a Heaven?"

"I haven't the least idea."

"But there are souls."

"Believe me when I tell you, Kylie, that I do not know."

He wore that sincere expression again, and I did believe him. So much so that I leaned over and kissed him. He blinked, confused.

"You're staying, aren't you?" I scooted closer till I could have been in his arms if he merely moved his hands. "You don't have to leave, you know."

I decided not to wait for an answer. I snuggled down into the hollow of his shoulder and finally felt his arms slide around me, yanking me toward his warm, naked body. He said nothing as he held me. I soon drifted off and began to dream, but thank God not about ghouls or zombies.

I woke once in the middle of the night to someone nibbling gently on my neck. A hand did some exploring, and when I rolled to my back, male lips joined the roving hands. Entwined, we coupled again, slower this time, with words whispered in a language I didn't recognize and gentle kisses peppered over my body.

When I awoke in the morning, spread out on the mattress as I was wont to do, he was still there beside me, sitting up and looking at me. I stretched. "Good morning."

"Good morning," he said tentatively.

"You have a funny look on your face. Haven't you ever spent the night with your human conquests before?"

"No."

His stark answer made that languid feeling slip away. "Oh? You've never slept all night with anyone?"

"I don't sleep."

"I didn't mean that… Wait. You mean you don't ever sleep? At all?"

"No."

"Then what did you do all night?"

"Listened to your breathing. Sensed your dreams. Replayed in my mind our encounters with the Draugr and the ghoul. Speculated as to where Andras might strike next. Counted your eyelashes."

"All night?"

"Yes. Well…except for a certain interval…"

I smiled. "How many eyelashes?"

"Five hundred and fifty-three."

I gently raised my hand to his face, stroking his cheek. His beard stubble never grew any longer and was never shaved. "What must it be like to be a demon?" I said softly, almost more to myself than to him. "To never sleep, never eat. No past…and no future."

He shook his head, frowning. "It is what it is. I was created for a purpose, and I fulfill it."

"Except that you're undermining it."

He cocked his head. "How so?"

"Well." I toyed with the comforter, not looking at him. "You *said* you weren't going to eat my soul. And you're trying to help us find a way to stop the Booke once and for all."

"I never said I would do the latter."

It was my turn to sit up. I grasped the covers to my chest. "Yes, you did. You said you'd help me to close the Booke for good."

"I think you are mistaken."

"Erasmus, we have to! We can't keep letting it ruin other people's lives."

"May I remind you that if the book is no more, then so shall I be."

A sharp sting in my heart made me take a breath and push my hair behind my ears. "I said I'd find a way around that. I don't want you to not exist."

"How very thoughtful."

"I mean it." I clasped his hand. His fingers entwined with mine for only a moment before slipping away.

He looked taken aback. "Why should you care?" he said quietly.

"I just do, okay? I mean…" I huffed an exasperated sigh. "You get under my skin."

Tentatively, he took my hand back, examined it, turned it over. "Yes, an apt description. I believe you have 'gotten under my skin' as well."

"I bet you say that to all the Chosen Hosts."

He looked at me with the sincerest expression I think he'd ever worn. "No, I don't."

I carefully took my hand back and glanced at the clock. "I have to get up. Get washed and dressed…and stuff. You, uh, do whatever it is you do in the morning."

I slipped out from under the covers and shivered as I grabbed my robe at the end of the bed. He watched me curiously as I tied the belt around my waist and made my way to the bathroom.

I leaned against the bathroom door after I closed it, my heart pounding. And here I thought that *he* might be taking advantage of *me*. It was clearly the other way around. He was the innocent. After all, he was only conscious when the Booke was open and causing destruction. He hadn't really time to form an opinion for himself on anything, let alone humanity. No wonder he was so screwed up.

I suddenly felt very bad for him. And for his strange life. He didn't want to die any more than I did. But if the Booke was gone, he'd be gone, too.

I took my thoughts with me into the shower, and when I got out wrapped in a towel, Erasmus was no longer in the bed or the room. I got dressed and hurried downstairs. The coffee was brewing in the drip, and he had turned the lights on in the shop. I took a moment to look around. It was all still here. My shop. Its overstuffed wing chairs, the tables with displays and urns for tea samples, the shelves with teapots and accessories, the antique buffet with its drawers of herbs. Everything was in its place, except for what he'd sold yesterday. And when I did a quick inventory, it seemed that he *had* sold a lot. He hadn't made any receipts, so I'd had to extrapolate from what was missing, but it turned out he was quite the persuasive salesman.

I found him in the pantry, dressed in his usual dark shirt and trousers again with that long, black leather duster. He had a cracker in his hand, of all things. He hadn't noticed me, and I quickly hid behind the door to watch him. What in the world was he doing?

He lifted the saltine to his nose to sniff it, then grimaced in disgust. Carefully, he opened his mouth, crunched down, and slowly chewed, eyes drawing down to slits. All of sudden, he heaved and spit cracker spatter into his palm. He stuck out his tongue and wiped it with his hand.

He was trying to eat solid food. For me. To save *me*.

I turned away, overcome with emotion, and squeezed my eyes shut. The tears came anyway, so I balled my hands into fists and pressed my nails harshly into the fleshy parts of my palms.

"What are you doing there?" he said, eyes narrowing.

I wiped hastily at my eyes and turned to face him, plastering on a smile. "Nothing. What are you doing?"

He hid something behind his back. "Nothing."

I smiled secretly as I exited the kitchen for the shop. *You can't fool me, Erasmus Dark, you old softy.*

* * *

I BEGAN MY day counting out the till and showing Erasmus how to use the tablet register, though he didn't seem to be absorbing the information. He kept sneaking looks at me. "Erasmus, if you're going to help, you have to use the register."

"I don't see why. It seems unnecessary."

"It isn't. There's tax to collect and inventory to maintain."

"I don't like your machine."

"Well…how about this?" I opened a drawer and pulled out an old school receipt book. "If you sell something, you write it down here. The item, the quantity, the number on the tag, and then the price. Can you do that?"

He took the receipt book and looked it over. "I suppose."

"You know, you seem good at this. Are you really not using magic on people?"

"I am naturally beguiling."

"Oh, really?"

"Yes. Haven't you noticed?" He grinned slyly.

I ignored it. "Maybe you could mind the store, then, while I see if I can't get Ruth Russell to come over here. It's time we get into her head."

"What? If you think you can order me around just because we—"

"I'm not ordering you around. I'm just asking for a favor."

"I should go with you."

"Why?"

"Because I don't trust her."

He had a point. But I hated to keep closing the shop.

The door opened, and the bell above it jangled.

"Jeff." I greeted him with a genuine smile. "What are you doing here?"

He glared at Erasmus. His eyes didn't wolf out, but it seemed like they wanted to. "Thought I'd let you know how it's going at your grandpa's place. See if you needed any…help."

"You're just in time, then. Erasmus and I have to leave. Could you watch the shop?" I grabbed my coat from the hall tree and jammed my arm in the sleeve.

"Wait. You're taking off? With *him*?"

"Yes," said Erasmus in his oiliest voice. "As you know, I stayed here *all* night."

"Enough, you two." I sensed Jeff was just barely holding on to his humanity. Yup, his ears were getting pointy. "Jeff. Ears."

He snarled, but the wolf ears began to recede.

"It would be a great favor."

"Okay, Kylie. But only because I owe you."

Erasmus let me go through the door first, but I turned just in time to catch him give Jeff the same forked-finger *I'm watching you* treatment that Jeff had given him the night before.

"Must you?" I asked wearily when we were outside.

"I haven't the least idea what you're talking about." He scanned the skies and took my arm.

"No! We have to go by car."

"Why?"

"Because it's a bit far to walk, and she'll get suspicious if we show up on a stroll in the middle of the work day."

He muttered something unintelligible and turned toward the Jeep.

CHAPTER SEVEN

I PARKED THE Jeep in front of Ruth's sprawling house with its perfectly manicured lawn and blazing gold trees in full fall raiment. We walked up the flagstone pathway and stood on the porch. Before I rang the bell, I elbowed Erasmus, pointed to the door mat, and toed it aside. A mandala done in glass tiles lay beneath it. The design was one that Nick had showed me online. It was supposedly for protection from evil.

He nodded sagely while he waited beside me, hands clasped behind his back.

I rang the bell. It wasn't long till Stella, Ruth's maid/housekeeper/ majordomo, answered the door. "Is Mrs. Russell expecting you?"

Never in a million years. "Not really. I hoped to catch her at home."

Stella paused to think. Last visit she had me wait on the porch. This time she thought better of it and let us in. She eyed Erasmus with a sultry blink of her lashes.

Did he have that effect on everyone? Why was I suddenly noticing it now?

Erasmus did a ballet of skirting the mandala, edging against the wall and leaping over it to land on the threshold. If Stella noticed she didn't say anything.

We waited in the warm foyer beside a table adorned with an enormous spray of harvest flowers, wheat sprigs, and tiny pumpkins. I noticed we hadn't been allowed into the living room.

I glanced at Erasmus. He was as calm as could be, even as he surreptitiously sniffed the air. Looking for other demons and black magic perhaps?

Ruth came down the stairs at a good clip for a mature woman. Her skinny legs were again exposed under a knee-length skirt and sweater ensemble. "Why, Kylie. And…friend." She looked Erasmus up and down.

"Sorry, this is my, um, old friend, Erasmus Dark," I said, coughing a bit to hide his name. "He was with me at the cemetery…"

She didn't put her hand out to shake, and neither did he. They simply stared at one another.

"Well," she said at last. "What an unexpected surprise. Won't you come in?"

"Actually, we were just passing by and I told Erasmus—didn't I say, Erasmus?—that we should call on Ruth and invite her over for—"

"Dinner," he said.

"Dinner?" I whispered out of the side of my mouth.

He glanced down his nose at me.

I turned a smile on Ruth. "Dinner."

"What a lovely idea," she said, though the expression on her face said otherwise.

"Tonight," he said, looking at her intensely now.

She didn't seem to be affected by the old demon charm. But she nodded in a *let's get this over with* sort of way.

"Very well. Tonight then. About what time?" She was already escorting us to the exit.

I didn't dare glance at Erasmus. "Shall we say seven?"

"Seven it is." She opened the door.

What's your hurry?

"See you later, Ruth." I grabbed Erasmus' arm and hustled him out. The door couldn't seem to close fast enough.

"Shoot. I didn't think she'd actually agree," I muttered as we walked down the path to the car. "Now I'll have to cook something. Hey, should we invite the rest of the coven? I think that might be a good idea. That way they can really gauge her, see if she's hiding something."

"You seem to already have decided."

"I don't suppose you cook."

"Since I don't eat, there is very little need for me to cook."

"Souls are best served raw, huh?"

He scowled. Okay, so that wasn't in the best of taste, having your food talk back to you. It was only a little gallows humor to cut the tension.

"You know," I told him as we got into the car, "she has a portrait of Constance Howland in her bedroom."

He stopped pulling the seat belt over him. "She does?"

"Yeah. And she's always changing the subject or interrupting whenever old Constance is mentioned." Constance was the last Chosen Host before me…in 1720. She was an ancestor of Ruth's—and also of mine, as it happens. Constance Howland's well-documented court case for witchcraft wasn't spoken about among Moody Bog's elite. Until I came blundering in, that is. If Ruth was so ashamed of Constance, why keep a portrait of her in her bedroom?

I turned to Erasmus. "Tell me about her." I wasn't going to take any evasions from him anymore. He was as bad as Ruth. At least now I was pretty sure he hadn't been lovers with Constance, which made me feel marginally better. It was not the done thing in the eighteenth century for a decent maiden fully churched to carry on with a demon. Or so I imagined.

Erasmus stared out the windshield at the perfect fall day. It was as if the stagehands had gotten the cue to distribute just the right amount of spinning fall leaves into the air, with a deep blue sky and bright clouds in the distance.

"She was like you in many respects," he said quietly, carefully. "Fierce. Strong. But she never entirely put her trust in me." He glanced my way. "Which was, all things considered, what one would expect. She worked alone. She insisted that I *not* help her. Her religious instincts forbade her from working *with* me, you see. It could have gone better for her if she had. She might have lived longer."

His monologue cut off when he seemed to realize what he said. He frowned. "I did *try* to help her."

"But you chased her off a cliff." It was on the old engraving that had started me on this journey. The one Karl Waters had in his museum. The one Ruth Russell refused to acknowledge.

"I did not."

"But you did." My voice was unsteady. Unlike Constance Howland, I kept forgetting who he really was. "You said you did."

"I *said* that I was there on Falcon's Point when she died. I was trying to help her. She insisted on running away from me."

"So, are you saying it was an accident?"

"No. It was suicide. She knew that this would close and seal the book. What she didn't realize was that its closure was only temporary…until you came along."

"Sh-she killed herself."

"Yes."

"Did they *all* kill themselves?"

His mouth curled into a snarl. "Some of them. Those that the creatures didn't get to first."

My heart suddenly squeezed tight. "Those that didn't…did *you* kill them?"

He looked out the window for a long time. I could tell he didn't want to say. But he seemed to screw up his courage to face me. "Yes."

I sucked in a breath. I didn't…I mean I really hadn't…

It was a long time till I was able to speak. "Thank you, at last, for your honesty," I said hoarsely. Facing forward, I rested my hands on the steering wheel, swallowing down the sour taste in the back of my throat. My stomach clenched. I wished I hadn't asked, didn't know.

"You fear me again. I can smell it."

"Of course, I do. I keep forgetting who and what you are."

"It doesn't change the fact that I have no intention of hurting *you*."

"But don't the Powers That Be expect it?"

He said nothing to that, just stared out the windshield again. And I found myself unaccountably feeling sorry for *him*. After all, this was his job. This was literally what he was created for. And now, suddenly, after centuries of having it work as it was supposed to, he had begun to question it. He was just as much a pawn as I was. Doomed to play out the same scenario like some hellish Groundhog Day, over and over again.

I couldn't bring myself to comfort him, so I started up the car instead.

Pulling off of Mill Pond Road, I meandered slowly through Moody Bog's better neighborhood, filled with mini-mansions and wide lawns. A thin dog, like a greyhound, was loping along the grass, leaping over hedges and trailing something—maybe laundry—over its neck and back. Except when I looked closer, I realized it wasn't a dog at all. My throat thickened, but I managed to croak, "Ghoul!"

Erasmus suddenly vanished beside me, and here I was with no crossbow. I rolled down the window and waved my hand around, but it just wouldn't come. I pulled over, scrambled out of the car, and went to the trunk. I grabbed a tire iron from my spare and took off after them.

I couldn't believe it. Here the ghoul was, just running around in the bright light of day. Then my heart panged. Where was the school? All those kids! They were all sitting ducks in the daytime. Is that where it was going?

Erasmus was catching up to it, which a good thing because I was getting winded. He managed to corner the little bastard at a rock wall. The ghoul could certainly leap over it if it wanted to. What was its game?

I got to them and raised the tire iron. It cowered away from Erasmus and then turned its bulging eyes pathetically toward me. What was I going to do, after all? Beat it to death? Maybe one good whack… But I knew I couldn't.

The hairs on the back of my neck prickled. When I spun, I caught a flash of skin suit and white wings and leapt out of the way, landing hard on the grass.

Andras swooped and banked and then, like a bird of prey, was on me again. I swung the iron and made contact. He screamed and grabbed his hip. He banked again but sloppily this time, yet it didn't seem to discourage him. He dove.

I swung and missed, and then *I* screamed as talons sank into both shoulders and lifted me off the ground.

The iron dropped from my hand, but I whipped around as hard as I could, no matter how much it hurt, trying to dislodge him. It was agonizing, but I couldn't let him carry me off or drop me if he got any higher.

Hands grabbed my feet and yanked. The talons dug deeper, and I gritted my teeth over my scream. I knew it was Erasmus trying to pull me from his grasp. I beat the clawed feet and scratched them for all I was worth.

Our combined weight must have been too much for him. The toes loosened, and I was suddenly tumbling toward the earth. Chosen Host skills reared up at the last minute, and instead of taking a noser and breaking my spine, I somehow flipped and gracefully touched down on my feet, my legs like springs.

I stood, wobbling for a moment before my legs gave out and I landed on my backside. Erasmus knelt and scooped me up.

"Kylie! Are you all right?"

"I…I think so." I groaned as I touched my tender shoulders. There was blood on my coat. My blood. "I guess I'm bleeding a little."

Scanning the skies, I sat there, recovering and relieved. Andras was gone. But so was the ghoul.

"That's the second time Andras screwed up my chance to get the ghoul." I didn't bother mentioning that I had no intention of smacking the little scrapper with a tire iron. I don't know why, but the crossbow seemed more…impersonal.

"I wish I had my crossbow," I said.

"It's *my* crossbow, and you're out of range."

"That's what I figured." I looked around the quiet cul-de-sac. No alarms. No one coming out of their house to ask questions. We were surrounded by lots of sheltering trees. I could only hope that they had blocked our aerobatics.

Erasmus gave me a hand up to steady myself. But then he didn't let me go, giving me one of those intense glares.

"I can't help what I am," he insisted.

Apparently, he wasn't letting go of our discussion in the car. I tried to keep all emotion from my face. "And I can't help what *I* am."

"Dammit, Kylie. I never imagined there would be a Chosen Host like…like you."

What could I say to that? "Yeah, well. We're all dealing with life's little surprises, aren't we."

I turned away, but he grabbed me again, drawing me to him and planting one on my lips. I was unresponsive. At least…I feigned disinterest.

He pulled back and studied my face. After a moment he let me go and scowled. He stalked sourly toward the Jeep, yanked open the passenger door, and sat sulkily.

I hobbled to the car and sat gingerly, pulling the seatbelt oh-so-gently over my hurt shoulder. Sitting in the car, a strange feeling came over me. I felt anxious, as if I'd forgotten something, as if it were right on the tip of my tongue.

I was just about to turn to Erasmus to ask him when my phone rang.

"Hey…Ed."

Erasmus was immediately on alert. He sat up but tried to look casual and as if he weren't listening to every word.

"Kylie. I thought you'd want to know what we found out last night."

"Yeah, go ahead."

"Well, not much. I mean, it wasn't as if I could discuss it with George or the coroner. They concluded some animal had somehow dug up Lexy and Dan Parker's graves. Smelled the recently buried, I guess. Now, about Dan Parker…"

"We know it was a ritual. A very bad one. And we think it might have been the one that summoned Andras."

"The guy with the wings."

"That's the one."

"You said not to go off on my own without consulting you. So I'm consulting. Should I arrest Doug?"

I turned to Erasmus. "What do you think?"

"You're talking to that demon guy, aren't you," said Ed sourly.

"Yes, I am. And what difference does it make to you? We're on a break, aren't we?"

He made some grumbling noises.

Erasmus considered. "Your constable can certainly ask him about it, but I fear this is beyond their abilities, even if Shabiri helped them. But…I should ask Shabiri instead. She might have some insight, though I don't know if she will help."

"Did you get that?" I said to Ed over the phone.

"Yup," he said in that clipped tone that meant he was annoyed.

"But I still have my suspicions about Ruth Russell," I put in.

"What? Kylie, that's ridiculous."

"No, it isn't. And by the way, she's coming over for dinner tonight. I think you should be there." I rubbed at my shoulder, wondering what in the world I could cook under these new circumstances.

"Ruth is coming over for dinner…at *your* place? How'd you manage that?"

"I just asked her. Doesn't that seem suspicious in and of itself, her agreeing and all?"

"I…it's…what?"

I stared at the phone in frustration.

"Kylie, I think you're making too much of this. Maybe she's just trying to get over you breaking into her house—"

"I didn't break into her—" I calmed myself and said more quietly, "Ed, just be there tonight, okay? Please?"

I could hear the surrender in his voice. "Okay. Does that Erasmus guy have to be there?"

Erasmus leaned over and spoke loudly into the phone. "I wouldn't miss it for the world!"

"Everyone's going to be there. Seven o'clock. Bye, Ed."

Erasmus had a wide smile on his face.

"This isn't funny," I muttered, starting the engine.

CHAPTER EIGHT

WHEN I TOLD Doc about the dinner, he suggested I invite Reverend Howard Cleveland from the First Congregational Church of Moody Bog—the little white clapboard church off the green. He thought Reverend Howard might be a tempering presence if Ruth got upset about the coven being there, and he wasn't wrong. At least Ruth liked Reverend Howard, who thankfully was delighted to accept my invitation.

Jeff had puttered about the shop all day, quiet and sullen. I didn't know how to comfort him, so I thought it best to simply leave him on his own. Jolene arrived at her usual time, throwing occasional curious glances at Jeff, perhaps wondering if he was going to shift. I wondered about that too. Seraphina had made him a wolfsbane potion to keep his wolfy tendencies under control, but it didn't look like it was working.

It was almost time for Ruth to show. I had decided to cook a New England pot roast dinner, because it could cook by itself for several hours and feed a roomful of people. I had hoped that the comfort food would cause Ruth to slip up and say something useful…or incriminating. And the meat was soft, which was good; my shoulders wouldn't have to work too hard chopping and slicing. Even after Erasmus helped me bandage them and declared that I would recover, they still felt sore. Who knew Chosen Hosting would involve so many scars?

There was an awkward moment when Ed arrived. He did lean down and tentatively kiss me on the cheek, but then his face reddened, and he quickly escaped in the direction of Seraphina, who was serving cocktails.

She sidled over to me once Ed was chatting with Doc. "Looks like something is amiss between you two. Is he having a hard time adjusting to the truth behind Moody Bog?"

"You could say that. We're taking a break."

"Oh dear. I was afraid of that. Maybe I should talk to him."

"No! I mean…" I glanced at Ed, who was shooting his own surreptitious glances at me. "I think he's got to work it out."

"Well, that may be. But might it have more to do with the presence of…" She nodded toward Erasmus, who was standing in front of the fire, brooding.

A regretful pang jarred my chest. "That's probably got a little to do with it, but I'm a free agent, Seraphina. I never told him we were exclusive."

She sipped her white wine, dark purple lipstick staining the glass. "Here in Moody Bog, we're a little on the old-fashioned side. Very traditional." She laughed a little. "Coming from *me*, I know that's something!" She was dressed in her usual boho-chic garb, with layers of patterned chiffon over linen and velvet and four belts around her waist. Her eyes were made up with a smoky liner, and the usual panoply of African necklaces and bracelets adorned her limbs.

"I'm not *that* out there," I said morosely.

She put her arm around me. "You're not. But I suppose you're also fresh blood to this little community. I'm surprised more young men haven't come knocking on your door."

"What would I do with them?"

She raised a brow.

"You know what I mean. With all this other stuff going on."

"I know," she said softly. "I suppose, all things considered, Sheriff Ed is taking it well."

"We need him."

She gave me a particularly pertinent look. "Yes, *we* do."

I slurped my wine and was about to check on the pot roast when a knock on the door stopped us all. Through the window, I saw Ruth standing on my porch, looking perturbed. I scrambled to the door and greeted her with a warm smile.

She glanced at the coven inside the shop with pruned lips. "I had no idea it was a dinner party with your…friends."

"It was a last-minute decision. Come in, Ruth. Would you like some wine?"

Doc made a beeline to take her fur-trimmed coat. "It's nice to see you, Ruth."

"Fred," she said to Doc. "You do keep some unusual company these days."

He laid her coat over his arm. "Well, I don't believe in stagnating, Ruth. I find it rather invigorating to make new friends and have new experiences."

"Yes, that sounds very *you*."

There was a second knock on the door.

Ruth seemed relieved. "Reverend Howard," she said.

"Ruth. Good to see you."

Erasmus was hovering, so Reverend Howard smiled and put out his hand. "I don't believe we've met. I'm Howard Cleveland. Please call me Howard. Are you one of Kylie's friends from out of town?"

Erasmus stared at his outstretched hand but didn't deign to take it. "Yes."

Reverend Howard waited for an introduction that was never going to come. I intervened and shoved Erasmus closer. "This is my old friend Erasmus Dark, from California."

"Erasmus Dark? That's quite a name, isn't it?"

"Do you get many people questioning the substance of *your* name, mundane as it is?"

"Erasmus!"

But Reverend Howard laughed, even as Erasmus turned away from him. "Well, he sure told me!"

"I do apologize for Erasmus. He's sort of…quirky."

"You don't have to apologize. People are so insidiously polite to me all the time it's rather refreshing getting the cold shoulder." Still chuckling, he excused himself to talk to Ed.

Besides on opening day for the store, I was hosting my first party, and I suddenly felt bad that it wasn't under better circumstances.

I felt a presence at my elbow and was surprised to see that it was Nick. "The fly is in the web," he said dramatically in my ear.

"True. Let's just observe for now, then spring a few traps. Carefully."

He nodded and crept away, like some cartoon detective.

I was beginning to wonder if inviting the coven was a good idea.

Reverend Howard sidled up to me once he'd gotten a chance to get away from Ruth. "I applaud your attempt at offering an olive branch."

"Let's just hope it doesn't blow up in my face."

"Ruth isn't really a bad sort. She wants good things for this village. And she gives generously."

"I'm trying to appeal to her better nature."

He smiled diplomatically and sipped his wine.

I glanced over toward Jolene, who was walking around with a tray of appetizers. When her tray was empty, she came up next to me. "I don't know why you thought this would be boring for me. I'm learning a *lot* by listening."

"There's a word for that, you know."

"But isn't that why you invited everyone?"

She had a point.

It wasn't long before I called everyone to the table. Erasmus, for propriety's sake, took a seat too. In fact, he was on one side of me with Ed on the other. It couldn't have been more awkward, except for Jolene grinning at me from across the table. I used passing the vegetables to Ed as an excuse to ignore her.

Ed leaned toward me. "I don't know that this was such a great idea."

"I have to know what she knows. And I'm hoping she'll break down if she's around people she's acquainted with."

"Well, Doc seems to be trying his best."

If I didn't know better, I'd think Doc was flirting with her. He was certainly turning on the charm. Of course, he'd known her the longest.

I was also glad Reverend Howard was there as moderator, if we needed one. And I had a feeling we might.

"Listen, Ed," I said quietly, "have you found out anything about Dan Parker from Doug? I assume you talked to him."

Unconsciously, he touched his left eye, and it was then that I noticed a little bruising under it. I assumed they'd had a very heated conversation. "Let's say I'm not entirely convinced he had anything to do with it."

"Then that *does* leave Ruth."

"You're getting ahead of yourself, Kylie," he said, cutting a chunk of meat with the side of his fork.

"But it has to be her. I don't know anyone else in town so intimately entwined with all this."

He chewed, made a yummy sound deep in his throat, and then swallowed. "Are you sure it wasn't that Shabiri person? I should probably talk to her."

"I mean it, Ed. Be very careful when dealing with her."

A shadow passed over me, but it was only Erasmus leaning in. "I'm curious as to all the whispering coming from this quarter."

"None of your business," Ed snarled.

Erasmus smiled as he dabbed his napkin into the corners of his mouth, even though he hadn't eaten anything. "Why, Constable Bradbury. That sounded suspiciously like jealousy."

I elbowed Erasmus hard. He coughed before he recovered. "Knock it off," I said out of the side of my mouth. "We're concentrating on Ruth, remember?"

I watched her. She ate as if each morsel were an exercise in patience, cutting her roast into miniscule pieces, sticking them with the tines of her fork, and slowly putting the fork between her teeth. Boy, did I ever want to spill hot gravy in her lap.

"More gravy, Ruth?" I asked, offering the sauceboat.

"No, thank you. It's delicious."

"Thank *you*."

"Yes, Kylie is a wonderful cook," said Ed, eating his food with relish.

"I'm certain she is," muttered Erasmus, looking down at his full plate forlornly. He pushed the food around but of course wouldn't touch it.

"Salt?" asked Reverend Howard, offering the cellar to Erasmus.

He shied back, scowling.

I reached across him to take it. "Erasmus is cutting down on salt," I said hastily. Salt was a good way to cage a demon. There was no way he could even touch it.

I sprinkled it over my own food and set the container down in front of Ed.

Something glinted at me under the chandelier light, and I looked up. Ruth's gold locket. When I thought about it, she seemed to wear that locket a lot. "That's a lovely locket, Ruth. Family heirloom?"

Her hand went to it immediately, protectively, just as mine did to the demon amulet around my own neck. The one I had snatched from Erasmus. "Yes. A very old family heirloom."

"A Founder's heirloom?" I asked as innocently as I could.

"Why yes. It belonged to my...to *our* mutual ancestor, as a matter of fact. Constance Howland."

Doc's cutlery clattered to his plate. He shook himself and picked them up. "Forgive me," he said. "I've...well, I've just never heard you voluntarily mention her name, Ruth."

She picked up her wine glass and twirled it a bit, until the red wine caught the light and sent shards of ruby across the table-cloth. "Yes, well. It seems the thing to do nowadays. What with Ms. Strange in town and all."

"I never realized before that my people were from Moody Bog," I said. "It was so long ago that I used to spend summers here. With my grandfather."

"Is that so?" said Reverend Howard, leaning on the table. "I'll be darned. Whereabouts was that? I know pretty much everyone in this village, and I would've thought I'd know your grandfather's name. Strange, I assume?"

"Yes. Apparently, they were Founders as well."

Reverend Howard blinked dumbly at me. "Is that right?" He scratched his head. "I...I can't seem to recall ever seeing that name..."

"It must have been some sort of conspiracy," I said with a forced laugh, "keeping our family name out of the archives. But I did some digging at the library, and sure enough, they were there."

Giving Ruth a surprised look, he turned back to me. "I'll be darned. Well! What a wonderful thing. Welcome back, Kylie."

He hiked his glass in a toast, and I raised mine in response.

Erasmus poured more wine in my glass when I set it down.

"So Ruth, what's inside the locket?" I asked then took a sip of wine.

"I don't know," she said, carefully encouraging a white potato slice onto her fork with her knife. "I've never been able to open it. Jewelers have tried but they were concerned with damaging it."

"Well, what a mystery," I said. "I'd be dying to know."

"Some of us have the patience and endurance not to worry over it."

I picked up the gravy boat again with a clenched hand, but Ed plucked it out of my fingers and set it aside. He frowned at me. I would have stuck my tongue out at him if we had been alone.

It was now my fondest desire to get that locket in my hands and pry it open. Because I was sure there was a powerful hex inside it. When I glanced at Doc, he was staring at her locket thoughtfully.

* * *

EVERYONE WAS ENJOYING the iced cherry cake I had made with their coffee in the main room. "It's so warm and homey in here," said Ruth, looking around. "I suppose if one *had* to have a shop, this would be a good one to have."

As backhanded a compliment as I had ever received. I smiled as if her words hadn't been slightly insulting. "Why thank you, Ruth. What sort of shop would *you* have…if you had to?"

She looked around again. "Oh, I don't know. An antique shop, I should think."

"I do have a lot of antiques. They came with the building. Funny, I would have thought the owner would have gotten them all out of here before they sold the place." I paused. "Wouldn't *you* have been the owner, Ruth? I mean…this was Constance Howland's house."

She fiddled with her locket. "I believe my holding company was in charge of the sale. To tell you the truth, I hadn't thought about this place in years."

The truth? I doubted there was much truth in that statement. "Well, I found some lovely things that I incorporated into the design. This buffet, for instance. It makes a great shop counter, and the cubby holes in this hutch are perfect for the herbs."

"Yes. I had little use for most of it. It was left on purpose."

I just bet you did. Which got me to wondering about the Booke. Had she known it was there all along?

I suddenly felt its presence in a strong flush of heat. I hoped it would behave itself and not suddenly appear in the middle of our cake and coffee. I concentrated on it, willing it to stay where it was.

"You're thinking about the book," said Erasmus in my ear, startling me.

"How could you tell?"

"I am its Guardian. I am connected to it."

"I know I've got to get that ghoul and I will, but there are other more pressing matters right now. For one, we've got to get Ruth's locket. I think it might prove interesting."

"I'll hold her down, and you snatch it from her neck."

I stared at him. "No! We will *not* be doing that."

"No?" He looked disappointed. "You always insist on doing things the hard way."

"It's the human way, I guess."

Jolene was waving at me. I gave her a nod. Time for plan B.

Jolene grabbed the coffee pot and made a beeline for Ruth. "Mrs. Russell, would you like more coffee?"

"Yes, I would. Thank you…Jolene, is it?"

"Yes. Say, I was wondering. I was studying designs in Hindu culture, and I was sure I noticed a mandala on your porch…"

Ruth studied her over the rim of her coffee cup. "I don't know what you're talking about."

Jolene kept shooting uncertain glances my way and began to stutter. "I…I was certain you had one. It's in glass tiles? But usually there's a mat covering it."

"Oh, that! That was something my husband had put in. A decorative thing for the entry. I always thought it was called a medallion. You call it a—what was that?"

"Mandala. If it's for decoration, why do you cover it with a mat?"

"You're an unusual girl, aren't you? In high school? Why would you be so absorbed with a design element on *my* front porch?"

Smooth, Ruth. I had to hand it to her. Deflection. So I took it up.

"I'm afraid it's my fault," I said. "I told Jolene about it. She's studying different cultural motifs in design, and I thought it might have some sort of meaning."

She squared on me. "Why?"

I shrugged. "I don't know. People put things, like design elements, in certain places for a reason."

"Do they? As I said, I'm afraid that was my husband's idea, and we can't ask him now, rest his soul."

Well, that shut it down. I gave a tiny shrug to Jolene.

I put my coffee cup and plate aside, then moved next to Ruth on the sofa. Gesturing toward her locket, I said, "I just can't get this locket out of my mind. Would you mind if I took a look at it?"

"I wish you wouldn't. It's very old and very valuable…and very dear to me."

"It must be. I don't believe I've ever seen you when you weren't wearing it."

"How very observant of you." She clutched it for a moment before slipping it inside her sweater. Damn.

This was getting us nowhere.

Erasmus leaned down over the sofa and said in my ear, "I still think my way is better."

Everyone started at a bang at my back door.

I looked to Ed. Both he and Erasmus stilled and then, at the same time, stalked toward the back.

I followed. My hand itched for the crossbow, but I kept reminding myself that we had mixed company.

We three went through the kitchen where I could see shadowy shapes through the dark windows. "Draugr!" I hissed.

"I'll take care of it," said Ed and Erasmus at the same time.

Ed grabbed the doorknob, but Erasmus covered his hand. "Don't. Not yet. Let me lure them away."

Heavy brows furrowed over Ed's eyes. "But you can't get out either."

Erasmus grinned…and vanished.

Startled, Ed blew out a breath. "Ass," he muttered.

I saw a shadowy figure at the door swing back their arms—surely to knock an axe through it—when they jerked to a halt and turned around. Erasmus was as good as his word—he *was* luring them away.

"Now what?" I glanced at the closed kitchen door. "You can't be firing your gun while Ruth and Reverend Howard are here."

"Well…get them out."

"How am I supposed to do that? 'Evening's over everyone. Out!' Not quite neighborly."

"You're going to have to do something." He lifted up his sweater and grabbed the gun out of his shoulder holster.

"You've been packing all night?"

"Of course. With all the weirdness going on around here, I'm never going out unarmed again."

"Oh. I guess I didn't expect—"

"Said the lady with the crossbow."

"I'm not getting it out now." I took another nervous glance toward the closed kitchen door, when Nick pushed it open.

"What's going on? Do we have 'company'?" He added air quotes.

"I'm afraid so. But I'm trying to convince the sheriff to not go all Wild West on it."

Nick looked at the gun. "Yeah, maybe the gun is not the best idea."

Ed seemed to be losing patience. "I don't suppose you have a better suggestion."

"Well…as a matter of fact, I do. Do you have any hair spray?" Nick asked me. "Anything in a compressed air container?"

"No hairspray. Will non-stick cooking spray do?"

"Yeah." We rummaged in the pantry together until I found it and handed it to him.

"Have you got a match?"

"I see where you're going with this," said Ed. "I've got a lighter."

Nick handed the can to Ed, who readied himself at the door.

I looked curiously from one to the other. "Are you trying to make a flamethrower?"

Nick nodded. "I think it will work. I mean, if bullets only stop them temporarily, then fire might do a more permanent job. At least until we can figure out a spell. And fire is a basic element. I'm pretty sure it'll work to take down a zombie."

The kitchen door opened again. I was about to lose it.

Jeff this time. "I smell them." He lifted his chin and sniffed the air. It was uncomfortably close to what Erasmus did. "I've got an itch to go after them. I can help."

Ed glanced at him sidelong. "You mean..." He made a vague gesture. "Do that...wolf thing? I thought you had to wait for a full moon?"

"Seriously, dude?"

"Well I..." Ed blew out an exasperated breath. "This is still new to me!"

"Me, too. Just went wolf last week, you know. So let me help. I don't think they'll go after me. Part demon now, I guess."

"What could you do?"

"Hunt them down. Corral them. While you hit them with that mini flame thrower. That is what you have planned, right? Or is there another reason why you're holding a spray can and a lighter?"

Ed nodded, screwing up his courage again. "Okay, then," he said, hand tensed over the doorknob. "Let's go!"

CHAPTER NINE

JEFF DOFFED HIS clothes, and when he sprang forward, he was a blond wolf streaking toward the shadowy figures in the mist. I couldn't see Erasmus, but somehow he was luring the Draugr away from us and into the woods. Nick hesitated in the doorway until I shooed him back inside. There was little he could do. It was up to Ed. I felt naked without my crossbow and cold down to my toenails. I hadn't grabbed a coat, but neither had Ed.

I hugged myself as we moved carefully through my backyard, past the glider swing and through the gate. I looked back at my house—its lights blazing warmly, the muffled sounds of people talking, the clink of forks on plates. Like nothing was happening. As if there wasn't a Viking zombie apocalypse going on in the woods nearby. How I longed to go back inside.

"This is what you've been doing for the past two weeks?" asked Ed, never looking away from the end of his...spray can. He held the lighter at the ready in his other hand.

"Pretty much. Only I usually have my crossbow." I ran my itchy palm down my pant leg. I knew—with an irritating shiver—that if I opened my hand even a little, it would soar through the house and out to me. Should I risk it? It was upstairs. It might go out the window. But then I reminded myself that the bolts had no effect on the Draugr. They would only be helpful if the ghoul or Andras were around, too, to take advantage of the distraction.

The Booke's pull was strong, so strong that I had to raise my hand. When the sash to my window snapped upward, I looked back and saw the crossbow coming toward me. I was seized with a hot, churning anticipation, the way one feels when waiting at the airport for a loved one to arrive and you finally see them. That kind of feeling. No matter how wrong that was, I still welcomed the sensation of utter satisfaction when the cold metal and warm wood slapped into my hand.

The crossbow was from Erasmus' world. And the more I welcomed it, the closer I felt to that mysterious place. I could almost sense its denizens through the wood, like the echo of a vibration.

"Kylie!" Ed hissed.

Had I zoned out in chthonic crossbow bliss? Embarrassed, I hurried to catch up to him.

"I thought you weren't going to get that?" His gaze ran curiously over the alien weapon.

"I...couldn't help it. There might be other things out here." I glanced to the skies. It was a cloudy night, so there weren't any stars. In a way, that was probably better for spotting the odd winged being stalking me from the heavens. The crossbow had armed itself with an unfamiliar bolt. Like Ed, I was ready, with the crossbow butt against my shoulder and its arrow pointing toward the gloom ahead.

We made it into the woods, where the air seemed still, and the mist was waist high. The smell of death and decay lingered. I could just make out movement when I peered into the darkness. And I definitely heard growls and snapping jaws. Jeff!

What strange bedfellows I'd made. Jeff, Erasmus, Ed...If I thought about it too much, I'd sink into the surrealness of it all. But we had Draugr to hunt, so I needed to focus. If I could.

A twig snapped. Ed and I both swung our weapons in that direction. Nothing. But I could sure smell them.

"It stinks like a dead body," said Ed.

"That's them, all right."

"When we see them, I want you to get behind me."

I hefted the crossbow. "Really?"

He cursed under his breath and nodded. "Sorry. Old habits."

I heard a series of sounds—a thump, the clang of steel, a wild rustling in the leaves, growls and snarls—to our left. I ran.

"Goddammit!" said Ed, hurrying to catch up to me.

Jeff had a Viking on the ground, jaws clamped to its neck. I've never been so proud of my ex in my life. I wasn't too worried about him, because like Erasmus, they wouldn't try to attack him. I think. But Ed and I were fresh meat, and as soon as the wind changed…

I saw them turn toward us from every place in the forest. All the ghostly figures in the distance stopped, raised their undead faces to the wind, and smelled the humans.

"Here we go," I said under my breath. The crossbow was obligingly armed though I knew it wouldn't stop them for good. I raised it as they started marching toward us, swords and axes in hand.

Ed shook the can and held it up, lighter ready.

"Any time, Ed," I urged.

"They have to be close enough. This thing won't go far."

"How far?" Because they were trudging ever closer. Their smell was pretty strong now. Looking at their dead eyes and through their cheeks to the backs of their throats was making me a little queasy.

One warrior raised an axe above his head, flesh hanging off his arm. He wore a dented helmet and a ragged cloak over his boney shoulders. He dragged one foot that seemed twisted, like his ankle had been broken off. And then he opened his mouth—more like released his jaw that fell to his chest—and let out an unholy scream, like the yowl of a cat caught in a trash can.

I took a step back. A ghoul or a succubus I could take, but not this undead thing. I'd never be able to sleep again.

He was getting within axe distance.

I took another step back, glancing at Ed. "Is he close enough now?"

"Let's find out." He flipped open his Zippo, flicked the flint wheel, and got a flame. Holding the spray can at arm's length, he depressed the nozzle and lit it up. It sputtered a flame only about a foot long—spectacularly unimpressive. But it did manage to catch the Draugr's cloak on fire.

The creature noticed right away and began flapping his scrawny hands at it. Then it spread. He kept slapping himself, trying to douse the flames, but soon was screaming in earnest. The others stopped to watch him.

He dropped his axe, raised his face to the sky, and went up like a Roman candle. I didn't think it was possible, but he smelled even worse, especially the burning hair on his head and the pelt on the shoulders of his cloak.

Ed tossed the can at him and grabbed me. With his body sheltering mine, he pulled me down behind a log. The can exploded, fire hitting the two nearest Draugr. Now three were on fire. The others drew back with worried looks on their faces. They tightened their skeletal hands on their weapons and withdrew, leaving their companions behind. Soon the three left were just piles of melted flesh, burning down to charred bones.

WereJeff padded forward and watched them reduce to blackened stumps, his eyes lit with the last of the flames. There was dark blood on his snout.

I disentangled myself from Ed and stood, looking at the smoking remains. "Go home, Jeff. Get yourself cleaned up… and dressed."

He looked at me like an obedient dog, growled once at Ed, but did as told, trotting back toward the house. The Draugr retreating into the woods took their smell with them. I didn't think they'd return tonight.

"Why'd you throw the can away? It was working."

Ed ran his hand through his hair. "It had a distance of one foot. That is not an effective weapon."

"Then you've got to get the flamethrower from the station."

He gave me an incredulous look. "We don't have a flame-thrower. What kind of police force do you think we are? No station has a flamethrower."

"Well…around here they should!"

We both watched the pile of smoldering bones to make sure they didn't get up again. Ed ensured they wouldn't by pounding on them with his boot, cracking the fragile bones into small pieces. He was getting soot all over his trousers, but I wasn't about to complain.

When he glanced at me again, it looked like he wanted to say something. That's when Erasmus blundered through the brush.

"Forgive the interruption," he sneered, "but I think there is a house back here that experienced the Draugr's visitation."

"Oh, no."

Ed firmed his jaw and followed Erasmus. I gave one half-hearted look back at my house and its dinner party going on without me, before I trailed after them. The crossbow had unarmed itself, and I held it down by my thigh as I trotted forward.

A small house—some old clapboard thing from the thirties—sat on a ridge some ways away. It wasn't more than a badly shingled roof, a shed out back, a doghouse, and a rusty umbrella clothes line. All was quiet, despite it being maybe nine o'clock. The lights were off…and something else was off too. The roof of the doghouse was smashed in the middle. And I didn't see Rover anywhere. Just a chain that looked to be…cut.

A tricycle lay on its side in the front by the concrete walkway. And the door was wide open. No. Not open. Axed open, the remains in splinters in the front entrance.

Ed got out his gun and straight-armed it with two hands, just like cops on TV. "Kylie, stay back," he said. I looked down at my crossbow, but it hadn't armed. I hung back anyway.

He stepped into the darkened doorway. "Police! It's Sheriff Bradbury! Mr. Warren? Mrs. Warren?"

The utter silence unnerved me. I was waiting for the jump scare I knew was coming. I should have stayed outside with Erasmus, but I couldn't make myself do it, so instead I crept in after Ed, holding the crossbow in my hands like a club.

"Kylie," he said quietly. "Be careful. I think…" He leaned over near a lamp and switched it on. Oh, how I wished he hadn't.

The family had been about to sit down to dinner. There was a stone-cold casserole congealing in a glass dish. A half-filled glass of juice rested on the table. The jug beside it was overturned, leaving a purple-stained tablecloth. Someone must have been pouring a drink when chaos arrived. Chairs were overturned, including one with a booster seat strapped to it. Pictures that had hung on the wall lay shattered on the floor. The wall was smeared with blood.

And there were Mr. and Mrs. Warren lying on the floor. Their bodies had been crushed. There was no way I was looking for the kid. Or the dog.

Ed holstered his gun. It was obvious we were alone.

He bent down over the bodies and frowned. "Looks like their ring fingers were…bitten off? Anyway, they're gone." He looked at the remains of the woman and pointed to her neck. I didn't come close. "I think she had a necklace. I see a mark like they yanked it off."

"Gold," said Erasmus, suddenly beside me. "They were looking for gold. They think it is their treasure."

I looked around for anything that might have been gold, not that I knew these people or their belongings. I hadn't even known that this house was all that close to mine, hidden by thick woods. There was a bare spot in the middle of the fireplace mantle. Maybe some sort of award had been there, plated with gold. Gone now.

Ed moved away from the couple and began looking under tables and down the hallway. "Dammit," was his brief exclamation when he must have found the child. When he came out, he looked grim. "I have to call this in."

"With all of these deaths, won't George get suspicious? I mean, do you have to call in the state troopers for this?"

"I guess I'll just tell George I already talked to them. Jeezum, I hate lying to him." He got out his cell and hit the call button.

Erasmus rested his hand gently on the small of my back. "Hadn't we best leave this place?"

"I guess you're right."

We walked outside to the porch where I inhaled the night. I did not smell death, though it was near. "Why, Erasmus? Why all this? Why the ghoul? Why you? What's the purpose of all this?"

"Need there be a purpose?"

"Yes! It would help to make sense of these deaths, these poor, innocent people who didn't have to die." His eyes glittered in the darkness. Softly, I asked, "Is it my fault they're dead? If I hadn't opened the Booke…"

"This is not your doing."

"Directly, maybe. If I hadn't opened the Booke, then Doug and his stupid gang wouldn't have all this power. They wouldn't have Shabiri. Those people wouldn't be dead from a succubus and a kelpie. Jeff wouldn't be a werewolf—"

Arms enclosed me—warm, sheltering. His dark voice in my ear made me shiver. "And you wouldn't have me."

I wanted to stay in his arms, but it was suddenly colder there. I gently pushed him back. "I don't have you." I poked his chest. "This tattoo here says I don't."

"I made my vow to you."

"And it's only as good as the Powers That Be says it is."

He trembled with fury. His coat smoldered, but his mouth stayed tightly shut. Because he knew it was true.

Ed came into the doorway. "George is on his way. I'll have to stay here to wait for him." He flicked his eyes toward Erasmus, then into the distance.

I got the message. Without a backward glance, I trudged back through the woods. Erasmus walked silently by my side.

* * *

WHEN I GOT back inside, the party was breaking up.

"There you are!" said Reverend Howard. "Water heater all right?"

I must have had a blank look on my face, because Nick stepped in with, "I told them that you had to see to it. It makes a helluva noise when it acts up. Oops. Sorry, Reverend."

"I do know all about Hell, Nick." He smiled. "It's getting late and I have work in the morning. Thank you, Kylie for a most enjoyable evening."

"Yes," said Ruth belatedly. "It was surprisingly entertaining. And the food was lovely."

I suppose that was the best I could get out of her. We still hadn't learned anything, though I was now more certain than ever that Ruth knew more than she let on.

"Thanks for coming. I'm sorry I was AWOL for part of it. But a water heater waits for no man. Or woman."

"It's good to be a handy woman," said Ruth in a shockingly agreeable manner. "It's not good to have to rely on others. Sometimes what we have to do is best done alone."

"Uh…yeah. Yes, that's my philosophy, too. It's what brought me here to Maine."

Ruth gave me and my shop another appraisal before stepping into the night. Reverend Howard and Doc walked her to her car to see that she got in all right…despite her speech.

I waved as she and Reverend Howard both drove away. The coven wasted no time ushering me back inside.

"What happened?" cried Jolene from one of the wingbacks, tucking a leg under her.

I sank onto the ottoman. "It was awful. This family up there in the woods. The Draugr got them."

Seraphina gasped and pressed her hand to her mouth. "Oh no!"

"Erasmus said they were looking for gold. It looks like they took their wedding rings—fingers and all—and any other gold things in the house."

Doc scooted closer to the edge of the sofa. "The Warrens, you mean? Not…the child…"

I nodded. Everyone fell silent.

Jeff was standing in the doorway, dressed again, though he'd forgotten to put on shoes and socks. It seemed that he never remembered shoes anymore.

"I can hunt them," he said fiercely. "I can find them wherever they are. But I don't think I can kill them."

"The fire did that," I said. "But we need something better, something more reliable than a spray can and a lighter."

Jolene grabbed her tablet from her nearby bag. Her hands were shaking. "I think we can devise a spell. Something with fire. Supernatural fire would be even better."

Nick knelt beside her. "Yeah. I figured that because fire is one of the four elements, it would be pure enough to get rid of them. But fire made from a spell could be even more effective."

"That's dangerous ground," said Doc. "We're surrounded by woods."

"But that's why we need a supernatural fire," said Jolene. "We can control it, direct it. And we can command it so it doesn't touch the trees."

"True." Doc got up and walked toward the fireplace, staring into the flickering flames. Fire could be a comfort, under the right circumstances. I loved a fire in my fireplace. But I was feeling less sentimental about it if it could get rid of these damned Vikings.

"I'm concerned about Ruth's locket," Doc went on. "To tell you the truth, I never gave it much thought before. I've seen it on her for years, but now I'm worried."

"So you're finally suspicious of her, too," I said without a shred of gloating. Well, maybe a little gloating.

"I'm not afraid to admit that I am…worried."

Nick sighed. "It would have been nice to get a good look at it."

"Look all you like," said Erasmus. He held up his closed hand and when he opened it, the locket and chain dropped, swinging like a pendulum.

I sprang to my feet. "How did you get that? You didn't hurt her, did you?"

"What do you take me for? I simply…vanished it from her neck."

"She's going to notice, and I am damn well not going to be caught with it. She'll call the cops on me for sure this time."

"I'm certain your constable will not arrest you."

Seraphina moved in to snatch it from Erasmus' grip. He sneered, almost growling at her, but Seraphina only had eyes for the locket. "This is very strange. I've made a practice of knowing about historical jewelry from all sorts of periods, but I don't recognize this style from the early 1700s."

I came closer and looked it over. It was gold, about the size of a quarter, rectangular, with a filigreed cover. But she was right. It looked old. Far older than three hundred years ago. It wasn't as delicate as one would expect from something from the eighteenth century, or even the seventeenth century.

When Seraphina turned it over, there was strange design etched on the flat surface, something with squirrelly lines and dots and swirls—not unlike Erasmus' tattoo. At first it looked like a design, but after a while it resembled some kind of writing. Seraphina showed it to Jolene, who snapped a picture of it with her tablet. "You can find out what this means, can't you, dear?"

"I'll do my best." She began tapping on the keys immediately.

"No," Seraphina went on. "I'd call this more…dare I say it? Babylonian. What in the world was Constance Howland doing with this?"

CHAPTER TEN

AN ANCIENT LOCKET from an extinct civilization? I reached out and almost touched it. "Really?"

Doc came up on the other side of Seraphina. "May I?"

She handed it over. Doc examined it, turning it over and over in his fingers. "I'll be darned. You're right, Seraphina. I don't know why I never noticed it before. Definitely Babylonian or thereabouts. Surely Constance Howland didn't have anything like this."

"She did."

We all turned to look at Erasmus. He stood with his hands behind his back, his ever-present duster coat hugging his calves.

Doc gestured toward him with the locket. "You *saw* her wearing this?"

"Yes."

"Do *you* know what it is?"

"No."

"Did she…acquire it *after* she met you? Like Kylie's amulet."

"It's *my* amulet, and I…don't know."

I pulled his amulet from my sweater and held it up. He always winced when he saw it. "Is it like this? Did she get it from you?"

"No. I merely recall seeing it on Mistress Howland."

Doc shook his head, staring at it. "And she always wore it?"

"Not always. She wasn't wearing it when she died."

"When you pushed her!" said Nick.

I held him back. "It's okay, Nick."

"As I explained to Miss Strange, I did *not* kill her. She committed suicide."

"Oh, what a load of crap!"

"Now wait a minute, Nick," said Doc, holding up his free hand. I had wanted to look at the locket, but for some reason I didn't want to touch it. "If she wasn't wearing it when she died, she clearly knew she was going to come to her end. She must've set the locket aside. It must be important for her to ensure it was passed down to her descendants."

Seraphina took the necklace up again and held it to the light. The filigree was more than a design element. It was cut through— you could see to the backing or whatever was inside it.

"Can we open it?" I asked.

Seraphina tried to no avail and gave up with a shrug.

"Let me see it," said Nick. He took it to the counter and tried to pry it open with the letter opener beside my register.

Jolene snatched it from him. "This is almost 4,000 years old, you goof!" She lifted her glasses to her forehead and looked at it up close. "Kylie, do you have a magnifying glass?"

"Should be one in the drawer by Nick."

Nick pulled the drawer open, rummaged around, and handed it over contritely. Jolene brought the locket to the lamp and looked through the magnifying glass. "It doesn't actually look like it *does* open."

"Ruth seemed to think so," I said.

Suddenly it was thrust into my face. "Maybe only a Chosen Host can open it."

I didn't touch it. "Maybe only descendants of Constance Howland."

"If that were the case," said Doc, "then Ruth would have been able to open it. Why are you hesitating, Kylie?"

"Because…" I didn't know why. All I knew is that I suddenly didn't want to touch it. I backed away a step.

"Kylie," said Doc, studying me. "What is it?"

"I don't know. I just…don't want to touch it."

"You wanted to before."

"I know. But now I don't."

"Does it…frighten you?"

"No…"

Nick hugged himself, even though it was warm in the room. "This is getting weird."

"Why don't *I* try," said Jeff.

Everyone looked at him as if they had forgotten he was there. And in truth, he tended to always stay in the shadows. New behavior for him. He used to love being the life of the party.

Doc offered it to him, and he took it carefully, frowning at the squiggles. "Why does it say this?"

Doc slid around the furniture to stand next to him. "Jeff, can you read what that says?"

"Sort of." He screwed up his face. "*The Almighty Sin-Muballit guards what is his.*"

We looked at each other.

"You know," I said, quietly, filling the silence, "maybe we shouldn't open it until we know what it is. Look at all the trouble I caused by opening the Booke."

"Don't open it," said Erasmus.

"Why not, Mr. Dark?" asked Doc.

"It is as Kylie says. Until we discern its function, it would not be wise to open it."

"Does this relate to the book, Mr. Dark?"

"I don't know."

Nick made a disgusted sound. "He's lying."

Suddenly Erasmus was in Nick's face, backing him into the wall. "What do *you* know of me, whelp? I am older than that locket. I am eternal. A demon of the Netherworld. I don't have to listen to your whinging."

"Erasmus," I admonished. I pulled him by the shoulders away from Nick, who was panting and clutching the wall.

Jeff hunched over and began to growl.

"Everyone," I said loudly, "just calm the hell down." I glared down Erasmus and Jeff. "Jeff, *you* take the locket."

His growl stopped, and his sneer disappeared. "What? Why?"

"Because it doesn't seem to affect you. You can guard it." I took a deep breath. "Now who is Sin-Muballit, and do we have to worry about him?"

Jolene smiled. "For once, no. Sin-Muballit was a king of Babylon in the Amorite Dynasty. He was the father of Hammurabi. You've heard of him, right? The guy with the code? It predates the Ten Commandments. Anyway, it just means that—if this inscription is true—it's from about 1740 BCE."

"Oh." I stared at it suspiciously, trying to discern its secrets. I was willing to bet they weren't anything good. "What would this have to do with…us? The Booke?"

"Seeing that Ruth had it," said Doc, "I can't think that it *would* have to do with the book. But then again, Mr. Dark here says Constance Howland wore it."

"A family heirloom," I muttered. "I can't see a Puritan woman wearing a Babylonian necklace. Unless she didn't know what it was. I wonder how she got it." I turned toward Jeff. "And why can Jeff read this? I thought he could only read demon languages."

Doc rubbed his chin. "That puts a new face on Babylonian, doesn't it? Perhaps it's an offshoot of demon languages."

"All human languages are an offshoot of demon languages," said Erasmus in a bored tone. "We were here first, after all."

He didn't seem to expect the stunned silence that greeted him. He shrugged and leaned back against a post, hiding his expression behind the shadow of his hair in his face.

"Uh…Jolene?" I said, thinking maybe a change of subject was a good idea. "Have we found out anything more about the ghoul?"

She swiped across her tablet. "Nothing new. It seems pretty

mundane, as far as other-worldly creatures go. I mean, it might hunt kids, but it usually likes them when they're already dead."

"Yeah. Why would the Booke spit out this guy? It's not all that dangerous. Not like a kelpie, or a werewolf."

Erasmus was sulking. Even with his arms crossed tightly over his chest and his nose in the air, he managed to say, "I have yet to determine why the book chooses what creature to disembark."

"That's helpful."

He glared at me. "Is it?"

"That was sarcasm, genius."

His sulk got sulkier.

"Well, I guess it doesn't matter. I've still got to get rid of it. But it sure seems that each time I encounter it, Andras shows up to spoil my party."

"Now that *is* interesting," said Doc thoughtfully, but he didn't say anything more.

"We also have to find a way to take down Andras. Jolene, start studying what it takes to kill a demon."

She flicked a glance at Erasmus before tucking into her tablet.

A knock at the door had us all sit up straight. Ed stood in the open doorway, with Deputy George behind him. "Looks like your evening is broken up."

"Only some of them have left," I said, urging him in. "We still have coffee. How about a cup, Deputy Miller?"

George came in and doffed his Smokey Bear hat. He flicked a glance at Nick. "Don't mind if I do, ma'am."

"Can I tempt you with some cake?"

He snatched a glance at Ed, seemed to see it was all right, and nodded.

Nick offered him a chair, and a warm smile, both of which George barely acknowledged.

"Ed, why don't you help me in the kitchen?"

Ed followed me and shut the door behind us. "He insisted on going with me. I couldn't shake him."

"That's okay. What did the coroner say?"

"Hard to avoid seeing axe and sword marks everywhere. Right now, it's murder from random thugs with farm implements. But this is getting serious, Kylie."

"I know." I paused. "Hey, where do the bodies go around here?"

"Mortuary. Up by the cemetery."

"That means the ghoul will go there."

"Aw, Christ. You aren't going to hunt that thing tonight, are you?"

"I *have* to."

I couldn't quite discern the complex emotions in his eyes. There was weariness, certainly. But also maybe a bit of pride. And a healthy dose of exasperation, of course.

"You know I have to," I said softly. I was also a little proud of him, too, putting aside his obvious discomfort with the two of us together but helping anyway. It warmed me inside.

"This new paradigm sucks."

I smiled. "Yeah, I know."

"Look, Kylie…" He stepped forward and took my hand. "Maybe I was a bit hasty and selfish…"

The door abruptly opened, smacking Ed in the shoulder.

"Oh!" said Nick. "Sorry, sheriff. Can I help?"

I grabbed the coffee carafe and handed it to Nick. "How does George like his coffee?"

"Cream and sugar," said Nick and Ed at the same time. Ed frowned at Nick as he ducked his head and slipped through the door.

"How does he—"

"He's a barista, remember? Here's the cream and sugar," I said, shoving them into his hands. "I'll cut him a slice of cake. You want another one?"

Ed accepted his second plate of cake, and soon we were all together in the main shop, drinking more coffee, while Ed and George devoured their slices. How they could eat after what they'd seen made me shake my head.

George set his empty plate aside. "That was sure good, Ms. Strange."

"You can call me Kylie, George."

"Yeah." He flicked another glance at Nick as he rose.

"Hey, deputy," said Nick. "Can you help me with the plates?"

"Sure, Mr. Riley."

Ed got in close once they were in the other room. "Quickly! What happened with Ruth? Find out anything?"

I sat back and rubbed my eyes. "We found out that locket she wears is Babylonian with some weird demon language inscription on the back."

"Babylonian? What's she doing with something like that?"

"Well, unless Moody Bog was founded in 1700 *BC*, I'd say Constance Howland had some very interesting connections."

"How do we know your ancestor had that?"

Jolene piped up with, "Mr. Dark saw her wearing it."

Ed glanced slowly at Erasmus, who gave him an equally sneering glance in return. "I forgot. The demon's been around a while."

"More than 'a while,'" snorted Erasmus.

"*Anyway,*" I said, intervening, "we have to find out its purpose. In the meantime, I want to go over to Doug's with you tomorrow."

"I'm not taking you there."

"Well…then I'm going by myself. I just thought you'd rather be there to make sure there was no funny business."

"Kylie, I do *not* want you going over there."

"Ed, you don't seem to understand the dynamic—"

"*I'll* go with her," said Erasmus, a smug look on his face.

That did the trick. "If he's going, I'm going."

"That's what I asked in the first place," I muttered.

The kitchen door blew open and a smiling Nick strolled in, pulling down the hem of his shirt. A few seconds later, George came through…with tie askew.

I motioned to him with some hand signals. Wide-eyed, he got the message, straightening his tie and tucking in his shirt.

"Look at the time," said Nick. "Maybe we should get out of your hair, Kylie."

"Nick is right," said Doc. "But we'll all be back tomorrow afternoon to work on the, uh, project."

"Project?" said Jolene. "Oh! *Project*!"

Spell, they meant. Something to get rid of the Draugr.

I had decided to question Doug myself about them. Maybe I could hammer into his head once and for all that whatever bad thing he did affected everyone else. Maybe he didn't care. But I had to believe that the family who raised Ed had to have instilled the same sense of fair play and goodness in his brother, too. Somewhere deep, *deep* inside.

But for now, we'd need to get over to the mortuary. And I wanted back-up this time. "Hey, Jeff. Need a ride home?"

He did that head-cocking thing that dogs did. It was…disturbing. "You offering?"

"Yeah. Erasmus wants to come, too."

Both Ed and Erasmus looked at me suspiciously.

CHAPTER ELEVEN

IT WAS JUST Erasmus, Jeff, and I in my Jeep. Erasmus had assumed he'd be sitting shotgun as always. When Jeff got there first, there was some pushback.

I didn't have time for this. "Just get in the car, Erasmus!"

He muttered something in a guttural demon language that I didn't understand, but that Jeff clearly did. He spun in his seat and glared. "I *heard* that!"

Buckling himself in, Erasmus merely smiled.

"Why are demons such dicks?" said Jeff, settling in.

Through the rearview mirror, I saw the smile disappear off Erasmus' face.

"I hope you've figured out by now," I said, ignoring their antics as I pulled into the street, "that we aren't taking Jeff home right away."

"Since you've got your crossbow, I sort of figured." Jeff looked at the locket and put the chain around his neck. "Good thing this isn't silver."

"Yeah. So are you okay with helping me with this ghoul?"

"That's what your friendly neighborhood werewolf is for."

"I appreciate it." I said, adjusting my grip on the steering wheel and making the turn toward the cemetery.

"Yeah. You know what the funny thing is? I always wanted a dog but figured I didn't have the time. Now I've got the best of both worlds, I guess."

He had the right to be sour about it. But it did make me feel guilty.

I followed the sign for the mortuary. Though the gates were closed, nothing was locked. You had to hand it to small towns.

I followed my headlights through the mist up the drive to the mortuary building. I figured we'd go toward the sign that said "back entrance." I doubted many bodies came through the front door.

I parked the car, killed the engine, and sat, listening to the night. Peering into the sky, I wondered if my personal assassin was near.

Swinging to the back seat, I grabbed the crossbow. "That's wicked," said Jeff, admiring it.

"I guess. Erasmus, I have a feeling that Andras is waiting to pounce. I think he's using the ghoul to find me somehow. Maybe they made a bargain."

"Yes, I was wondering that myself. It is not beyond the scope of a demon to use such tactics. I know very little of Andras except by rumor. But a ghoul is little better than a dog. They wouldn't have the capacity to bargain."

"Then how is Andras using it?"

"He is said to be particularly devious and unrelenting. My best guess is that he is simply following him."

"Great. How do I kill him?"

"You don't."

"Demons *can* be killed, can't they?"

He squirmed a bit. "This is not a comfortable topic."

It was Jeff's turn to smile, and he turned around in his seat to give Erasmus his full wattage. "Don't tell me you're scared?"

"I know Kylie would never use these methods on me. You, on the other hand…"

"Jeff, could you wait outside?"

"What? Just as it was getting good?"

"Please. I need his help."

He blew out a breath. "Okay. I'll sniff around outside, see what I can find." He meant that literally, of course. He got out of the Jeep and started removing his clothes. I turned away and saw him morph out of the corner of my eye. A blond wolf padded away into the shadows of the building.

I turned and faced Erasmus. "He's gone now. Can you tell me? Do you…trust me?"

His eyes narrowed, and his scowl was world class. "You cannot kill a demon easily. Your Wiccan spell should have killed me, but it did not. Perhaps it wasn't done correctly. Certainly being speared through the chest with iron would disable a demon and send them back to the Netherworld. And it isn't easy to escape the Netherworld."

"That's why demons need to be summoned."

"Precisely."

"So why can *you* pass through over and over?"

"Because of the book. It serves as a gateway. Which is why other creatures can come through it as well."

"That's right. It's a gateway. And it seems to strengthen spells and other gateways. That other vortex that the Ordo opened."

"Shabiri assisted with that, no doubt."

"You made that special arrow. Poisoned it by…by sticking it in your eye. Will that kill Andras?"

"It might."

"Will it be enough to send him back?"

"It…might."

I threw my head back. "I wish you had more definitive answers."

"So do I. I'm sorry. I've never been required to do such a thing before."

I swung open the car door and stepped out. It was bitterly cold. Each night seemed to be getting colder, and I didn't like the look of that mist. Erasmus seemed to think the Draugr were laying low now, but I didn't trust any of these Netherworld denizens.

I clutched the crossbow and moved with Erasmus to the door. It was dark. No lights or even motion sensors around. I guessed little Moody Bog generally didn't have trouble with vandalism or break-ins. At least, until a certain party from Hansen Mills came to town.

I got my phone out, turned on the flashlight, and shined the light on the door. "How do we get in? Do you have a special breaking-in trick?"

He smiled and vanished. And then someone was opening the door from the inside. Before I could run, I realized that it was Erasmus.

"Well, that's handy," I muttered, trying to mask my doubling heartrate.

"This is very strange," he said, frowning. "Why do you keep your dead in such a place?"

"Uh… It's just a place to keep them before the funeral."

He didn't seem convinced. I ignored him to look around outside. "Jeff!" I whispered as loud as I could. "Jeff!"

Out of the mist came a four-footed shape—a blond wolf. He stopped before me, stuck out his tongue, and panted.

"Do you want to come in or stay out here?"

Somehow, I expected him to say something, but of course, he couldn't in wolf form. Instead, he trotted past me inside.

I peered down the darkened hallway. "Now what?" I whispered.

Jeff's ears pricked up. He gave a deep growl and crept into the darkness. Erasmus took up the rear guard as I readied the crossbow. And looky there. It had armed itself.

Never in a million years had I imagined creeping around what was essentially a morgue in the middle of the night. With a demon. And a werewolf. So okay. There were a lot of "nevers" to go around.

Both Erasmus and Jeff kept lifting their noses, presumably following the scent of the ghoul. We passed a time clock, a break room, and then turned a corner. Over a big double door hung a sign saying, "Morgue." I really didn't want to go in there, but where else are you gonna go when a ghoul needs to snack on a corpse?

I motioned for my companions to stay quiet as I carefully pushed on the door. Relieved it made no sound, I looked around at the stainless-steel wall of refrigerated doors. Slabs, I guess. One had been opened and rolled out. I knew it was the child, because the ghoul was bent over it and had taken on the appearance of a four-year-old boy in torn jeans and a striped shirt.

I raised the crossbow, aiming square in the middle of its back. It hadn't noticed me yet. And it was making lip-smacking eating noises, messily devouring the kid that the Draugr had killed. Except that the ghoul itself looked like a kid. And I couldn't shoot, even though I could feel Erasmus beside me urging me on.

I had to be sure. I had to know.

So I cleared my throat.

The ghoul stopped. When it moved its head to listen, I cleared my throat again.

It sprang into action and leapt to the side, leaving me a clear view of the child, naked, laid out on the stainless-steel tray. His guts had been torn out. Some ribs poked upward through the gore—broken, bitten through. I quickly looked away before the queasiness took over and tried to breathe out of my mouth. That way I couldn't smell it, the thick tang of metal in the air, of blood.

Jeff began to growl behind me.

I turned. "Jeff, you…" But his eyes. They weren't the normal wolfy eyes. They had turned red, and he was looking at me, lips snarled back, teeth bared, saliva dripping from his jaws.

I backed away. "Jeff?"

"It's the blood," said Erasmus. He stepped forward and pushed me behind him. "The blood drives them mad."

"But it's Jeff."

"It's a werewolf, Kylie. You must never forget it."

"What do we do? I can't shoot him. I won't."

Erasmus said nothing before he pounced. He grabbed Jeff's furry neck, holding off the barking and snapping muzzle. Jeff went wild, as if he were a real wolf, snarling and scratching. Erasmus bared his own teeth, too numerous for a human mouth. His mouth suddenly stretched unnaturally wide and then all his teeth were sharp shark teeth. Barely escaping the snapping jaws, he pushed the werewolf, struggling, toward the double doors until they were out in the hall, where the growls and screams bounced off the walls and echoed.

I locked the door behind them, pushing up the deadbolts into the lintel. When I turned back, the ghoul was in the corner hissing at me, still looking like the Warren child. There was no way out.

"You shouldn't have done it," I said. But was it to the ghoul… or to me? *I* opened the Booke, after all. *I* brought these things to Moody Bog. *I* killed that child.

I wiped my sleeve over my suddenly wet eyes but kept the crossbow trained on the ghoul. "You're not getting away this time."

It hissed again, and I could tell it was ready to spring away. Maybe up to those transom windows.

I lifted the crossbow, and with my trigger hand against my cheek, I fired.

The bolt soared true and pierced the ghoul right in the chest. It screamed, and the mask of the Warren child shed like Jeff's blond fur. It was the ghoul again, bugged eyes rolling in its head. It scrabbled at the arrow, but a beam of light was already shooting from the hole. More beams of lights began to tear through its body.

A transom window shattered and the Booke of the Hidden appeared before me, quill pen at the ready. It lay open to the next empty page, and I dropped the crossbow and picked up the quill. Jabbing the point of it into my left palm, I used the pooled blood to write on the blank page.

I first saw the ghoul on the street in front of my shop, and I pursued it to the cemetery…

I didn't even know what I wrote. I just kept writing, telling the story of the ghoul and what I knew about it. Every time I looked up from the page, I saw each word tear another hole through the ghoul, or the gateway, or…whatever. I didn't really understand it, but I kept writing until it disappeared completely into a painfully bright dot of light until that, too, was gone with a pop. The Booke slammed closed and fell to the floor.

And then my legs gave out. I sat beside the Booke, nursing my hand from all the pokes I had given it in the last few weeks. I was going to have to pick a different spot to get my blood, I decided vaguely, when Erasmus appeared in the room with a puff of dark smoke.

"Kylie, what happened?"

I showed him my bloody hand and gestured toward the Booke.

"You sent it back already?"

"Yeah. Come to think of it, didn't that seem a little too simple?"

He didn't say anything, but we both turned when the doors rattled. Jeff snarled and howled from the other side.

"How do we turn him off?"

He stalked over to the body on its tray and looked it over dispassionately, then shoved it back in the drawer and slammed the door. There was a little blood and...*stuff*...on the floor, and he knelt to scoop it up. He vanished, and immediately reappeared.

The snarling and howling suddenly stopped, replaced with whining.

Erasmus crossed to the door. Before I could shout for him not to open it, he did. The wolf bounded in right for me. I cowered, covering my head, but instead he nudged me, whining. He closed his mouth gently on my wrist without piercing the skin and pulled me toward him, then began to lick the blood away. I almost snatched my hand back—I certainly didn't want Jeff getting a taste for my blood—but Erasmus stopped me.

"He's only trying to heal you, Kylie. He's attuned to you. He knows you've been injured."

"Jeff," I said with a tremble to my voice. "Jeff, shift already. Be Jeff again."

The wolf stopped. He looked at my face, cocking his head to the side, when the fur started to shed in great handfuls. I thought I was used to it by now, but I wasn't. I wasn't used to watching his face shrink back from a muzzle to a human nose and mouth, from ears that were wide and pointy to two shell-like protrusions on the sides of his head, from back legs lengthening and twisting to human legs.

He sat beside me, holding my hand. Naked.

"I'm sorry, Kylie," he said sorrowfully. "I don't know what came over me. I smelled the blood and suddenly I wanted to kill. I'm so, so sorry."

"We…we have to work on that, I guess. I thought the potion you take is supposed to…"

"I didn't take it today. I thought I could learn to wean myself off of it."

"Did Doc say you could?"

He looked away. "I just thought I could."

"Well…now we know you can't."

"I fucking *hate* this!"

I put my arms around him. Ironically, as a man, Jeff didn't have a lot of body hair. I rubbed his smooth back and tried not to think about his nakedness. After all, I'd seen him naked plenty of times while we were living together.

"It's not your fault," I kept repeating. But in my head, I also kept saying, *It's mine.*

He wiped at his face and drew back. "So you got the little dope, huh?"

I looked back where the ghoul had stood and nodded. "Yeah. That was it." We both glanced at the Booke on the floor.

I should have been celebrating. But I couldn't help but feel it had been anti-climactic. Far too easy. Almost as if the ghoul had been a kind of placeholder for something worse. I had only a split second of waiting for the other shoe to drop when it did.

The wall with the transom windows exploded. I was flung back along with the bits of glass and broken cinder blocks, as something landed in the room.

CHAPTER TWELVE

IN THE CLOUD of dust and debris in the air, I got the merest glance of a giant winged creature. For a second, I assumed it was Andras, but... I blinked and narrowed my eyes.

Baphomet!

He roared with a weird half-cow, half-otherworldly sound, before resting his gaze on me with a frown. And when he pointed right at me and opened his mouth, it was like the voice of doom.

"Kylie Strange," he said, in a deep booming voice. "I am angered."

He was big, bigger than the last time we saw him. He filled the height of the room, his wide bat wings touching from wall to destroyed wall. How had he not been noticed out there? His tall, twisting horns stood straight up from his head, and his human-looking male torso was incongruous to the goat head. He flexed his pecs as well as the muscles in his arms that tapered down to human hands with black talons instead of fingernails. His torso transitioned into shaggy goat legs and black cloven hoofs. And all of him was massively oversized, like a statue in a temple.

My heart was throbbing and pounding in my throat. I didn't think I could talk my way out of this, but I sure tried. "I...I'm sorry. I didn't know who you were. I thought you were just another…*something*…from the Booke." My voice sounded tinny and pathetic to my own ears.

He cast a glance of disdain toward the Booke of the Hidden lying on the floor. The Booke didn't seem to care about his presence. In fact, I could feel exactly what the Booke thought of him, and it wasn't impressed. *Easy for you to be brave,* I thought at the Booke. You *can't be destroyed like* I *could.*

Baphomet pointed toward the floor. "Bow down to me, and I'll consider your fate."

Jeff had shifted back into a werewolf, snarling with his blond hackles up, and Erasmus shied away toward the wall. When I looked to him for what to do, he was at a loss.

Hey, if it would get us all out of this alive, I was all for a little humiliation. I got down on one knee, when Jeff suddenly howled.

Baphomet stepped forward, his cloven hoofs clacking on the linoleum floor. "Keep your beast in check."

"Jeff!" I hissed desperately. "No!"

He growled but stayed beside me. I was afraid he'd leap at any moment, and I didn't know how to get across to him that you didn't attack gods. I had done it before with my crossbow, and he'd broken it. In fact, he was staring at it with annoyance—a strange expression to see on a goat face.

Well, I must be terrified if I'm making these comments in my head, I thought. Because I pretty much *was* terrified. Too terrified to speak. I finished getting down on both knees and hung my head, but I still kept a tight grip of the crossbow. It was armed with God knows what.

The god moved forward again, moving past me to glare at Erasmus. "Demon. You anger me, as well."

Erasmus said nothing. He kept his head down and looked at the floor. I didn't like seeing him so cowed. He was supposed to act superior to everyone around him. This was not the demon I knew.

Baphomet sneered and snarled, "I never liked you and your book."

Still Erasmus said nothing.

The god took a step forward, reared back, and kicked Erasmus with that hard hoof. If Baphomet had been the size of a man it might not have hurt so much, but he was ten times bigger. Erasmus crumpled, and I jerked toward him.

Talons suddenly dug into my scalp, and I was yanked up by my hair. I screamed.

Erasmus moved toward me, and Jeff barked.

"Kylie Strange," growled Baphomet, turning me this way and that, glaring into my face with those weird goat eyes. I grabbed his wrist trying to spare my poor scalp and hair. He glanced at Erasmus, then back at me. "Why aren't you dead by now, Kylie Strange?"

"I've…got a job to do," I gritted out.

"That's never stopped the demon before." He chuckled. "Maybe he's not done playing with you yet. You *are* very amusing."

I lifted the crossbow and shoved it into his stomach.

"Kylie, no!" cried Erasmus.

The god looked down…and we locked gazes.

I fired.

He howled in pain as the bolt shot through him, and he dropped me. I tumbled to the floor and rolled toward Erasmus. He grabbed me just as another winged beast descended from the broken roof and set upon Baphomet.

Andras.

He scratched and clawed, but it was like swatting at a hummingbird. Baphomet was so much bigger, yet Andras was so much angrier. "She's *my* kill!" he cried over and over.

Erasmus didn't stick around for the floor show. Everything vanished. I felt the strange coldness as we transported to the car.

I stood unsteadily, stunned at what had just occurred, when a blond wolf burst through the door. As he ran, he shifted into a naked man, scooped up his discarded clothes, and jumped into the car.

"Go, go, go!" he yelled, slapping the outside of my Jeep through the open window.

He didn't have to tell me twice. I slammed the car into drive and tore out of there. Amid the cries and howls coming from the mortuary, no one would notice the squeal of my tires.

Erasmus was suddenly in the back seat, twisting around to look behind us.

"Thanks, Erasmus," I said breathily. "That was fast thinking."

"You never should have shot him again."

"He was already angry enough to kill me. How much deader could I get?"

"There are things he could do. He's a god. He can prolong your agony. Keep you barely alive enough to suffer in torment for years."

"Oh." That didn't sound good.

I gripped the wheel, driving like a bat out of hell, fish-tailing all over the road. When I dared look back through my rearview mirror, I saw something tear through the sky and then felt the deep boom of explosions. Crimson and yellow flashes sparked over roof tops in the distance, and smoke billowed from different parts of town.

"Baphomet is angered," said Erasmus.

"What's he doing?"

"He's wreaking havoc throughout your village. I have seen him raze entire cities to the ground."

"What? He can't do that!"

"He can. He's a god."

"What can we do?"

"Keep driving!"

I slammed my foot down on the accelerator and squealed down the wet streets. Cranking the steering wheel hard at the last minute, I made a dicey turn at Alderbrook Lane. The Jeep titled precariously before finally righting itself. Out of the corner of my eye I saw Jeff grip the grab handle above the window with both hands as he slid around his seat. No one had had time for seatbelts.

Then he stared out the windshield, blinking. "What's that glowing thing?"

I looked, trying to catch a glimpse of what he was seeing and nearly sent us off the road. "What do you mean? I don't see anything."

"Those glowing lines."

"He means the ley lines," said Erasmus.

"Wait. You can *see* them, Jeff?"

"Yeah. Like a greenish glow heading up the hill toward the house."

"Ley lines," Erasmus said again. "Lines of power."

We didn't say anything else until we made it to my grandpa's house. Behind us in Moody Bog, the fury in the sky seemed to have calmed. It didn't look like Baphomet was bent on destroying everything. At least, not yet.

As if we hadn't just escaped certain death, Jeff was studying the ley lines I couldn't see. "They're glowing," Jeff said in wonder as I parked the car.

"Didn't you see them before?" I asked.

Erasmus got out of the Jeep. "He is becoming more and more attuned with the Netherworld. He can already read demon languages. He's become more creature than man."

"Don't say that." I grabbed Erasmus and pulled him aside as Jeff made his way to the darkened porch. "He's having a hard enough time with all this," I whispered harshly. "Don't start calling him a…a monster."

"But that is what he is."

"Then what does that make you?" I left him there and stalked up to the house. I was glad he didn't follow.

Jeff turned on a light, belatedly realizing he wasn't wearing the trousers he was clutching. He turned his back to me and slipped them on.

"He's right you know," he said softly. "I am a monster."

"No, you're not. You're a man with a…a werewolf problem."

He snorted and looked over his shoulder at me. "You always did see the best in people."

"I try."

"I didn't deserve you."

"You screwed up, that's for sure. But that's over now, right? We've both moved on."

"You have."

He studied me for a long time. A brief look of sadness flitted across his face before he turned away and dragged himself to the kitchen. "Do you think that winged guy will follow us here?" he asked from the other room.

I trailed him into the kitchen. "It's protected by the Forget Me spell. And the ley lines, I think." I got out my phone. "But I've got to call Ed. Tell him what's going on."

Ed answered on the third ring. "I can't talk now, Kylie. There's been some explosions in town—"

"I know. It was Baphomet."

He paused. "Baphomet."

"Yeah. I pissed him off, and he took it out on the town. I don't know if anyone is hurt. It's all my fault."

"Are *you* all right?"

"Yeah. Just shaken."

"Are you in a safe place?"

"At my grandpa's old house."

"Stay there then. Is there anything I should look out for? Is Baphomet coming back?"

"I don't know, but keep your eyes peeled, Ed. Stay safe."

"Okay. I have to go."

"Go help them." He clicked off.

I still couldn't believe that a vengeful god was after me. Why I couldn't believe that over everything else, I didn't know. But the smoke from the explosions was drifting this way. Or I imagined it was. I thought I could smell the destruction.

Jeff looked at me for a moment before poking his head into the old-style, rounded fridge. "You want a beer?"

I nodded. I could sure use one.

He twisted the tops off of two brown bottles, and handed me one. I drank a long sip of the cool liquid. Jeff leaned against the fridge, bare-chested, bare-footed, and definitely buffer than I remembered him. The advantages of being a werewolf.

"I'm sorry about earlier," he said, shaking his head and looking at the floor. The gold locket glinted from his chest. "It was like I didn't know you anymore. Like you were just…meat."

I shivered. "You already apologized."

"I thought I could beat this thing, you know."

"Jeff, you have to think of it like a disease, a condition that you have to learn to live with. And you've also got to take your medicine."

"My medicine," he muttered, taking another swig of beer.

"The wolfsbane? You should maybe take it now, since you missed a dose."

He ran his free hand through his shaggy blond hair. "Yeah. I guess you're right." He opened the cupboard and took out a decorative bottle that had Seraphina's handiwork all over it. He pulled the cork out with his teeth and spit it aside. He knocked the bottle back, drank, and made a face, before washing it all down with another swig of beer.

"Bad, huh?"

"Like cat piss. And worse…since now I can actually smell cat piss in every damned bush I pass."

"I'm sorry."

"It's not your fault."

"Except it is my fault. I opened the Booke. What's happening out there right now is all my fault." We both heard the whine of sirens in the distance, getting closer.

He moved fast, grabbing my shoulders. "You gotta stop blaming yourself. Anyone would have opened the book."

"Not anyone. I was destined to. I'm from a long line of Chosen Hosts. Back to Babylonian days."

"That's still not your fault." He drank again, and so did I. "It's just our bad luck we were where we were. The wrong place at the wrong time. But how I wish I could go back. I've lost everything, haven't I? I can't even go back to my shop."

"You might. As soon as you learn to control it, you can probably live a normal life."

"Alone, you mean. I'm a monster, remember?"

"I don't know. I mean…think about it. There are probably lots of werewolves out there that no one knows about."

"Seriously?" He cocked his head and considered. "There might be. That's weird to think about."

"Yeah. And maybe with your heightened senses, you can find them some day. Maybe even…I don't know. Get to know them. Maybe…find a girlfriend."

"We can get a nice doghouse somewhere."

"Jeff."

"Sorry. Yeah, you might be right. I should stick with my own kind."

"I didn't mean that. I just thought you might want to see if they were around. Get some support. Learn some tricks to keep it all under control."

He drank thoughtfully, one hand resting on the fridge. "I would like to go back to California," he muttered, "but there's also something about these woods…"

"I don't think you should dwell on your wilder side, Jeff."

He looked at me with a sour expression before tossing the empty bottle toward his recycling bin and grabbing another from the fridge. "There are…things out there, you know? Things I've never seen before."

"What do you mean?"

He gestured with the beer bottle. "Like your friend says. I'm attuned now. I can see…*things*, creatures. They live here. They've always lived here, side by side with men. Creatures."

"Like…what? Fairies?"

"I don't know what they are. Some don't mean any harm. But some aren't so nice. I don't know why exactly but I get a bad vibe from them."

"Erasmus never mentioned them. Did they come from the Booke?"

"I don't think so. My impression is…they've been here all along."

"That's…weird."

"No weirder than the rest of this."

"I guess." I knocked back the bottle.

"Look, Kylie, I know I've got no business lecturing you about your love life—"

I bristled. "That's right, Jeff."

"But I've got to tell you. Do *not* trust that Erasmus guy."

"Jeff…" I sighed and retreated into the living room. The rug had been vacuumed, the sofa dusted. The pictures on the walls had been straightened and cleaned. You wouldn't have known the place had been empty for the last twenty years.

I sat in the rocker. I had spent many an evening on Grandpa's lap in that very rocker, with him reading or singing to me. I looked around, hoping to see his ghostly apparition hovering in the shadows.

Jeff stood in the archway between the living room and the foyer. "I'm not kidding, Kylie. There's more to him than meets the eye. He's keeping some kind of secret."

"I know his secrets."

"Oh, really? Which ones?"

"Like the one that…well. He's supposed to…eat my soul. Like he did for all the other Chosen Hosts."

His eyes widened. Maybe I should have broken that news with a little more grace. "Whoa. Christ, Kylie. Why do you let him stick around?"

"Because he promised he wouldn't."

"And you believe him?"

"I think he's in love with me."

Jeff's mouth dropped open while I clamped mine shut. It was the first time I'd said it out loud, the first time I'd allowed myself to even think it.

Jeff trudged into the room and sat on the sofa. He sat there a long time, just looking at his beer bottle, tearing little pieces off the wet label. "And…are you in love with him?"

"I don't know, Jeff."

"Seriously? Dude, you gotta focus on the sheriff, not the demon."

"It's not that simple."

"Bullshit. You know what I see? I see typical Kylie bullshit, looking for something exotic, something romantic, and not being practical."

"Said the guy who cheated on me multiple times."

Jeff took a swig from the bottle and put it down empty on the coffee table. "Yeah. Okay. But I wasn't the only one wanting a fantasy. You did, too."

"I was working hard at the shop. Maybe I didn't have time to baby you."

"I'm not saying it was your fault—" He put his hands up in defense. "I'm not. And not just because you have a crossbow," he muttered the last thought. "But I'm saying that your head was not in the game. Maybe you were secretly planning to escape way before your mom got sick. Maybe you had already decided to leave long ago, open your own shop, and make your own plans without me. Because sometimes I sure felt like you were already gone."

I twisted the beer bottle back and forth by the neck. "You did? Really?"

"I knew I was already losing you. And I didn't know what to do or say."

I stared at the rug. He was right. Thinking about it now, I could see where I had begun to pull away. Maybe it was because of Jeff's hijinks, but part of it had started long before that. Was it me…or was it the Booke, pulling on me from all those miles away?

Even now, the Booke drew on me, its absence draining me. I knew it was safe, back at my shop. I knew exactly where it was. I knew it hadn't feared Baphomet or Andras or any*one* or any*thing*. And as the days drew on, I was feeling closer and closer to it. What did that mean? Was I going to become so obsessed with it that one day I wouldn't be able to focus on anything else?

"Kylie?" Jeff said again.

I looked up. Blinked.

"You're in your own world again. This is what you used to do in our shop."

"I did?"

"Yeah."

Oh, God. Maybe I *had* pushed him into someone else's arms— No! I refused to take responsibility for that! He was a grown human being and perfectly capable of controlling himself. Except that he hadn't.

"I'm sorry if I did that, Jeff, but it's no excuse for the things *you* did—"

"Dude, I know. I'm owning it, okay? But you gotta own it too. Something's up with you. Something's always been up with you. Maybe it *is* that book."

"Maybe it has been. How the hell do I get it out of my life?"

"It's gotta go. You have to get rid of it, destroy it."

"If only we could."

"Your coven will find a way. They are some pretty straight-up dudes. I trust them."

I bit my lip. If anyone could, they could. But I couldn't help remembering that if the Booke went, so would Erasmus.

The demon in question was suddenly standing in the arched doorway. Even with the light on above him, he always seemed to be in shadow. "Are you ready to go home?"

"She can stay as long as she likes," said Jeff with just the hint of a growl to his voice.

With narrowed eyes, Erasmus lowered into a pouncing stance. "Don't think you can win a fight with me, *dog*."

Jeff shot to his feet.

"Jeff! Don't take the bait."

Jeff's ears grew, and his nose took on a particularly snouty look. "Maybe you should go, Kylie. Only one monster at a time."

I grabbed Jeff's hand and squeezed it until his face was normal again. "It's going to be all right, Jeff. It will. You're Jeff. Not anyone else."

He shook himself and seemed calmer. "I'll see you tomorrow. Maybe the coven should come here. The ley lines make it safer."

"That's a good idea. I'll suggest that to Doc tonight."

I moved away from him, but he grabbed *my* arm this time. "Don't fall for his bullshit, Kylie. You've got a good head on your shoulders. Think with your head, not with your heart."

I nodded and gently pulled away.

* * *

ERASMUS WAS QUIET on the way back to the shop, searching the skies through the windshield.

"Is Jeff really more creature than man?"

He still hadn't answered when I pulled up in front of my shop. "Is it such a terrible thing if he is?" he finally asked.

"Yes! He's human. He was born that way, lived his entire life that way."

"I see." He sat for a long time, still as stone. When it looked as if he wasn't going to reply, I got out of the car and quickly unlocked my front door.

When I looked back, he had at least gotten out of the car, but he was still standing on the gravel outside. His long coat hung around him like a cloak.

"Um…are you coming in?"

"No. I think it wise I patrol tonight. See if I can't find where Andras is hiding. If he survived his encounter with Baphomet, that is."

"Oh. Okay. Well…good luck."

He gave me a long, lingering look, then vanished in a wisp of smoke.

* * *

I LOCKED UP, making sure all the windows were shut and the back door was secured, before pulling out my phone. I texted everyone about what had happened tonight and recommended that we meet at my grandpa's house tomorrow.

There had been too many distractions, and we still had a lot to do. Like learn more about the locket. I was glad Jeff was guarding it, but I also worried about the guy. His life had changed drastically in the last week and a half, and it was a helluva thing to have to reconcile. Strangely, it seemed to have matured him like nothing else had. If he had been like this when I'd met him…

No use thinking about that. And Erasmus was wrong. Even if Jeff was half wolf now, he was still a man. A man with a wolf problem, not a wolf with man issues.

I checked my phone one last time for any texts and noticed I had a voicemail. I clicked on it and heard Ruth's agitated voice on the line.

"Kylie, it seems I have misplaced my locket that you were so admiring. It might have fallen off in your shop or in the parking area. If you would be so kind as to look for it and return it, I'd be obliged. Good night."

Oops. Of course, she would have noticed. How was I going to hold her off? We'd all have to come up with a plausible lie. I didn't want to think about it now, so I trudged upstairs.

The Booke was leaning against the wall in the stairwell. I walked past it and did my nightly routine.

After I dressed myself in a long-sleeved pajama tee and sleep pants, I stepped toward my bedroom window to look down into the yard. A lone figure strode past my half-fence like a ghost wandering the plains. It was Erasmus, of course. I was glad he was on patrol. We had narrowly escaped with our lives tonight. I didn't know how long our luck would hold out. Surely it was only because I had help. Other Chosen Hosts had gone it alone and look where it had gotten them.

In bed with the lights out, I couldn't help but think about the Booke, its presence almost palpable in the back of my mind. I could *feel* it on the stairs. What had made it close up and become inactive in previous centuries? Was it because the

Chosen Hosts back then had captured all the baddies and sent them back? How *could* they have? Surely the Booke's supply of monsters was unlimited. No, there was only one conclusion I could draw. They had died, ending the Booke's cycle for that period. Yes, I decided with a chill in my bones, it had to have been the death of the Chosen Hosts. No wonder it had never been truly stopped for good.

And what had killed the Chosen Hosts? Some had been killed by the creatures themselves, Erasmus had told me that. But others had either committed suicide—sacrificing themselves for the good of mankind—or been killed by Erasmus himself.

How many Chosen Hosts had there been—Generations' worth? Centuries' worth?—that he'd killed, whose souls he'd eaten?

Had it been their deaths that had closed the Booke…or their eaten souls?

I rolled over away from the window and stuffed my arm under the pillow, blinking into the gloom of the bedroom. If it was their souls that triggered the closing of the Booke, then why didn't he just eat them right away? Did they need to…ripen? Were they tastier when they'd been allowed to hunt and chase the baddies? Did Erasmus even know? Or did the Powers That Be simply tell him to wait…wait…until a time of *their* choosing?

Dread made my belly squirm.

What if they ordered him to do it now? Would he?

I don't know how I fell asleep amid all the thoughts whirling around in my head, but I did. But I woke in the middle of the night, eyes wide and body alert. Something was in my room.

I opened my hand for the crossbow and it came to me. And when I quickly aimed it into the night, a hand simply pushed it out of the way.

"It's only me," said Erasmus in the dark.

"Jesus Christ," I gasped, relief shooting through me. I lowered the crossbow and switched on the bedside lamp. "What are you sneaking around for?"

"It's what I do."

He stood at the side of my bed, looking as he always did—stern, alert, stoic. His dark clothes and his black leather duster covered him. And he was looking at me curiously, the way he always seemed to be looking at me. He said he'd never had a Chosen Host like me before. Never met one who had friends willing to help, who stood up to him toe to toe, took his amulet right off his neck, and demanded a chthonic crossbow. What weapons had these former Chosen Hosts used if not the crossbow? Spears, axes, swords?

"Is everything all right?" I asked. "What did you find out?"

"Nothing. I could not find him. But I sensed him. He's still alive."

"That's too bad. It would have been nice if Baphomet had taken care of at least one of our problems. Should I pray to him to do that, do you think?"

"Don't. And don't mention his name again. How many times must I tell you?"

"Sorry. Forgot."

He huffed a breath and then looked about the room. "Well… I'll…let you get back to sleep."

Really? With all that hanging over my head. Sure. Why not?

I rubbed my eyes and slipped back down on the bed, pulling the covers up. "Whatever."

But he lingered. Slowly, he leaned over, paused, then bent further to kiss me. I let him. And then I reached up, kissing him deeper.

He put a knee on the bed. The mattress sloped downward as he slid his arms around me, lifting me toward him. After the kiss, he drew back only inches from my lips. "I mustn't keep doing this."

"No," I agreed. "You should leave."

"I should." He dipped down to kiss me again. I clutched at the collar of his duster. "I should go."

My lips lingered on his. "Or…" I said softly, "you *could* stay."

"I could."

I ruffled the coat collar. "You'd have to take this off."

"And you'd have to remove that ridiculous outfit of yours."

I looked his duster over. "I wouldn't start calling what *I'm* wearing ridiculous."

His affronted expression made me chuckle.

But he took the coat off anyway.

CHAPTER THIRTEEN

ERASMUS WAS GONE before I awoke. He might be a terrible demon in every other way, but he was certainly good at...*that*.

Thinking lingeringly about last night, I showered, dressed, and went downstairs to open the shop for the day. I hadn't expected Jeff, but there he was. Again.

"Hey, Jeff," I said as casually as I could. "I know you're stuck here for a while, and I don't mind loaning you some money occasionally when you need it—"

"But you can't afford to hire me. I know. I just don't have much else to do. I already cleaned up your grandpa's place, and I'm kind of going stir crazy. As for money, my shop and the rentals are doing okay, at least that's what my bank account says. And you putting me up at your grandpa's house is saving me loads of expenses, so...if it's okay with you, I don't mind helping out. For free, you know. I still feel I owe you." He smiled. It was that old Jeff smile. I had no doubt he'd be able to charm the female customers as much as Erasmus did.

I shrugged and went back to looking over the herb inventory. This was my life right now; the man I left California to get away from was now working at my shop in Maine.

After a while, I checked my watch. Ed was supposed to come by so we could go over to see Doug. I was steeling myself for that encounter. The Ordo wanted to be so big and bad but really, how bad could they be? They were two-bit bikers from a small town. They wanted to seem scary, but I just didn't think they could pull it off. If the Booke hadn't given them special powers, they might have just faded into the woodwork. Now they were in everyone's faces, summoning Baphomet and performing other dangerous black magic. All the while remaining completely clueless.

At least the Booke gave my coven power, too, so they could work to counteract the damage the Ordo was doing. What would happen when the Booke was finally closed again? Would that power vanish? I kind of hoped so. But maybe I'd never know. *No, Kylie, don't think that way.* I wasn't going anywhere. If anything was getting retired, it was the Booke. We all had to get *that* into our heads.

"Did you call the coven?" asked Jeff, startling me out of my reverie.

"I texted them. I kind of hoped I could leave the shop to you this afternoon so I can get over to Grandpa's place when Jolene gets off school."

"Seraphina too?"

I stopped. "Jeff…she's old enough to be your mother."

He shrugged and gave me one of his crooked smiles. "She's still got it going on, though."

I shook my head. Jeff Chase never changed. "I'm waiting for Ed to pick me up. Remember, we close at six. Then you can come on over to Grandpa's."

* * *

ED WAS FIFTEEN minutes late, but he finally arrived with his fur-collared coat and Smokey Bear hat. He acknowledged Jeff with a chin raise before looking down his nose at me. "This is against my better judgment."

"Then it's a good thing it's not up to you."

Burn, mouthed Jeff from across the room. Ed sneered at him and followed me out the door.

He drove the Interceptor slow and easy up the highway. "Last night," I asked, "what was the damage?" I had been afraid to find out.

"It wasn't pretty. Three farms. Houses blasted nearly down to the foundations. Only one survivor, and he's barely holding on."

"Oh my God."

"I managed to convince everyone it was probably a gas leak. Crews are tearing up the roads now. People are being evacuated. I'd feel better about it, but some aren't going far enough away. Just to their neighbors' houses. I wish I could get everyone out of harm's way."

"Me too. Can't you get the county to—I don't know—declare a state of emergency?"

"I tried to suggest it, but they'll want proof, and of course, there isn't any."

"You've done the best you can."

"Is this going to be a nightly thing now? Is he going to swoop down and snatch people off the streets?"

"God, don't say that! I hope not. But… I just don't know."

He gripped the steering wheel and frowned. "Can I just say right now that I hate that book of yours?"

I did too. But of course, my emotions were warring with each other. I hated the Booke with all my heart…and wanted to grow closer to it. *So* fucked up.

I sat there, quiet, lost in my own thoughts. Ed was too, I guess. I certainly didn't relish going into Hansen Mills, but we had to. I almost wanted to take Jeff with us, so he could follow the ley lines. Erasmus told me he'd only be able to see them at night. Of course, Erasmus could see them all the time. But he wasn't with us either.

We didn't pass many cars coming from the other direction, which made it a leisurely cruise through the dense growth of trees on either the side of the road. Dark pines cast their shadows interrupted by the bright splash of hornbeams, alders, and maples. It was all so beautiful. I couldn't fully enjoy it, wondering what lay beyond the trees. Worrying that at any moment Baphomet or Andras could come after me and hurt the people I had come to care about.

"Andras showed up last night too and attacked Baph—uh, Goat Guy, and we just slipped away while they were fighting. The good news is that I got the ghoul last night. Wrote it in the Booke and everything. The coven is going to meet tonight at my grandpa's house on Alderbrook Lane to go over our next steps."

"Where?"

"It's that street that doesn't exist…unless you think about it hard enough."

"Oh, yeah…" he said dreamily. "God, that's weird."

"It's a spell."

"I can still hardly believe that stuff exists and that it works. But…I've sure seen a lot in the last few days." He flicked a glance at me. "How are you holding up?"

"Okay, I guess."

"I suppose…that Erasmus guy is—"

"I don't think you want to finish that sentence."

He lightly touched the brim of his hat. "Yes, ma'am."

Doug's place was just up a dirt road—a mobile home with a barn. Both were in poor shape, especially since we sort of trashed the barn the last time that we'd been here. Though it wasn't entirely our fault. Goat Guy had a lot to do with it. But there was Doug's brand-spanking-new bike parked out front. And it looked like he was alone, which was good news.

We pulled up, Ed refraining from hitting the lights and siren. His jaw was stiff and tight when he got out of the car, grabbing the rifle from its holster in the seat. It looked like one of those semi-automatic army-issued guns I kept seeing on TV.

"Really?" I asked. He said nothing and gripped it by the barrel, carrying it by his thigh. I rolled my eyes and followed him to the mobile home door.

"Police. Open up, Doug." Ed pounded on the door.

I could hear approaching steps before Doug threw the door open. "You're two weeks early for trick-or-treating, Edward. And it's a lousy costume." Then he noticed me. "Hey, sweet thing. Now *you're* welcome to come in. Don't happen to have that book on you, do you?"

"Nope."

Doug stepped aside as Ed pushed his way through. "I don't suppose you've got a warrant."

"To visit my one and only brother?"

The place smelled like dirty carpet and skunky weed. There were the remnants of a joint in an ashtray. Doug smirked at Ed's frown of disapproval. "Hey, bro, it's perfectly legal in the great state of Maine."

"I'm aware."

"So what do I owe the pleasure? Gonna illegally turn over my place again?"

"Kylie wants to talk to you."

"Oh really?" Doug sat down on his Naugahyde recliner and leaned back, hands laced behind his head. There was an enormous big screen TV on the wall and an old-timey popcorn machine that looked like a cart next to it. Both looked brand new.

"Come into some money, Doug?" I asked, glancing around.

"It's just good old-fashioned hard work, sweet thing."

"I'm not sure that I believe that. What is it you do for a living again?"

"I resent the implication. I'm a man who repairs cars and rebuilds engines. It's patient and precise work."

"You are so full of shit, Doug," growled Ed.

"Bro, that's just the kind of attitude that will send you to the hospital with an early coronary. You need to relax more. Get yourself some therapeutic vegetation." He gestured toward the bag of weed beside the ashtray.

"No thanks."

"Don't knock it till you've tried it. How about you, Kylie? Or does your boyfriend here disapprove?"

I pulled up a footstool and sat…and then was sorry I touched it. "Look, Doug, we're here for a reason. You haven't come across a stash of gold lately, have you?"

Something passed through his eyes but he hid it in his jovial manner. His smile was broad under his mustache and beard. "From a Leprechaun? Who even says 'stash of gold' these days?"

"I don't care where you got it. I don't care *that* you got it— new bike, big screen TV, bags of weed. All I know is what comes with it. You ever go out after sunset, Doug? You and your Ordo pals? Have you noticed the mist lately?"

His smile faltered. "What are you talking about?"

Ed tightened his grip on the rifle. "Remember the Warrens? They're dead now. All of them. Down to the dog on the porch."

Doug scrambled up from his chair. "What are you talking about? We didn't have anything to do with anything like that."

I pushed past Ed. "They're dead just the same. And the ones you stole the gold from, the Draugr? They're ancient zombie Vikings. They want their gold back. Whether you found it or conjured it or whatever, you have to give it back before anyone else gets killed."

He stared at us incredulously. "Zombie Vikings? I know what *I'm* smoking, but what are *you* smoking?"

"Cut the crap, Doug," said Ed, "and listen to her, for pity's sake."

He waved his hand at us and retreated to his dingy kitchen, in all its seventies goldenrod glory. "We didn't steal anything." He opened the fridge and popped the top off a can of beer, slurping up the overflowing froth.

"Then where'd you get the money?" asked Ed, standing over him in the doorway.

He shrugged. "A little here, a little there."

I folded my arms and did my own glaring. "You got it from Shabiri."

"You called?"

Scared the hell out of me. But there she was suddenly behind us, catsuit and all.

Ed held his rifle at his shoulder, aiming. Shabiri gave him a silky appraisal like she had the first time she'd seen him.

"Where'd you get the gold, Shabiri?" asked Ed. It was likely the same tone he used in the interrogation room. I wouldn't have wanted to be on the other end of that.

Doug's eyes widened. "How do you know about her?"

"Kylie filled me in. On a lot of things."

"Well...shit."

She made a point of walking all the way around him, examining him. If a guy had leered at me the way she was leering, I'd be calling the cops. He really had no choice but to lower the gun, not that it would do any good anyway.

"You didn't say please." She poked him in the chest.

Maybe he wouldn't slap a lady, but *I* wasn't above it. "Spill, Shabiri," I said. "We've been dealing with Draugr."

Her salacious smile vanished. "Draugr? Darlings, that's nothing to joke about."

I might have knocked Ed sharply out of the way to get in her face. "No shit. People have died. Give back the freakin' gold, already."

She exchanged a sly glance with Doug before she shrugged. "I don't know what you're talking about."

I reached out and grabbed Doug's demon amulet, dragging him forward by the chain. I squeezed it and twisted. Shabiri cried out, cringing. "Stop touching that!" she snarled between gritted teeth.

Doug snatched it back out of my grip. "Hands off, lady." Vaguely, I remembered when Doug tried to steal *my* amulet...and got a burned hand for his trouble. I looked at my palm. No damage.

The roar of bikes echoed out in the yard. Looked like the rest of the gang was pulling up in front of the mobile home. I saw Charise swagger off her new bike as Dean and Bob made their way up the steps, barging in.

Charise swept in after with leathers similar to Shabiri's. "We saw the police car—" She smiled and looked Ed up and down. "Look who's here!" she said cheerfully, until she spied me wiggling my fingers at her. "Oh. You too?"

Ed's body language looked all kinds of uncomfortable. *What? Please don't tell me—*

"Your old girlfriend's here, *Edweird*," said Doug, frowning. "I guess this is awkward. New girl, old girl."

"Shut up, Doug," he muttered.

I stared at Ed. His reddened cheeks said all I needed to know.

Charise sat on the arm of the chair where Doug was sitting and leaned into him. "I don't go for cops anymore."

Shabiri shook her head and hung back, eerily similar to how Erasmus would have behaved; staying in the shadows but missing nothing.

Ed threw his shoulders back, rifle across his chest in a show of force. "Listen up, everyone. We know damn well you all came into some money. I don't care where it came from, but you've got to give it back. We're being attacked by what Kylie calls the Draugr. They're undead Vikings, and their sole purpose is to protect their magical hoard of gold. And when they don't get it, they kill. An innocent family was slain, all because of your greed. So whatever you have to do, bring the gold to the police station, and we'll return it to them."

Everyone was silent…then burst out laughing.

"Right, Ed," cackled Charise. "That's just what we're gonna do. Bring gold to the police station. I mean, *if* we had it."

"That's dumb, even for you, *sheriff*," said Dean of the pentagram tattoo.

"I'm not kidding. If I have to trash every one of your houses, I'll do it."

"Get a warrant, maybe," said Bob, smiling at Charise.

Ed stomped over to Bob and grabbed him by the shirt, hauling him only inches from his face. "I don't do warrants for supernatural shit. I just barge in and do what I have to do, get it? And if it means beating your ass to a pulp, I'll do that, too."

"Okay, okay," I soothed. "Ed, we can go about this more reasonably."

"Back off, Teen Barbie," said Shabiri, nudging me aside. "I like this rough and tumble sheriff. It's oh-so-sexy when he takes charge. Dougie, how come you never told me about him?"

"I didn't know you cared. Well, look at this big happy family. It's too bad you can't stay, bro."

"I'm staying right here until you turn over that gold, Doug."

"And *I* have a bone to pick with you," I said.

Doug grinned. "Anytime, baby."

Charise frowned. Bob looked ready to swoop in and comfort her if only she'd notice.

"Your goat god is trying to kill me. Are you concerned at all that he's loose and ready to strike at anything he doesn't like... including any of you?"

Doug's jovial expression dimmed. "I call that your problem."

"No, it isn't my problem. It's *your* problem. Or more accurately..." I spun and pointed at Shabiri. "It's *her* problem. This gold belongs to the Draugr. She's brought them down on you, and you don't even know how much you've been played."

"No, sweet thing." Doug rose, all humor wiped from his face. "I'm not being played. I'm just getting my own back."

It happened so fast no one was prepared. He snapped his hand out and grabbed Ed's rifle. But even as Ed tugged it, Doug cold-cocked Ed square in the jaw. He went down like a crumbling wall. I lurched forward to catch him, but Shabiri sunk her talons into my arm and yanked me back.

"Tie him up," said Doug, turning away with a wince and rubbing his knuckles.

Shabiri kept a death grip on my arm as she slammed a hand over my mouth. "We can't have you calling for Erasmus, can we?" she hissed in my ear. "Anyone got any duct tape?"

CHAPTER FOURTEEN

ED AND I were quickly duct-taped to chairs, though Ed was sort of out of it, lolling next to me. Shabiri had made sure my mouth was covered. Charise had placed a big piece of duct tape over my lips with smirking satisfaction. The whole thing was ridiculous.

"Shabiri," said Doug. "What is the Draugr?"

"Nothing to worry about."

He grabbed the demon amulet with the green stone eyes and held it up to her face. "Maybe I want to worry about it. What the hell are they?"

She sighed and leaned against the wood-paneled wall. "They are undead warriors who guard their gold hoard for all eternity. Anyone who stands in their way gets crushed to death."

"So, this gold you helped us get." He flicked a glance at Ed. The sheriff was coming back to his senses and seemed mad as hell about the duct tape on his mouth. "Where did it come from?"

"I told you not to worry about it."

"And I told you to answer me. Are the undead out there killing people?"

"What do you care, Doug? I thought you wanted to be feared. I thought you wanted to be respected. Everyone respects a man who holds their life in his hands. You're going to have to put your big boy pants on to earn the respect you claim to want. You're going to have to do some bad, bad things."

He scowled. "I know that! I don't care. Who are these people to me? It's just…what if Charise had been caught by these guys. It would have been nice to have a heads-up."

"Oh, excuse me," she said, tossing her hair over her shoulder. "Let's *certainly* not get *Charise* of all people consumed by undead Vikings."

"Hey, bitch." Charise pointed her talon of a finger in Shabiri's face. "Shut your damned mouth."

Shabiri blinked slowly before darting her hand out around Charise's neck and lifting her up. Charise scrabbled at Shabiri's hand with everything she had, but Shabiri easily raised her higher, one-handed, as Charise choked and kicked her feet uselessly.

"Put her down, Shabiri," said Doug in a stern tone.

"Doug, tell your side-thing that she needs to treat me with a tad more respect."

"Put her down."

Shabiri turned toward him, her eyes beginning to glow a bright green. When she smiled, her mouth was far wider than it should have been with more teeth that were sharp like a shark's. "You can only order me around so much, dear Doug, before I *snap!*" She shook Charise, whose face was turning blue.

"*Please*, Shabiri…" he said.

The demon seemed to relent and slowly lowered her before letting her go. Charise fell to the ground, grabbing at her neck and gasping.

Doug was too busy facing off with Shabiri to notice Bob on his knees, with his arm around Charise, wiping away her tears.

"That's not how this works," said Doug, eyes narrow, fists trembling at his sides.

"Are you sure?" Shabiri wasn't winded. Of course not. She was a demon. "Are you sure you know *anything*, Doug?"

He marched to the kitchen, grabbed the salt shaker, and heaved it at her. She vanished with a curl of black smoke. The shaker hit the front door and shattered.

Doug ran a hand over his mouth and beard, before pivoting to stare at Ed.

"Well," he said after a time, "it looks like we have a difference of opinion. How do I know that these Draugr are out there doing what you say they are?"

Ed and I gave him withering looks. *Kind of hard to answer, Doug, when our mouths are taped up.*

He must have realized it, too, because he stepped forward and tore off Ed's tape.

"You hit me, you son of a bitch. I'm charging you with assault on an officer."

"Blah, blah, blah." Doug mimed a talking puppet with his fingers. "Later, I'm sure. What are Draugr?"

"Kylie knows more."

"I'm not taking off the gag. She might call her demon."

Ed looked at me then. And I could see the swirl of emotions in his eyes. *Her* demon. He took a deep breath. "I saw them. I fought them. They're…really undead. Walking corpses. Zombies. They have swords and axes, and they aren't easy to stop. And they're still out there. They go for anything with gold. Anything. They bit off the fingers of the Warrens to get at their wedding rings."

Charise gasped and reached for the cache of gold necklaces at her throat.

"Yeah," said Ed. "Anything. But if they get their hoard back, maybe they'll stop and…go back to wherever they came from."

"They could be from Kylie's book."

"They aren't. And what is she saying about Baphomet? Did you really summon him?"

Doug looked defensive. "Look, maybe we got a little ahead of ourselves with him. We thought he was doing things for us. Turns out it was really Shabiri. I guess…she kind of goaded us into summoning him. We didn't know…" He rubbed at his beard.

"Did you hear the sirens last night? That was your pal Baphomet. He wiped out the Harrisons, the Norrises, and the Greeleys. Their whole families, all in one go. That's *your* fault, Doug. You summoned him. God knows how many others he'll kill."

"What? You're lying."

"He killed them all! Blew them up. Their houses are nothing but cinders. Chris Norris was the only survivor, and over sixty percent of his body is burned. He's gonna wish he didn't make it."

Doug wore an expression of shock and terror. "We just want the book," he said distantly.

I hoped he saw me roll my eyes with all the disdain I could muster.

"I'm pretty sure Kylie must have told you that the book is attached to her…with all the problems that come with it."

"I can't believe she told you."

"She kind of had to when the assassin demon showed up right in front of me."

"What assassin demon?"

"Seriously? You might as well confess to that, too. Because when I get out of this, I am going to kick your ass so hard, you'd be lucky if there's anything left of you to throw in jail."

Something hardened in Doug's eyes, all the empathy seeming to wash away. "Then maybe we shouldn't let you go."

"You haven't got the balls."

"Oh, yeah? You know, you've been a thorn in my side all my life. I wouldn't mind if you just disappeared."

"And what would you tell Mom and Pop? You are a piece of work, Doug. Oh, it's all very biblical, but I repeat: you don't have the balls."

I screamed behind my tape and rocked my chair violently back and forth. *Ed, you are such an idiot! Don't bait him!*

They both stared at me like *I* was crazy!

"So these zombies," said Doug, back to business. "What about them? Are they out there right now?"

Ed shook his head. "They come out at night. They rise when the sun sets and disappear when the sun rises."

"Fine. So, if we put the two of you outside, maybe with a little gold chain on you, they'll come?"

Ed gritted his teeth. "Don't even try it."

Doug clapped his hands together. "Sounds like a plan to me!"

I threw my head back on my shoulders. Great. Just great. I fall into the middle of sibling rivalry and get eaten by zombies because these two can't shut the hell up. I scowled as hard as I could at Ed who suddenly refused to look at me.

We sat taped to our chairs while the Fantastic Four played video games and drank beer all afternoon. The scintillating conversation was just about killing me with boredom. And I was achy and sore and hungry. I wondered if Jeff would worry about me being gone so long. Or Erasmus. But I was with Ed so I was safe, right?

Ed turned to me and said quietly, "I'm sorry about this. I didn't think Doug would...I'm sorry."

So much I wanted to ask. Especially about Charise. What did Ed ever see in her? Maybe it was just what happened in small towns where there weren't enough girls to go around.

"Looks like the sun's going down." Doug rose and stretched. Something I longed to do. "And there's a mist rising. Let's see what happens when we put the bait out for the zombies. Take 'em, boys."

Dean and Bob managed to grab Ed, chair and all, and drag him outside, knocking him down each stair as they went. Doug and Charise lifted me, Charise's nails biting into my arm, the be-yotch.

They placed us right outside the mobile home in full view of Doug's big living room window.

"Oh, and we'll need this." Doug snatched the necklaces off of Charise's neck. She yowled her unhappiness. "Shut up, Charise. I'll buy you better ones." He dropped them over my head and crouched in front of me. "You know, that spear you stole from me, Gáe Bulg, the Spear of Mortal Pain? It won't seem to come to me anymore. That wasn't cool, girl. Not cool at all. If you get out of this alive, we'll have to discuss this further."

They left us there in the cold as the sky darkened and mist slithered over the gravel drive.

I kept pushing on the duct tape with my tongue, trying to dislodge it, while Ed concentrated on struggling with his bonds. I tried to communicate with my eyes and through muffled sounds. If only he would call out for Erasmus, maybe he'd come. But I supposed that was the last thing he'd ever do.

I glanced toward the picture window; the gang was all there, snug inside while we began to freeze. We both had coats on, but they did little to protect against the wind. Night was falling, and the shadows in the woods around us seemed to be growing denser with the dark. But it was that persistent mist creeping toward us that was making me most nervous.

When the sun abruptly dropped behind the hills, all was cast in gray. Did the Ordo really mean to kill us? Had Ed unwittingly goaded them to the next level?

I tried to move my arms in earnest, but they were taped tight to the chair. I glanced at the window. Charise was smiling. Dean's face was bright in anticipation. I guess he wanted to see zombies in the flesh or only half-believed in them. Bob looked vaguely interested in the proceedings. But Doug's expression was the most inscrutable. Maybe he hated Ed as much as Ed seemed to hate him. How could it have gotten so bad between brothers?

A movement at the edge of the woods caught my attention and I stilled, straining my eyes to discern what it was in the falling light. Maybe a deer. A squirrel. It didn't move again, which made me think it might have been my imagination until something else in a different part of the woods drew my eye. There was definitely something moving over there.

I screamed at Ed through my tape.

He turned and saw it too, then struggled hard and glared up at the window. "This isn't funny anymore, Doug. Something is coming!"

Doug moved closer to the window and looked where we were looking. Charise pressed her nose to the glass, leaving greasy smears.

I heard branches and twigs snapping. Something was coming out of the shadowy mist. Oh, God. They were coming out of the trees.

"Goddammit, Doug!" cried Ed. "I'm not kidding!"

But Doug and company just stood at the window, watching it all unfold.

The forest seemed to tremble as they stepped closer. And then the first one breached the dense growth. I saw the boot step on the grass at the edge…and drag a large battle axe over the sharp line of dark and light.

I had to get free of this damned chair. The only way to do that was to break it, which was *definitely* going to hurt. I set my feet firmly to the ground and shoved back. Since my legs were also taped to the chair legs, it wasn't easy. I pushed down hard on the balls of my feet until the chair teetered back.

Come on, Chosen Host skills, I urged in my head.

I rocked forward again, and this time, when I shoved back, I planned to give it more momentum. Ed saw what I was doing and mirrored me.

One big shove and I was careening over. The chair smacked hard on the ground, which hurt my lower back but didn't manage to break me free. Dammit! Now what?

The Draugr with the battle axe was drawing closer. The axe blade dragged along the ground and over the gravel, making a scraping sound. More were coming out of the forest, all heading straight for us.

Even Charise, pressed to the window, had lost her smile. And Doug seemed shocked. I guess he hadn't quite believed it either. He signaled to the Ordo; they left the window and came out onto the front porch.

I struggled, trying to roll the chair and loosen its joints. Anything to dislodge the tape. I smacked into a big rock in his front garden—a place of weeds and dead shrubs marked off by a row of rocks of all sizes. One of the chair legs cracked. I heaved back and did it again. The leg broke off, freeing *my* leg. I snatched a glance over my shoulder and spotted the Draugr lumbering toward me, slowly raising his axe.

Chapter Fifteen

I ONLY HAD one leg free. Not as good as an arm. But with a leg I could at least maneuver the chair back toward the rock. I slammed it back, trapping my upper arm in the process. Did that ever hurt like a son of a bitch! But I thought I heard it crack...or was it my bone? Hopefully not. I needed my arm free. I rolled on my back, further cracking the chair so I could begin to loosen my arm.

Something made me turn just as the axe come down toward me. I ducked my head and rolled right at the Viking, taking his legs out from under him. My nose filled with the stench of rotted flesh. I wasn't quite free, though, and so I rolled away, trying to slam myself back again to crack the chair completely.

My arm was suddenly free. It snapped up without my telling it to, grabbing the axe handle I hadn't noticed whooshing toward me. My Chosen Host strength held the weapon at bay, while the Draugr breathed his foul breath right in my face. I stared up into his empty eyes—just open, gooey sockets—and gritted my teeth as I pushed the axe back and away. He looked slightly perplexed that I had been able to do that, but was winding up to strike again when his head blew off.

Bits of Draugr covered me. I swiveled. Doug was standing on the porch, smoke coming from Ed's rifle in his hand.

I reached up and tore the duct tape off of my mouth. "*Erasmus!*" I yelled at the top of my lungs.

Suddenly, a dark shape moved with lightning speed between the Vikings, cutting their legs out from under them. They fell like bowling pins. Doug fired again, aiming for their heads—maybe he watched a lot of zombie movies—and felled several, which was good since the ones Erasmus had stopped were already getting up again.

I was able to tear the rest of the tape off my body and jump to my feet. Ed was still struggling with his chair on the ground. He'd been doing the same thing I had done to try and get free. I stopped him and ripped off the rest of his tape. He kicked his chair aside and reached for his gun in his holster, since the Ordo hadn't bothered taking it.

Ed was aiming straight-armed at the zombie heads, too, backing away toward the porch. "Come on, Kylie," he urged. "In the house!"

Doug was still shooting as we shoved our way through the Ordo back inside.

My phone buzzed. I automatically grabbed it, worried some other thing had befallen the coven. When I saw it was Jeff, I put it to my ear.

"Jeff, is everyone all right?"

"Where are you? Everyone's here at your grandpa's."

"We ran into a little trouble with the Ordo."

"The who?"

"The guys who beat you up?"

"I'll tell Doc, then. You want our help?"

"Oh, shit!" A battle axe came swooping down at me. I feinted to the right and kicked out with my left foot. The zombie went down. Someone fired their gun right near my head. Now my ear was ringing.

"Kylie? What the hell's going on? Was that a gunshot?"

I pushed the headless zombie off of me. Eww. "Just a little problem with the Draugr. The Ordo is sort of helping."

"Kylie, I can wolf out and come help you."

"No! Just stay where you are. Stay!"

"That isn't funny."

"I didn't mean—"

"I'll tell Doc." And then he hung up.

Doug shot a few more rounds, then slid back through the door, locking it and shoving a chair against it.

"Sorry," he muttered. "I guess I didn't believe you."

I punched his arm. "You son of a bitch! You could have gotten us killed!"

"Not with *your* super powers, sweetheart."

I glanced out the window to my chair. It was splintered to pieces. "I did that?"

"And like super-fast."

But it hadn't been fast at all. Did my perception of time slow in Chosen Host mode? Weird.

Charise was suddenly in my face, hand out. "I want them back."

Her necklaces. I disentangled them from the amulet and threw them at her feet. "Take them. I don't want them."

Out of the corner of my eye I could tell she was winding up to punch me, but without even looking I stopped her fist in my hand. I tightened my grip and turned to her. Her dark red lips twisted with a wince. "Don't. Touch. Me." When I tossed her hand away, she nearly fell over.

"And as for the rest of you," I said, spearing them all with my glare, "do you believe us now? That those monsters out there are here because of you? They've killed…because of *you*!"

The Ordo exchanged glances.

"But…but Shabiri said…" Bob began.

Dean shook his head. "I think we listen too much to Shabiri."

I blew my hair off my forehead. "The first smart thing you've ever said."

"Shabiri has done a lot for us," said Doug.

Ed shot forward and grabbed his rifle out of Doug's hand. And then he decked Doug right onto his smelly, avocado-green shag carpet. "I can't even begin to add up the counts against you."

I straightened my jacket, still watching Erasmus kick Draugr butt, only to have the Vikings continue to get up again. "If the Ordo helps us now, that will go a long way toward forgiving the charges."

"No, it won't!" Ed was staring at me incredulously.

"We have bigger fish to fry, Ed. Draugr, Baphomet, Andras?"

Doug straightened, rubbing his bearded jaw. "Who's this Andras?"

"He's the assassin you sent to get me."

"We never sent an assassin. We figured our Lord Baphomet would do his will."

"Don't say his name," I muttered absently, thinking.

"Doug, are you really telling the truth this time?" asked Ed, gripping the rifle tightly.

Doug stayed on the ground, resting his arm on his upraised knee. "Yeah, I'm really telling the truth. I don't know this Andras dude."

If Doug hadn't conjured him, then that put it back on Ruth.

I watched out the window as the Draugr suddenly seemed to lose interest in Erasmus and the fight. They all turned away at the same time and trudged back into the woods. But now I worried about some other hapless farmhouse. Would another family end up like the Warrens?

Erasmus stood alone in the yard, shoulders heaving as he watched them depart. Then he turned toward the window. His eyes zeroed in on mine.

One minute he was out there, the next standing in front of me. He took me by the shoulders, hauled me in, and kissed me fiercely.

After a moment, Erasmus let me go…and Doug burst out laughing. "Oh bro! No wonder you're so butthurt and angry. Girlfriend's gone demon on you."

Ed scowled. "Shut up, Doug."

"Oh, I don't think so!" He tried to stand, but Ed shoved him back down with the butt of his rifle.

"I'm not kidding. Shut the hell up. The rest of you, on the floor with him."

Slowly, hands raised, they all sat cross-legged beside Doug. "Now get this through your thick skulls. You need to help us. You need to return the gold. Where is it?"

They all looked dumbly at each other.

"This is ridiculous," I muttered. "Erasmus, make Doug tell us."

Doug's eyes widened with alarm. "You...you can't do that. You're the good guy."

I folded my arms. "I'm a pretty pissed off 'good guy.' Erasmus?"

He grinned as Shabiri had, with a too wide mouth filled with too many teeth. "With pleasure."

"Shabiri!" cried Doug as Erasmus moved toward him.

Shabiri appeared in an instant, but she looked annoyed. "Got yourself into a pickle, I see." She smiled, looking Erasmus over in that lascivious way of hers. "Hello, Erasmus."

"Get out of my way."

"I'm afraid I can't let you hurt him. Demon code and all."

"He wears your amulet. Foolish of you to let him."

"Look who's talking? I notice that the human female has yours."

"That," he said looking back at me, "I don't mind."

She seemed taken aback, staring at him with her mouth agape. Erasmus hid his face in the shadow of his hair. Maybe he hadn't meant to blurt that out so blatantly. Everyone else was looking at him with some surprise, too.

I ducked my own head since Ed couldn't seem to stop glaring at *me*.

"You stupid, stupid fool," said Shabiri when she'd gotten her voice back. "Didn't I warn you centuries ago about that?"

"Are you going to get out of my way?"

"Well..." She glanced at her polished nails and rubbed them on her leather top. "I *would*, darling, but he *does* have my amulet, and I'm afraid I absolutely *must* protect him, though he scarcely deserves it."

"Hey!" cried Doug.

She turned to him. "You must admit, you asked for it. I mean, look at the mess you're in. The big, strong sheriff there has the drop on you. And you let Kylie get the better of you too."

"I am *trying* to get the book…"

"You're not trying very hard."

Erasmus, exasperated, grabbed Shabiri and whirled her around. "Why are you still forcing this imbecile to go after the book? I have told you time and again that it will yield you nothing. The book is solely the possession of the Chosen Host. No one else can use it. No one has the power."

"Not even you, darling?"

"Why won't you believe me? If I could free myself from the book, don't you think I would have done so centuries ago?"

She narrowed her eyes. "You really do believe that, don't you?"

"What are you talking about? It is what it is. It is far more ancient than you are…"

"You don't know! You let yourself be yanked around as if there's a ring in your nose, and you have no idea." She grabbed his arm and they both disappeared.

"What the hell just happened?" I asked.

"Looks like our demons are having issues," said Doug. He squared on me with a stupid grin on his face. "So, you and Erasmus. My, my. That must really burn your biscuits, Edward. That your girlfriend prefers demon action to you."

"We're taking a break!" said Ed between clenched teeth.

"Is that what you call it? I think the word you're looking for is 'dumped.'"

He looked like he was about to slam the rifle butt into Doug's face. Though I wouldn't have minded that one bit, it wouldn't get us the result we were looking for.

"Ed!" I said, stepping in front of him, blocking his advance. "We need to get the gold back to the Draugr."

He trembled in anger but took a deep breath and lowered the gun. Rubbing his hands over his eyes, he nodded. "All right. Okay. Doug? Are you ready to tell us?"

"Just to show that I'm not an unreasonable guy...it's in the crawlspace. There's an access door in the closet in my bedroom."

"Great." Ed pointed the gun at Dean. "You go get it."

"Me?"

"You don't think I'm going to let my brother get it and accidentally slip away, do you?"

Doug shook his head. "You don't trust me. After I saved your life."

"By first putting it in jeopardy? Get up, Fitch."

Dean rose and wiped at his leather chaps. "Such little respect around here," he muttered as he made his way into the hall.

"Kylie, why don't you go with him."

I nodded. Dean didn't seem happy about it, but I wasn't interested in what he thought. In fact, I wished that I had a little more Chosen Host skills at my disposal. Maybe a spell or two to zap his ass with. Or that spear.

I followed Dean into a back bedroom with an enormous bed covered by a gaudy bedspread. All the room needed was a velvet painting hanging on the wall.

Dean opened a closet stuffed with T-shirts, jeans, and boots of varying shades of brown. He knelt and pushed the shoes aside, searching for the trap door. When he found it, he looked up at me in surprise. He dug his hand through the carpet to grab the ring and haul it up. Peering in, he stopped. "I don't see nothing."

"Maybe you have to go down into the crawlspace."

Scandalized, he shook his head. "I don't want to go down there."

"What's the matter, Dean? Afraid of spiders?"

"There's stuff worse than spiders."

"I know. I keep having to kill them."

His eyes rounded as he looked me over. "Doug says a lot of stuff about you...that I'm beginning to think isn't true."

"Stuff? Like what?"

He shrugged. "That you're just a...a girl, you know."

I threw my hands up. "What the hell, Dean? This is the twenty-first century. Women can even vote."

"I know! It's just... Charise isn't anything like you. To tell you the truth, she's kind of a bitch sometimes."

"Well, thanks for the vote of confidence."

He ran his hand over his shaved head. "Well...I guess I'm going in. You don't have a flashlight by any chance, do you?"

"You've got a phone, haven't you?"

"Oh, yeah." He dug it out, clicked on the flashlight, and shined it down the hole. I looked over his shoulder. I guess I expected a Leprechauny pot of gold, but there wasn't anything there but a layer of fine dirt.

Dean set the phone down beside the square hole, and dipped his foot in. When he put his other foot in, he was only waist deep. He grabbed the phone and slowly bent to lower himself the rest of the way.

"If I don't come back, something probably got me."

"I won't let anything get you."

He leaned an arm on the carpeted floor. "Just for the record, if you were *my* girlfriend, I wouldn't let no demon kiss you." He gave me a significant look before dropping out of sight.

His words had been slightly disconcerting at first, but if it meant at least one of the Ordo was on my side, it was worth it.

After listening to him grunt and swear, I decided that waiting for him would be more tortuous than going down there myself, so I sat on the edge, dangled my feet down, and plunged in.

I followed the beam of Dean's flashlight as he whipped it this way and that. He pivoted, even bent over as he was, and shined the flashlight right in my eyes. "What are you doing here?"

"I thought you might need some help." I suddenly realized I wasn't fond of cramped spaces. But as I lifted my own phone and shined light into the far reaches of the underside of the mobile home, past the axles and stacked foundation cinder blocks, it seemed plain to me that nothing was here. Doug had lied. Surprise, surprise.

"I don't see anything," I said with a sigh.

Dean was more direct. "Bastard."

"Did you ever see it, Dean? This gold?"

He nodded, moving farther to the edges where the lattice covering the bottom of the mobile home was broken. "It kind of looked like an old pirate chest. With coins and jewelry and stuff. Charise couldn't wait to get her hands on it."

"Those gold necklaces she's got. Were they part of it?"

"I think so."

"Dean, why are you loyal to him? You know he's going to screw you over if it's to his advantage."

"That's not...necessarily true."

"Really?"

He looked right at me, then. "You don't get Doug, or any of us. You're from away. Things are different in small towns. We stick together. We stay put."

"I'm not disparaging that. Just the way you're going about everything. It was the worst thing you could have done summoning Ba—uh, Goat Guy. Did you really think that was a good thing?"

"You don't get it. We've been his followers a long time. Ever since Doug banded us together. We're a family."

"And where does Ed fit into it?"

"Sheriff Ed? He's the enemy! And he treats Doug like garbage."

Yeah, he did do that. But there was a history there, too. "They're brothers."

"I get it. I don't get along with my family either. But Doug is smart. He's got ideas. He got us all together."

"But can't you see the harm you're doing? Do you really want to kill people? People you've known all your life? Like the Warrens? And those other people that Baphomet killed last night?"

He turned away, scowling. "You can't think about that stuff when you've got ambitions."

I grabbed his arm. "That is such bullshit and you know it!"

He shook me off. "I know he promised to make us rich and he delivered."

"At what price? Do you really want that money—that gold—knowing that people will die? I don't know you, Dean, but I can't help but feel that this isn't really who you are."

"You're right. You don't know me." He walked away as dignified as a guy could be while crouched under a mobile home. I followed him quickly, afraid he'd block the trap door, though in that case it would be easy enough to kick through the surrounding lattice.

He didn't close the trap door, and I climbed out on my own without a helping hand. Dean looked divided—angry at Doug but trying to be loyal to him, too. Doug had introduced a lot of complications to the Ordo's lives that had probably been relatively simple before. But I realized from our underground encounter that if I could talk to each Ordo member individually, I could make a few cracks in their loyalty. Well, maybe not Charise's, but perhaps Ed could do that if he talked to her.

Dean stomped back into the living room and faced Doug, fists at his side. "It isn't there."

Doug looked from him to me. "The hell it isn't."

"Dean's right," I said. "It isn't."

He got up, ignoring Ed's threatening gestures. "Are you shitting me?"

"It's not there," said Dean, ready to throw a punch.

But Doug didn't look like he was acting. "What the hell…" He shut his eyes. "Shabiri," he hissed. "She fucking took it."

"Goddammit, Doug!"

"Edward! Listen to me for once in your damn life. She took it, okay? I never meant for people to die for this."

"No," he said sourly. "Just me."

"I wasn't gonna let them kill you. Only scare you a little."

"Oh, thanks. You're a real prince."

"I'm trying."

"Prove it. Call Shabiri back, then."

He nodded. "Okay. *Shabiri!*"

We all expected her immediate appearance. When that didn't happen, Doug and I wore matching expressions of horror.

"E–Erasmus!" I called.

Nothing. This wasn't good.

"Now what's happened?" I muttered.

Movement out in the yard caught my attention. Was it Erasmus? No, it was something else, something smaller. It was creeping up to some of the dead Draugr. Or *deader* Draugr, I supposed. The ones whose heads had been blown off. Something was bent over one body, doing something I couldn't quite make out.

I didn't bother to think whether it was a good idea or not as I marched to the door and threw it open. I stood on the porch, trying to see through the mist. It must have heard me, because its head snapped around and stared at me. Bugged-out eyes, wispy hair, green complexion. The ghoul?

My fears were confirmed when its features suddenly contorted and morphed into those of the Draugr. Unlike its lumbering, undead brethren, the ghoul hopped up and took off running on all fours.

"What the hell?" My hand itched uncomfortably for the crossbow, but it was too far away to come. "But it was back in the Booke. What's going on?"

By then, Ed had reached me and saw the little jerk flee. "Wasn't that the—"

"Yeah. The freakin' ghoul."

"But I thought once you wrote it in the book…"

"I thought so, too." I looked up at Ed. "I have to go. I have to meet with the coven."

Ed looked back into the mobile home. I couldn't let him stay here alone. We'd have to leave this for now.

Ed blew out a breath and stomped back inside. "We have to leave. More trouble. But you," he said, pointing his gun at Doug, then skimming it toward the rest of them. "You all have to find that gold. We *have* to give it back to the Draugr in order to stop the killing. Do you understand me?"

"We get it, Edward," said Doug.

I was heartened. If we could convince them about this, maybe we could make them understand about Baphomet.

I scanned the skies looking for him and Andras. Something had to be done about the both of them. And that ghoul.

As we went down the stairs, Doug came out to the porch. "Hey! Are you just gonna leave these dead…" He gestured vaguely. "These Viking zombies?"

Ed glanced around. There were about four dead ones around, including the one the ghoul had been dining on. "Drag them into a pile and light 'em up. It's the safest way."

"Are you kidding me?"

Ed smiled grimly. "Nope. Watch out for the others. Fire seems to stop them for good." He turned away, holding the rifle parallel to the ground as he stomped toward the car.

I hurried to keep up with Ed. "This will make us even, Doug, if you get that gold," I called to Doug over the hood of the car.

"Even, sweetheart? I don't know about that."

"It makes *me* even with *you*, I mean. It means I won't kick your ass."

He laughed for a second before he stopped, thinking about it.

As I got in, Ed couldn't hide the tiny smile at the edge of his mouth. He started up the Interceptor, and we peeled out of the yard.

The radio squawked with calls from dispatch. "Sheriff? Sheriff, you there?"

"I'm here, Patty."

"Sheriff, we're getting all kinds of calls about trespassers and troublemakers. Really weird calls."

"I'm on it, Patty. I, uh, just won't be available to radio for a while. I'll be monitoring, though."

"Should I get George to investigate?"

"No, don't do that! I'm on it. Locations?"

"Up near the Blackstone Farm, Norton Pond, and Oak Bog."

"That's a thirty-mile stretch. Well…I'll do my best."

"Dispatch out."

He slowly pressed the accelerator once we made it to the highway. "Must be the Draugr. And they're really moving."

I was quiet for a while until I noticed our surroundings. "Uh, Sheriff?"

He glanced at me. "Yeah?"

"I don't know where *you're* going, but I have to meet the coven." The Interceptor slowed to highway speed. "Oh. I forgot. Where was it again?"

"Alderbrook Lane."

"Oh, yeah." He looked for a spot to turn around and did so. Silence fell again, until I broke it with, "Charise, huh?"

His grip on the steering wheel tightened. "It was a few years ago. And it was only a couple of dates…that were mostly just for sex."

"Oh my God, are all men animals?"

"I don't know that I would be disparaging *me* for that," he grumbled, "but that's what she said she wanted. She wasn't my girlfriend, but everyone else sort of characterized it that way."

"Wow, are you ever dense. That's just what she said because she didn't think she could get you any other way. Why do you think she's with Doug now?"

"No. No. That can't be right…" I could see him working it out, his dark brows digging into his eyes. All at once he blurted, "Ah jeezum rice! I feel like such a heel now."

"Well…"

"How was I supposed to know?"

I shrugged and sat back while Ed brooded. Maybe I had used Ed for the same thing. Or maybe I had used Erasmus. I had no way of knowing. Or maybe I didn't want to think too hard about it. But it was what men did, wasn't it? Juggle several women. Why couldn't I juggle men? My life was a little too complicated to settle down now.

I stared out the window at the darkness of the forest, trying not to think at all.

Ed passed Alderbrook Lane, then slammed on the brakes, shaking his head. Logic couldn't get you out of the spell, and ultimately, I was gladdened by it. If we ever needed it, we still had a place to hole up where we couldn't be found. It was too bad it was so far from my shop.

My poor little neglected shop. How was I ever going to make a go of it if I wasn't ever there? But did it even matter when in the end I was going to die?

No, stop thinking like that, Kylie. No one's going to die. Erasmus won't eat my soul and I will defeat this damned Booke. I will.

And yet, I felt its pull getting stronger by the day. Sometimes I'd catch myself for minutes on end just thinking about it in a strange, dreamy way. And those moments were stretching for longer and longer amounts of time. Almost as if…it was pulling *me* between its leather-bound covers…

The car bounced, waking me from my musings. It clattered up the long dirt road and finally pierced the mist to come to the yard, where Doc's Rambler, Seraphina's Saab, and Nick's junker were parked.

Ed killed the engine and looked at the house through the windshield. "Damnedest thing," he muttered. "I really felt this hard pull to go in the opposite direction."

My grandpa's house. To me, it was a friendly haven from long ago—a quaint little structure with a porch, curtains in the windows, a gabled roof, and clapboard sides. I had spent childhood summers in Moody Bog that I now barely remembered, thanks to an ancient spell.

I got out of the car just as Doc came out onto the porch. "Kylie?"

"I'm here. Let's go inside. We have a lot to tell you."

CHAPTER SIXTEEN

THE COVEN LISTENED, wide-eyed, to my tale about the Ordo, what they did to us, and how they finally capitulated. All the while, Ed paced from the front door to the hall stairs and back again.

Then I told them about the ghoul, which seemed to upset everyone.

"But you wrote it in the book," said Jolene plaintively.

"I know. And it exploded like all the other creatures that went back into the Booke. Did I do it wrong? Could I have been mistaken?"

Doc slowly rose and moved toward the fireplace, where a warm and welcoming fire flickered. "I think you're ignoring the obvious."

"And what's that?" I asked.

He leaned an arm on the mantel. "It's a *second* ghoul."

"A second one? Then how many are there? And how will I know I'm done capturing them? This sounds like a nightmare within a nightmare."

Seraphina patted my hand and pulled me down to sit beside her on the sofa. "And what were you saying about Mr. Dark?"

"Oh, yeah. He and Shabiri disappeared together. After she hinted that he didn't have to be connected to the Booke."

"Would that be such a bad thing?" she asked kindly.

"He…he wouldn't be around to help me with whatever creature came out of it." That sounded feeble even to me.

"True, but he would also no longer be a threat to you."

"Remember," said Nick, "he wouldn't be tempted to eat your soul. I mean, I *assume* he wouldn't be. Right?" He turned to Jolene. She was wearing another of those knitted hats with animal ears.

"He'd have no reason to. I mean, from what I've been studying about demon lore and from what I could find in Karl Waters' archives on the Booke of the Hidden, it seems to me that a demon who was specifically tied to a thing or an object and then was released would leave in a hot minute."

A little breathless, I sat back. Yes, it meant he would leave. That was what I worried about the most. Even though he was pretty handy as a Guardian, WereJeff could do that task now. Jeff could protect me from Andras or even Baphomet and give me time to get rid of them. And then I'd be the only Chosen Host to have survived the Booke. In theory.

"I'm still trying to figure out how to close it for good," said Jolene. "There's a good chance we can figure it out soon. And if we do, then you won't have to hunt anything down anymore. And it wouldn't matter if Mr. Dark were here or not."

It matters to me, came the little voice in my head.

"It'll never happen," said Jeff. Once more, he was standing in the far corner in the shadows. Maybe it was more than just a side effect of being embarrassed by wolfing. Maybe the wolf *wanted* to be in the shadows, away from others. A literal "lone wolf."

Jeff pushed away from the wall and stepped into a pool of light, which gleamed on the locket hanging from his neck. "I've seen the guy's face. Do you know he hangs on every word you say? He'd never leave you."

As much as that thought warmed me, Ed's next words chilled me again. "But it's not safe having him around."

Then Doc was talking. "Safe or not, we need him. We're going to have to come up with a way to get rid of Andras. Mr. Dark is the only one who can protect Kylie from him."

"I wish Erasmus was here to help right now," I muttered.

"And so I am."

Everyone gasped at his sudden appearance. I jumped to my feet, my hand balled into a fist. Was I going to punch him? I sure wanted to. "Where the hell have you been?"

He shook out his leather duster. "I had something to attend to."

"No, you don't get to brush us off."

He looked around at our angry faces and raised an arched brow. "I don't answer to your Wiccans."

I grabbed the amulet and shoved it forward. "But you answer to me."

He looked around again before grabbing my arm and yanking me toward the kitchen.

Ed stepped forward and blocked him. "What do you think you're doing?"

"Having a conversation with the Chosen Host. So you can step aside…or I will make you."

"You and what army?"

A dark cloud came over Erasmus' face. When he flicked his hand, Ed slid across the room, as if there were magnets in his shoes, and slammed against the wall.

"Hey!" I said.

"You all underestimate me," said Erasmus with a sneer. "Now I am going to talk to Miss Strange and I suggest you leave us be."

"Kylie?" said Doc, concern on his face.

"It's okay." I gestured for him to stay put. "I want to talk to him anyway." Ed was peeling himself from the wall, rubbing his arm. "You okay?"

"Yeah," he said, seeming more humiliated than injured.

I grabbed Erasmus' arm and dragged *him* to the kitchen. As soon as the door clicked closed, I whirled on him. "Just what the hell was all that?"

His jacket was smoldering as he paced. "I'm not a plaything. I'm not their guide to all things Netherworld. I am a being! A powerful demon! And I will not be trifled with!"

"Whoa, whoa. Who's been trifling with you?"

He swept his arm toward the kitchen door. "All of them. They talk about me and sneer and use oaths. I am older than the stones they walk upon. I will be treated with respect!"

"Okay. Um…I don't think anyone is disputing that."

"*They* do. Your precious Wiccans."

"Listen, Erasmus." I approached him slowly, laying a hand on his arm. It seemed to calm him instantly. "They're scared. *I'm* scared. It's our way—a human thing—to deflect fear by making jokes. We make light of things."

"It's disrespectful," he muttered grudgingly. "I used to be feared. I was never laughed at."

"Well…I'll talk to them then. But *you* have to be nicer to *them*, too."

"I *will* not!"

I let him go to punch a fist at my hip. "It's give and take, pal. If you're rude to them then they'll be rude right back."

He considered it. "Is this part of your twenty-first century?"

"Yes."

"As far as centuries go, I don't much like it."

"Never mind. None of this explains where you were. I called for you and you didn't come. And you promised you would."

The ire on his features softened. "I…I know I did, but sometimes…"

"You promised. That means always. If you don't respond to my call, then I think something bad has happened to you."

His whole body language changed and his stiffened shoulders drooped. Smoke stopped puffing off of him as he took my hands in his. "I worried you. I'm sorry. I never meant to. There are just some moments, when dealing with others from the Netherworld, that I must…disappear. I needed to talk with Shabiri in a place we couldn't be overheard."

"So you didn't go to the Netherworld?"

"No. It is too dangerous for me now."

"Then…where did you go?"

"Somewhere in between. The Place of Waiting."

"Place of Waiting? That sounds ominous."

"It's not pleasant. But I needed to hear what she had to say."
I rested back against the counter and lightly crossed my arms, trying and failing to be casual about it. "What *did* she say?"

He sighed and walked to the other end of the kitchen, picking up a can opener on the counter and examining it absentmindedly. "She told me I didn't have to be tied to the book if I didn't want to be."

"And is that true?"

"I don't know. She made a compelling argument. But she is also an accomplished liar, as are most demons." He turned to look at me with a sly smile. "Sorry."

"I know who you are, remember?"

The smile vanished. "Yes." He turned back to the can opener, touched the sharpened cutting disc, and promptly sliced his finger. A bubble of black blood spilled over his skin. He stared at the blood, curious. But as soon as it started it stopped, the cut vanishing. He set the can opener down on the counter.

"How can you sever your ties to the Booke, and more importantly, would that help *me* sever mine?"

He raised his head again. "I hadn't thought of that."

"Well?"

"It doesn't seem likely. I shouldn't think it would apply to humans."

We stared at each from across the kitchen. "Erasmus," I began quietly. "Lately, I've been getting this feeling. I've been thinking more and more about the Booke at all hours of the day. I...I feel like I'm drawn to it, like I could get lost in it. Does this always happen to Chosen Hosts? I feel like...I'm losing myself."

He took a moment before he spoke, his eyes locked on mine. "Each Chosen Host comes to understand the book in a different manner. But it does draw them in. And eventually, they are consumed by it. It is...the beginning of the end."

I licked my lips, suddenly breathless. "We need to close the Booke for good."

"I do not have that knowledge. I doubt anyone does."

We both knew what would close it.

His jaw strained as he gritted his teeth. "I will not devour your soul. I already promised that."

"You promised to come when I called."

"Dammit, Kylie! That is the one thing you must believe of me."

"How can I? It's not just my death that closes the Booke. It's taking my soul that does it, isn't it?"

I didn't think his brow could furrow any more than it already had. "I honestly don't know."

"Have you ever *not* eaten the soul of the Chosen Host?"

His shoulders smoldered. "No."

"Then you *do* know."

He shook his head in denial, ignoring the unpleasant aspects of his existence that he'd never had to consider before.

"What if…you weren't attached to the Booke anymore? What would you do?"

His eyes lit with possibilities, then dimmed just as quickly. "I won't leave you to your fate."

"Are you sure?"

He said nothing. And boy, did that silence say a lot.

I pushed the hurt back. "Tell me what Shabiri said to you."

He took a breath. "There were…rituals I could perform. With the help of another demon."

"Her. It's because she wants the Booke. Why? The Booke is also a key. What could she use it for?"

"I don't know."

"Well, don't you think you should find out before we're all destroyed by her shenanigans?"

He looked to the side, trying to avoid my glare. "There…is something to what you say." But when he looked up again, he strode right up to me and took my face in his hands. "I'm sorry."

"Don't be sorry. Be cautious."

He leaned in, but then stopped to gauge my reaction. When it didn't seem like I'd bite his head off, he tilted in the rest of the way and kissed me. It was a relief to feel his lips again, how warm and soft they were. I wanted to succumb all the way, let his arms engulf me, and fall into the bliss of his mouth. But I couldn't. Not with everything on my mind. I kissed him back, but not with the ardor I wanted to give.

He drew away, looking at me skeptically, but he seemed to understand and dropped his hands away. "I will endeavor to discover what might be done with the book. I have my suspicions. I might need the help of the young one."

I smiled. "I'm sure Jolene will be happy to assist you. But there will be a price."

He frowned. It was his best expression. "And what is that?"

"She'll want to know all there is to know about demons."

He cracked a smile. No, I was wrong before. *This* was definitely his best expression. "That, I can pay."

"Come on. Let's get back out there. I'm sure they're all wondering what happened to us."

I pushed open the door, nearly hitting Ed. His face reddened at being caught eavesdropping, but he didn't apologize. I gave him a knowing nod and rejoined the dead-quiet living room.

"So, uh, Erasmus is fine, and he's going to be working with Jolene to figure out the properties of the Booke and why Shabiri seems to want it so badly. Is that okay with you, Jolene?"

Her mouth hung open. "Lord, honestly?"

Erasmus stuffed his hands behind his back. "I am prepared to answer as many questions as you can ask."

"Holy crow. You've got it, Mr. Dark."

"I'd be interested in overseeing that," Doc piped up.

"You wish to chaperone," said Erasmus, drawing out the word and managing to make it sound dirty. "Of course."

"But in the meantime, I would like to relay a message. Erasmus feels like he's not being respected, which is true. So we," I motioned to everyone present, "have to do a better job. In turn, Erasmus has also promised to be more respectful of all of you." I elbowed him hard. "Isn't that right, Erasmus?"

He scanned the group with mild disdain. "That is correct." He bowed, which seemed to have an effect on Jolene. Not so much the men.

"Now that that's out of the way," I said, "we've got a few immediate problems to take care of. There's still Andras, and Ba—uh, Goat Guy—" Erasmus shook his head wearily. "And the ghoul. It's back. Or there's a second one, as Doc suggested."

Erasmus snapped his head toward Doc. "A *second* one? Unusual." He had a thoughtful look about him.

"Not what I wanted to hear, but okay. I'll deal with it. Still. Andras is the biggest thing on my mind."

"I've been thinking," said Nick, clutching his beer bottle. "If Andras can be *summoned*, can't he somehow be…*un*-summoned."

Doc squinted. "That's a very interesting thought."

"I get what you're saying," said Jolene. She looked down at her tablet, swiping, typing. "There are all sorts of summoning rituals, but practically none for 'de-summoning.' Probably because once a demon has accomplished the task for which he was summoned, he would presumably just…disappear. I-isn't that right, Mr. Dark?"

"Quite. But I have never heard of a…*de*-summoning ritual."

"But I think if we can't find a ritual," she went on, "we can just invent one."

Erasmus' mouth curled in a smile. "Yes, of course. You are a very clever mortal. I will help you."

Jolene looked like it was her birthday and Christmas all rolled into one.

I hated to break up the love fest, but I stepped between them nonetheless. "And I was thinking about some sort of weapon. Or maybe a bolt for the crossbow."

Seraphina got up from the sofa to stand beside me. "I think Kylie's got something there. The poisoned arrow. But with the addition of iron and salt. That might work for immediate protection. But I also think that a ritual would be more permanent."

"Ay-uh," said Doc. "Permanent's what we want. And sending him back in an unconventional *conventional* way would bind him there, I think."

"Then Jolene and Mr. Dark will work on a ritual," said Seraphina. "And perhaps Kylie and Nick can work on an arrow."

"And I'll order pizza," said Jeff, reaching for his phone. "But I guess…I'll have to pick it up since no one can find this place."

Ed had nothing to add.

* * *

I COULD TELL Ed felt out of place as we each began to tackle our tasks. This was all new to him, after all. He stood aloof, looking over everyone's shoulders and pacing back to the window. What he could see in the darkness past the curtains was a mystery to me. There really wasn't much he could do. And I think he'd hit a brick wall where Dan Parker was concerned. He'd said that Doug wouldn't admit to it, and by the way the Ordo was acting about the Draugr and what they'd done, I'd be hard-pressed to believe they were capable of that kind of brutality.

Which meant Ruth. But she couldn't have done it on her own. And that meant she had help. Human help? Or demon? Or maybe a bit of both. I remembered the faces of the men around her at the Chamber of Commerce get-together. One was a gun dealer, a little smarmy. And the other…

Doc approached me. "I've been working on that pentagram you saw in the church. Because we don't have a picture of it, I can't be certain what it might have been for, but the seal at the Dan Parker murder has been easier to identify. I'm fairly certain that this was the one used to summon Andras."

"That's big, Doc," I said.

"Yes, but there's a problem. We don't know all the sigils that were used on the seal's hex circle. Dan's body covered most of it, and his blood covered even more."

"But wouldn't Ed have access to the police photos? The few photos I was able to take were probably not the best. The police must have taken pictures of it without the body."

Ed perked up and stepped forward. "I gave those to Doc, all that we had. But even in the photos without Mr. Parker's body, the blood obscures a lot of it."

"Didn't you clean it off of the seal?"

"What for? Kylie, the techs went on the assumption that the seal didn't really matter. There was no need to document every square inch of it. Beyond the chemical samples and type of paint used, that is."

I looked at both of them in turn. "Could Mr. Parker have drawn it himself? Or was he done in by Andras?"

"With what I understand of such a ritual," said Doc, "Dan couldn't have done it himself, and he couldn't have been alone either. I doubt Andras did it. It was likely done with a ritual knife."

Ed nodded. "Techs corroborated that. He didn't commit suicide."

"So…he *was* a sacrifice?"

Doc shook his head sadly. "Appears that way."

Seraphina made a worried sound. "Would he have known? I just can't believe dear old Mr. Parker would be involved in something like that."

Doc shrugged. "I just don't know, Seraphina. What do we really know about anyone in this village?"

It was a horrible thought either way, whether he was a willing victim or an unwilling one. Maybe he put that pentagram in the church. Maybe he was coerced into it. Maybe he even invited his killers into his home, not knowing what they had planned.

"Doc, could I talk to you for a moment?"

He followed me into the kitchen, and I made sure the

swinging door was closed. "Two weeks ago, at the Chamber of Commerce get-together, Ruth was with a group of men who, well, disparaged all the Wiccans."

He sighed and seemed to gird himself. "I'm not surprised."

"But what if *they* were in league with Ruth, forming another sort of black magic circle?"

"Do you think that's likely?"

"I never thought *any* of this was likely three weeks ago."

"Who then? Who was with her?"

"I don't want to be an alarmist or a gossip—"

"Now, young lady, you opened this door. It's best you just march right through it."

"Okay. It was John Fairgood, that gun shop guy. And, I hate to say this, but…Deputy George was with her, too."

"Hockey pucks. George Miller just has some conservative tendencies. I have no doubt that Mr. Riley will soon wean him from that."

Despite our solitude, I got in close and said quietly, "You know about them, then?"

"I have eyes, don't I? I certainly can't believe that George would do anything as heinous as a ritual murder."

"But he is a cop. He's used to all sorts of violence."

"If you have your doubts, I'd talk to Ed."

"Yeah. I guess I should do that, but he'll probably vouch for him like you did."

"And I'm sure Nick would do the same."

"But like you said, do we really know anyone? People have been fooled before. You always see it on the news. They interview the neighbors of that nice, quiet guy…who has a bunch of heads in his garage freezer."

"You've been watching too much television. And as for John Fairgood, well. Not to put too fine a point on it, I don't think he has the smarts or the capacity to get his hands dirty. But to make you happy, I'll do some digging. In the meantime, no more Chamber of Commerce for you!"

I decided I would heed Doc's warning as I watched him return to the living room.

Nick was trying to figure out how we were going to attach salt and iron to an arrow. I kept sneaking glances at him, wondering if there would ever be an opportunity to ask about George… and imagining just how that conversation would go.

"That will never work!" said Erasmus loudly. All heads turned toward him.

"It will!" cried Jolene. "Especially if we use the power of the rift back in the caves."

"That is extremely dangerous. If we should make a mistake, the rift would widen and encompass your world completely. There would be no stopping it."

Jolene stilled, gnawing on her knuckle in front of the demon. "The scrying stick." She crouched and reached into her Hello Kitty Witch bag almost up to her elbow when she remembered. "Doc, you have the scryer."

"I do, young lady, and I'm keeping it until we have a good reason to use it again."

"I think we can use it to manipulate the rift and keep it from opening more than it already has."

"I'd like to see any documentation you have on that."

He marched over to her as she sat on the sofa again, now flanked by Erasmus and Doc. It was the weirdest sight I'd ever seen.

No, I had to amend that. Jeff sniffing the air like a dog and leaning forward as if ready to pounce on all fours was the weirdest sight, especially when his ears began elongating. "Jeff?" I said.

"I smell them." He was heading toward the door.

"Jeff, what do you smell?"

"Draugrrrrrr…" he said, voice becoming a growl. His hair began to grow. He started pulling off his clothes, and everyone rose, dropping whatever it was they were doing.

I looked around. "How could they find us? We're under the Forget-Me spell."

"It could be random," said Doc, worried. "They could have just wandered here on their way somewhere else and sensed gold here."

Jeff looked odd because he hadn't completely shifted, though his clothes were dumped on the floor. He'd given up wearing shoes a while ago. He wasn't full wolf, but a weird in-between. A long sleek body with strangely configured legs as his thighs grew wider and his feet grew longer. And there, on his furring neck, was the necklace and locket.

"It's gold," I said, pointing.

"By Godfrey," said Doc. "They're after the Babylonian locket."

And Jeff was walking right toward them.

We couldn't stop him before he opened the door and morphed fully into a wolf, leaping out over the threshold.

I grabbed my coat from the hall tree. Before I could reach the door, Erasmus shot out of it. Jeff and the Draugr were already enmeshed in mortal combat.

Nick pushed me aside to run out into the yard. The growling and barking echoed loudly in the clearing, and then the Draugr howled. The others might hear him and come running…uh, shambling. He had to be stopped. "Erasmus! Make sure no other Draugr are on their way."

Ed was on the porch with his handgun. But every time he tried to aim, he pulled the gun away. He'd just hit Jeff if he fired.

Nick reached into a pouch in his hand and grabbed a handful of…something. Herbs and powders and whatnots. He started an incantation.

"Nick!" cried Jolene from the doorway. "It's not ready."

"Yes, it is. I've worked it out. But we've got to get Jeff away from the Viking."

"Is that the fire spell?" I asked.

"Yes. But it's gonna be explosive and I don't want to hit Jeff."

"Okay. I'll get him out of the way. Somehow."

Nick started his incantation again. I approached Jeff and the Draugr's fighting, scrambling bodies. The Viking was trying to use his short sword, but one of Jeff's clawed paws dug in to his arm and pushed hard against it.

The stench was horrific, the smell of rotting flesh seeming that much stronger as he fought.

"Jeff! Jeff, you have to get away! Let Nick and Ed do their work."

Jeff was still snarling and snapping at the Draugr's neck, while the Viking tried to get at the locket with boney fingers.

"Jeff!"

One of his ears twitched toward me.

"Jeff, you have to get out of the way!"

He turned his head—a fatal mistake. The Draugr darted his head forward and clamped his teeth to Jeff's neck.

Jeff whined a scream and let go of the Viking's sword arm. No longer blocked, the sword plunged toward him, when something dark darted forward. Erasmus? No, it was Nick!

Nick held fast to the Viking's sword arm, trying to wrench the weapon from its grip. It was enough of a distraction that the Viking released Jeff's neck. But now the wolf was biting anything that came his way—the Viking's arm, ear, rotting clothing— while Nick was struggling to break loose from between them. The Draugr's skeletal hand clamped onto Nick's wrist. Nick tried to shake it loose and finally slipped down to the ground, taking Jeff down with him. The Draugr stood over them, seeming to choose who to kill first. He raised his sword.

The Draugr's head blew apart. Ed was standing on the porch, his smoking gun still aimed in their direction.

"Oh my God!" Nick was screaming. "Oh my God!"

"It's okay, Nick." I rushed forward and knelt beside him, curling my arm around his shoulders. His face and shoulders were covered with pieces of rotting Viking head. "You're okay."

"No, I'm not." His bloodied face was twisted in terror, tears rimming his eyes. He was holding his arm. "He bit me."

"Oh! Let me see. It's okay. Their bite isn't infectious—"

"No," he wailed. "It wasn't the zombie. It was the *wolf*."

"Oh my God." I looked at Jeff. He was morphing back, and as soon as he was even remotely human-looking, the horror was plain on his face. His ears, still long and sharp, drooped, and his snout still protruded when he reached for Nick. "I'm sorry. I'm so sorry."

"The werewolf bit me," Nick kept saying.

Jolene had her hand over her mouth. Seraphina stood pale and frozen. Doc hurried down from the porch and bent over him.

"I didn't mean it," said Jeff, clumps of blond wolf hair falling off him. "It was an accident."

"He bit me. He bit me." Nick held his arm and yes, I could plainly see the punctures from teeth marks on his bleeding flesh.

I looked at Doc. "Doc? Is it bad?"

He clutched the arm and stared at the open wound but said nothing. "Let's get him into the house."

Ed holstered his gun and moved to help Doc lift Nick, who moaned and muttered in a feverish chatter as they maneuvered him inside.

Jeff, now naked and fully human again, stood in the yard, the headless Draugr at his feet. He grabbed my hand before I could follow the others inside. "Kylie, it was an accident. You believe me, don't you? I never would have…I mean I couldn't do that…"

I patted his hand. "I know, Jeff. It wasn't your fault."

"But I bit him. He's gonna be a—"

"We don't know that yet."

"He is, though. That's how it happens. That's what happened to me. I *am* a monster." He whispered the last.

"Jeff." I took his shoulders. "Look at me. You are *not* a monster. It was an accident."

"He might die," he said dully. "It might be better."

"Don't say that. If…if he's a wolf, too, you can help him. You know it's not the end of the world."

"No. Only the end of *his* world."

I thought he was going to trudge inside, but instead, he morphed back into a wolf, quicker this time, like turning on a switch, and leaped into the dark woods.

"Jeff!" There was only silence in response.

I hugged myself and hurried inside.

They had laid Nick on the sofa. He looked pretty out of it. Doc was bandaging his arm.

"Will he be all right?"

"It's not a fatal wound," said Doc. "But as for his being all right, I think you know the answer to that as well as the rest of us."

"He's…he's going to wolf out, isn't he?"

"I cleaned the wound as best I could, but…"

I dropped my face into my palm. "Oh my God." And this, too, was my fault for opening the Booke. I wished that I could run out into the forest like Jeff, run and run till I was exhausted. But I couldn't. I had the Booke throbbing in my consciousness, reminding me that I belonged to it. That everything from now on was about the Booke and only the Booke.

I wanted to scream. When the pull of the Booke felt at its strongest, I glanced wildly at Erasmus, who was suddenly at my side…and he knew. His eyes told me to follow him, and I did. I trudged into the hall, into the kitchen, and out the back door.

"Help me, Erasmus," I whispered. "Help me."

He enclosed me in his arms and the coldness went away, at least for a while. "I will do what I can. You must believe me, Kylie. I will help you."

"Don't disappear, okay? I couldn't stand it if you disappeared."

"I won't." He held me tighter. I inhaled his scent—wood smoke, cedar, and musk…and the faraway hint of sulfur.

CHAPTER SEVENTEEN

NICK WAS, FOR all intents and purposes, unconscious. He groaned from time to time as Doc kept checking him—under his eyelids, his pulse. Jeff was back from the woods, hovering. He knew. He knew what Nick was going through because he'd been there only a week and a half ago.

Jolene's eyes were red. "He lives with his folks. What are we going to tell them?"

"That's a fair point, Jolene," said Doc. "Jeff, I trust you won't have any objections to a roommate."

"No. No, anything he wants. I owe him." He shot a desperate look toward me.

"Of course, he can stay. He's going to need help."

"And I will need more help brewing wolfsbane," said Seraphina. "I hope Jolene wouldn't mind—"

"Anything to help," she said tearfully.

Erasmus stood aloof in the corner, watching all of us with critical eyes. But it was Ed I had to talk to. I tapped his shoulder and motioned for him to follow me. I noticed Erasmus watching us as we left the room. Once the kitchen door swung closed, I said quietly, "Ed, how well do you know George?"

He shook his head, perplexed. "I've known him since we

were kids. I mean not well, but we were both from Moody Bog. Hard not to know everyone in town."

"When I saw him at the Chamber of Commerce thing, he was sort of siding with Ruth. How much do you trust him?"

"With my life. I have to. What are you suggesting?"

"If Ruth sacrificed Dan Parker, she would have to have had help."

"No way. Not George. He might be a bit stiff and kind of a loner, but he is *not* like that."

"Well…he's not really a loner. He's…he's with Nick."

"What do you mean?"

O mighty detective. "I mean he and Nick are together. *Together* together."

He stared at me for another second before the penny dropped. "Oh! Jeez, I didn't know that. You know a guy for years and… Why didn't he ever tell me?"

"I don't know. Nick said that he's a private sort."

"That's for sure." He rubbed his chin and stared at the floor. "You just don't know people, do you?"

"Well, that's the assumption I'm working under. That maybe people in town are up to no good and we wouldn't know it."

"I can't believe it of George."

"You didn't know he was gay."

"That's different. *That* I can believe, but not this other thing."

"Putting that aside, what do we do about George?"

Ed looked back at the closed kitchen door. "You're asking if we should tell him everything?"

"He'll have to be told if he and Nick—"

"Now hold on, Kylie. If George isn't out, it isn't fair to drag him into all this."

"It isn't fair *not* to. What's he going to think when Nick suddenly falls off the radar? He's going to know something's up."

"Isn't that Nick's decision?"

"Nick's going to need all the help he can get."

"And what if George rejects him?"

I didn't want to think about that.

Ed rubbed his chin again. Looked like he needed a shave. The last thing I wanted was for him to look like Doug. "We've got to wait till Nick...wakes up."

"That might be a while. And wouldn't it help *you* if George knew?"

He shook his head. "But it's different now. How would *you* feel?"

I stiffened and the anger and hurt returned. "You mean he might say he wanted to take a break?"

Bullseye. Ed's mouth clenched. "I'm...I'm sorry for that. I felt a little overwhelmed. And for the record...it was a mistake." He made a beaten puppy face at me. "My timing is terrible. But I'm sorry I ever asked for a break. I don't want one anymore. But I'm afraid..." He looked toward the other room where Erasmus was. "Maybe it's too late now."

Was it? I thought about Erasmus—his literal smoldering looks, his kisses, the way he made love. And I thought of Ed, too, and his very human reactions and sensibility. And *his* lips, and the way *he* made love. I still didn't want to make a choice.

"*I* hadn't want a take a break."

"Then, are you saying there's...hope?" He hesitated, before finally lifting his hand and taking mine.

"We'll just have to see. Right now, I can't really think straight."

His hold on my hand tightened involuntarily. "You mean you still want to see...that guy? The demon?"

When I thought of leaving Erasmus for good my stomach clenched. "I might."

Ed wasn't happy when we left the kitchen together to check on Nick. Erasmus followed us with narrowed eyes.

Nick's moans were morphing into low growls. All of a sudden, he started whipping about. Doc tried to hold him down, but Jeff pulled him out of the way.

"Jeff!" he cried. "What are you doing?"

"Saving your life. Look!"

Nick thrashed as thick, black hair began sprouting all over him. He screamed as his mouth and nose elongated and darkened into a snout, while his ears grew into longer, pointed appendages. His whole body shook and cracked and changed. He growled and howled from the pain. It *had* to be painful, what was happening.

He tore at his clothes with the claws that were now on his fingers, and soon he flipped over onto his paws, crouching down on the sofa with back arched and hackles raised, a fully black-furred wolf. His green eyes snapped open. He looked about the room at us, lip curled back in a snarl, revealing sharp canines.

We all drew back. It looked like he was about to leap at any one of us, when Jeff shed his clothes and shifted in seconds into a wolf. He bared his teeth and bark-growled at Nick, who just as quickly cowered back, bushy tail curled under him.

There was some wordless communication between them, as Nick seemed to understand the pecking order in the…the pack, I guessed. Jeff was his alpha. What a weird thought.

As he cringed back on the sofa, his fur sifted off of him in big chunks and his face slowly contorted back to normal. I snatched the knitted throw off of the sofa back and tossed it over him just in time.

Sitting up and naked except for my grandmother's throw in his lap, Nick swayed, clutching his head. "Oh, shit," he sobbed. Seraphina was closest. She sat beside him and cradled him in her arms, letting him cry.

Doc ushered the rest of us away to the dining room. "Kylie, you'll need to get some supplies from the shop," he said quietly. "And maybe you should grab the crossbow while you're there. I think it's going to be a long night. Seraphina and Jolene will have to work through most of it to make the wolfsbane."

"Okay. I'll get Erasmus to drop me off."

The demon was still standing in the darkened corner. When I approached him, his countenance almost made him look like a stranger to me. I didn't know how else to describe it. "I need a favor."

"Of course, you do."

"What does that mean? I'm sensing some resentment. What's wrong?"

"Nothing. You made an agreement with your constable. Why should I resent that?" He crossed his arms over his chest.

"Why should you?"

"No reason whatsoever. What is the favor?"

"As usual, you don't know what you're talking about. I need you to transport me to my shop."

"Done." He reached out, and almost before the word echoed off my ears, we were there in a breathless wink of darkness and cold. He was gone again before I had a chance to tell him what a jerk he was being. Jealous much?

He'd put me across the street near the woods, and it was a good thing, because Deputy George's black and white cop Jeep was parked right next to mine in front of the shop. He and his mustache were outside the place in his heavy jacket and Smokey Bear hat, peering into the windows of my darkened place.

I casually walked across the street and hailed him with my hand raised…and realized I wasn't wearing a jacket.

He shined his flashlight in my face. "Oh. I was looking for you. You know, you'll catch your death like that."

I rubbed my arm while reaching for my key in my jeans pocket. "Yeah. Pretty brisk, these Maine Octobers." Unlocking the door, I switched on the light as I let him in. "Is there something in particular I can do for you, deputy?"

He turned the flashlight over and over in his fingers. "I was, uh, just, uh, checking."

Was I going to trust him? Ed did. But Ed hadn't known about all the magic before. Of course, Nick trusted him. Wasn't that enough to go on? "You were just checking what?"

He sighed and pushed up his hat. "The thing of it is, Ms. Strange—"

"Kylie, deputy. You can call me Kylie."

"Kylie," he said tentatively. "The thing of it is…Ruth Russell called me and asked if I'd come over here and ask you about a gold locket…" He trailed off. Plainly, Ruth accused me of stealing it and, knowing I was seeing Ed, she called on George instead.

That…that…*witch*! Except…"witch" was a relative term these days.

"You can tell Ruth—" I started but then stopped and calmed myself. With more aplomb, I said, "George, you can tell Ruth that I haven't seen the locket but I am still turning over my place looking for it."

He swiped his hat off his head and breathed heavily. "I tried to tell her that, but…" He shook his head. "She can be stubborn. And wicked mean."

I was glad to hear him say it. It didn't look like he was acting to me.

"That she can be." Though I felt a little guilty, because we actually *had* stolen it.

He'd said his piece and accomplished his mission, yet still he lingered. "Yes, George? Was there something else?"

"I, uh…I had an appointment with Mr. Riley, and sometimes he comes here in the evenings. I was wondering if you'd seen him."

It was an opening staring me right in the face. But should I say? Did I have the right to involve the poor, oblivious George in all this, and effectively out Nick without asking first? But this was a matter of life or death. Things were getting decidedly serious.

But how would he react to it all?

He was looking at me so expectantly that I had to say something.

Think before you leap, Kylie.

I leapt anyway. "George—can I call you George? George, maybe we need to sit down."

CHAPTER EIGHTEEN

GEORGE STIFFENED. "WHAT happened?"

"Nick's okay. But there are some things I need to tell you, to explain."

He wouldn't move. He was growing tenser and there was nothing I could say that could make matters any better. In fact, I was seeing now that I was making them worse. Too late now.

"I have to tell you some things. So...do you believe in magic, by any chance?"

"I believe in the gospel. That Wiccan magic is evil."

"Well...you don't think Doc is evil, do you?"

"What are you talking about? Where's Nick?"

He was really agitated. I couldn't blame him.

"I know you don't like all the Wiccan stuff Nick is involved in, but it's real, and he's a warlock—I guess that's the term—but he's only in it for good, not evil."

George walked in a circle, slapping his hat against his thigh. "I told Nick over and over not to mess with that stuff. Something bad happened, didn't it?"

"Well...yes. But let me explain."

"You don't have to explain. I told him the only thing he needed was our Lord and Savior, but he just wouldn't listen."

"George, you're getting ahead of the story. I need to tell you more."

"He wouldn't come to church with me. I mean, just as friends, you know. That's all I asked."

"I know you're more than friends."

He stopped. Without looking at me, he said quietly, "Who told you that?"

"No one needed to tell me. Then Nick, well…"

"Darn it!" He still wouldn't look at me. "It's bad enough I go around lying to everyone. It was supposed to be a secret."

"It is. But Nick trusted me. I'm hoping you'll trust me, too."

He seemed to gird himself and pivoted to face me. "What's happened?"

"First, I have to show you something." I concentrated, felt where it was in the house, and asked it to come to me. It wasn't like when the crossbow screamed across an open space toward me. It had more of a velvet smoothness, the soft arrival of someone you knew well.

The Booke didn't pop into existence. It came to me as if on a breaking wave, gently flowing downstairs and across the room. It hovered in front of me until I grasped it in both hands. The sensation was overpowering. I wanted to hug it to me, but I fought it, fought the need to have it even closer.

Instead, with much willpower, I set it on the table, pushing aside some tea strainers and teabag rests. When I looked up, George was staring at it, then at me. "It's a trick."

"No. It isn't. This is the Booke of the Hidden. I found it inside the wall of this building. It's very old. But I didn't know that when I opened it, I'd start a cycle of events that quickly got out of control."

"It's an instrument of Hell."

"I have no doubt about that. You see, it let out all these creatures that I have to put back. Creatures that have killed."

Harsh breaths coursed from his open mouth. He stared at the Booke but wouldn't come closer. Trembling, he slowly nodded. "And this has harmed Nick in some way."

He was buying it. As Erasmus had explained, those with a religious leaning accepted magic in these terms of good vs evil.

I dared not mention Erasmus. Not yet.

"Yes. It has. Out of the Booke came a werewolf. It first bit Jeff, my…my friend from California."

"Werewolves are real?"

"I'm afraid so."

"Is that what killed Karl and that cyclist? And Nicole Meunier?"

"Those were…other creatures. But yes. They came from the Booke."

"And where are these creatures now?"

I raised my hand; the chthonic crossbow whistled through the house and smacked into my open palm. "I killed them. With this."

He stared at the crossbow, eyes ready to pop out of their sockets.

"I've already told the sheriff about all of this. It took him a while to believe it too, but he does now. He's seen some of the creatures for himself. And he's helping us stop them."

"So what about Nick?"

"Well. I did kill the first werewolf, but it bit Jeff, so…so *he* turned into one. But he's a good guy. We're making a potion, more like medicine, so that he doesn't even try to…hurt anyone. He's safe. He really is. Except…it was an accident. And while he was protecting us from a creature, Nick got in the way…and he…he accidentally bit Nick."

His breath hitched. "He bit Nick?"

"Yeah. So now Nick—"

I hated the sound of his sob. It was a ragged, helpless sound.

"No," he said hoarsely.

"I'm afraid he's a werewolf now. But he'll be okay."

He took a step toward me so suddenly that I drew back. "What do you *mean* he'll be okay! He's a monster now! A beast!"

"He's not! He's the same old Nick. It's just that now, he… Look, think of it as someone with epilepsy. He can't help it, and you'll have to take certain precautions, but he's still the same Nick."

191

"He's not. He's not."

"George…"

He tried to push past me, but I grabbed his arm. "If you love him, you'll help him. He needs all our help right now. *We* love him."

"Those Wiccans." He hissed the words, all his anger compacted into his tight stance.

"Those Wiccans are with him right now, helping him, standing by him. I'm sure he would welcome you, too. He needs you now more than ever."

"But he's—"

"He's Nick. Now look. I'm here to bring this crossbow and some herbs so they can make his po—uh, medicine. Will you come with me?"

He said nothing. He seemed to have lost all momentum, hanging there as if a puppeteer had cut his strings.

He had to decide on his own. I left him to quickly gather the herbs for the wolfsbane and put them in a small brown bag. With crossbow in hand, I walked to the front door.

"Deputy, are you coming?"

He stood like a stone.

"At least see him."

He nodded slowly. He crossed the threshold, and I locked the door. He got in his Jeep, and I got in beside him. But he didn't put the key in the ignition. He merely sat there, arms limp by his sides. "This is probably a mistake."

"You never know. I can't believe you'd be with Nick if you really thought he was evil in some way. I've never met a gentler man than Nick."

He wiped his hand across his nose and sniffed. "Yeah." He started the car and pulled out of the parking lot. "Where are we going?"

"Alderbrook Lane."

"Where?"

"Just let me guide you. It's got a spell on it, so people forget it's there."

He gave me an *are you kidding me?* look but kept driving. "It's had the spell on it for over twenty years. I used to come here in the summers to visit my grandpa. It's his house. But the spell makes people forget. Even I forgot I was ever in Moody Bog before."

"What was the name of the street again?"

"Like that. It's Alderbrook."

His lips moved over Alderbook, repeating it silently as he shook his head in disbelief.

We almost passed it, but I told him to stop, to turn there. He looked at the street sign through the windshield and whistled softly.

He drove up the hill and parked in front of the house. "I never knew this was here. I must have passed that sign at the bottom of the hill a thousand times. Maybe a million. Never saw it."

"George." I faced him. "He might change while you're here. You know, shift into a…into a wolf. Please try not to look horrified. He already feels like a monster. I know Jeff does. And neither of them are."

"I don't know." He ran his hands absently over the steering wheel. "Maybe I shouldn't come in."

"If it were you, you know Nick would be there."

He nodded. His face was a mess.

We walked in together. Nick was sitting up with the throw wrapped around him. His face collapsed when he saw George. "No! Why did you bring him?"

"Nicky!" cried George as plaintively as I have ever heard. He lost all pretense, all stiff propriety when he lunged for him and enclosed him in his arms, sobbing on his shoulder.

Hair all askew, Nick looked bewildered but held George tightly, before he buried his face in the man's hair and breathed.

Doc hovered, but I urged everyone else away. We gathered in the dining room.

"He was at my shop," I said quietly in explanation as I dumped the crossbow and herbs on the table. "Ruth Russell called him to search for the stolen locket."

"She called George?" said Ed, with a tinge of hurt to his voice.

"I told you. He was sort of on her side."

"But you still brought him here."

"I went with my gut feeling."

"If your feeling is wrong, you've doomed us all," said Erasmus.

"I prefer to go with my gut. In most things."

"What do your intestines have to do with it?"

"Mr. Dark," said Jolene, tentatively pushing him out of the way. "We have to get to these herbs and make the wolfsbane potion. You can help, if you'd like."

"*Will* you help?" I asked.

He had a sour look on his face but relented and went with Jolene and Seraphina into the kitchen.

* * *

ED AND I stayed out of the way in the dining room, looking back through the arch as George and Nick talked furtively together on the sofa. George never stopped touching him, his neck, his hands, resting his palm on the side of Nick's face. Nick was starting to look better, not so deathly pale, and he hadn't morphed at all. Maybe George's presence helped.

"Boy, I just never suspected those two," said Ed. "I wonder how long that's been going on." He put his arm around me. "That's a good thing you did there. Nick doesn't look so sick anymore."

"I'm sure it's the wolf in him making him stronger, but I'm also pretty sure that love and acceptance go a long way."

"I'm going to have to ask George about Dan Parker."

A pang in my chest broke the mood. No matter what George had done now, we had to clear him fully.

"I agree. You can use a bedroom upstairs."

"I don't know if I should do it here. Maybe more conventional surroundings like the station would be better."

"This place is forgettable. It's safer here."

He considered. "All right."

"Besides," I said, rolling my stiff shoulders, "I've got a Draugr to burn."

"Shit, Kylie, I'll do that."

"I'll get Erasmus to help me."

Before he could say *that guy* in that disgusted way again, I pushed into the kitchen. Seraphina and Jolene really looked like two witches, stirring an iron kettle over the stove. I guess Grandpa had practiced his share of Wicca, too, because that sure looked like a cauldron to me.

Erasmus was overseeing them, but I had the feeling they could handle it without him.

"Erasmus," I said softly. "Can you help me?"

"It's my fondest desire," he said in his snarkiest tone.

He followed me out just as Ed and a perplexed George were going up the stairs.

"You can cut the sarcasm," I told him, grabbing my coat and opening the front door.

"Sarcasm? I detect no sarcasm in my tone."

"Bitchiness, then."

"Do you *dare*—"

I whirled on him. "Yes, I dare. Stop being an ass."

He crossed his arms over his chest. "I haven't the least idea what you're talking about."

"I didn't break up with you in favor of him. If you and I even *have* a thing." I stepped outside, shivering at the cold.

"A 'thing.' Such imprecise language these days." He adjusted his collar. "You are my lover. Is that what you mean? Is that what you…remain?" The last was cautious, tentative. He was so not fooling me.

"Yes."

"And your constable…*knows* this?"

"Yup."

"And here I thought the Netherworld was a dangerous maze to navigate."

"I need your help to burn the body of the Draugr." I stood out in the yard and looked around. "Now…what happened to it?"

He pointed. "I don't think that will be necessary."

In the light from the house shining through the windows, I saw what was left of the Viking. Its body had completely collapsed into a foul-smelling slime. Even the armor, that had once been fairly shiny, had rusted down to mere metal fragments, sinking into the muck and the mud. A good rain would wash it all away.

"Once it was truly dead, the magic holding it all together vanished."

"That's convenient."

He looked down at it, sniffed once, and turned away.

"Erasmus."

"Yes?"

"What can you tell me about Andras?"

His mood altered, anger dissipating. He seemed to remember that my life was in danger. He couldn't seem to help himself from glancing up into the cloudy sky.

My breath blew around my face. It was incredibly cold, like ice crystals were in the air. I fluffed my down jacket and hunched into the upright collar.

"As I said, he is clever and determined. He won't stop until he's achieved his goal."

"Where does he come from? I mean, I know from the Netherworld, but what sort of mythology is attached to him? Can it help us defeat him?"

He snorted. "Mythology? That's what humans call it. We simply call it history." His eyes scanned the skies as he spoke. "They say he once had the head of an owl, but that was only a helm in the *shape* of an owl—though, admittedly, he does have a distinctly owl-like quality with his wide eyes and beak-like nose. He is a slayer and fighter and once ruled over thirty legions of demons."

"He doesn't do that now, does he?"

"No. I daresay, if he did, you'd be dead by now. No, he lost favor over the centuries. He once had a mount, a black wolf." He grinned, but it slowly waned when I didn't so much as smile. "He's a minor demon now and resentful of it. When someone needs an assassin, they often summon him."

I began to slowly walk around the perimeter of the house, trying to keep warm. "And would *you* know how to summon him?"

He walked beside me, hands in his coat pockets. I knew he didn't need to keep them warm. He must have picked up the habit from watching humans. "A seal, sigils, blood sacrifice."

"That much *I* know. But specifically. What kind of sigils?"

"Ah. I see. For your *de*-summoning. I'm sure your junior Wiccan can find the answers."

"It would be helpful if we could hurry this along." I couldn't help glancing back into the woods around us. Any change in the shadows made my heart race.

"And he was using the ghoul to bring you right to him. Clever."

"And now there's a second one."

"And that disturbs me."

"Why?"

He stopped at looked at me intently. "Because I'm fairly certain…there is only one such ghoul in the book."

"So wait. If there is only one in the Booke—and I have no reason not to believe you—then Andras—"

"Somehow brought the same ghoul *out* of the book. And I know that this is impossible."

CHAPTER NINETEEN

IT LOOKED LIKE we had a big problem. I gathered the Wiccans sans Nick, who George was fussing over. We retreated into the dining room, keeping our voices low, and I told them what Erasmus had said.

Doc worried at his lip with his fingers. "This is very alarming. If Andras could get the ghoul out of the book—"

"Then he can get anything out of it," I said. "Anything I've already put back in it. The werewolf, the kelpie, the succubus…"

"That's not good," said Jolene.

"No. It isn't. We've *got* to get this guy."

Seraphina tapped her nail on the table. "Is Shabiri helping him?"

Erasmus grunted. "It's a possibility. She wants control of the book. With Andras' help, she just might get it."

"I…have an idea," I said. "Would you all excuse me for a minute?" I walked around the table and grabbed Ed's arm, pulling him along to the kitchen. I dared not look back at Erasmus.

Once the door was closed, I bit my lip. "So…George checks out?"

"As far as I can tell. He was pretty shocked that I'd accuse him. Then he got mad. But…now that I've seen him with Nick… well." He shook his head. "He looks like a different guy. I can't believe he'd do anything like that."

"Good. Because I have a plan. It's going to be dangerous, and it might mean taking you out of circulation for a while. George will have to be in charge of the law and order around here."

He gave me a sidelong glance. "What do you have in mind?"

When I told him, the whole house likely heard his yell. But after some convincing, he sourly agreed.

* * *

GEORGE QUICKLY DROVE home, tried to return to Alderbrook Lane, got lost twice, but was eventually able to bring over new clothes for Nick. After, he wouldn't leave his side, even when Jeff showed him the spare room.

"Looks like you might have an extra roommate tonight," I said to Jeff.

Jeff shrugged. "As long as it makes Nick comfortable, I'm all for it. But it's starting to look like a frat house here."

"How are *you* holding up?"

He ran his hand through his hair. "Okay, I guess. Feeling guilty as hell. I didn't know I'd be making recruits. What if—you know—in the middle of the night, what if Nick shifts and accidentally bites George? I don't know how this alpha thing works or if they'll both listen to me."

"Seraphina said they gave Nick a double dose tonight. He'll mostly sleep." I yawned.

"Looks like you could use some sleep, too." He glanced at the clock. "It's three in the morning. You can't run a shop this way."

"I don't even know anymore, Jeff. What's the point of pretending everything is all right and there'll even *be* a future?" I paused to gather myself. "Look, if…if something happens to me, I want you to have the shop. As long as you still let Jolene work there."

"Whoa, girl, don't talk like that. You're gonna get through this. You've got all of us watching your back."

"And two of my friends have been turned into werewolves. What next? Will I get one of you killed?"

"Kylie." He took me in his arms and rested his cheek against my head. "Babygirl, you sure know how to whip up the drama."

"I didn't want to. I just wanted a new start, a new shop…"

"And everything will be okay. You'll see."

A low growl sounded behind us. Jeff moved with speed and grace, pushing me behind him while he spun and partially shifted, pointed ears pricked and snout full of sharp teeth.

But it was only Erasmus. "Step away from her," he growled again.

I thought Jeff would challenge him, but he only laughed. His ears receded, and his snout shrunk back to normal. "He's the jealous sort, isn't he? Stand down, Frodo. Mordor's not going anywhere."

Erasmus frowned.

"Besides," said Jeff with a dark smile, "isn't this a Sheriff Ed night? Since you can't seem to make up your mind—"

Great. My love life was the stuff of jokes now. "We're *not*…" I took a breath. "Good*night*, Jeff."

He waved and trudged up the stairs. Seraphina had offered to stay, too, but Doc decided that between Jeff and George, they could handle things.

I could tell that everyone was exhausted. We'd worked on everything we could think of. Erasmus had spent a lot of time with Jolene, going over possible rituals and discussing the Booke's unique qualities.

I had a plan that I hadn't told the coven about. I preferred asking for forgiveness rather than permission.

But it was time to turn in. Everyone retreated to their various cars, with Seraphina steering a sleepy Jolene toward her Saab.

I turned to Erasmus. "Can you take me home?" He frowned at first, until the realization hit him.

"Not your constable?"

"Has your transporter mechanism suddenly broken down?"

"No. But I—"

"You don't appear to be listening." I stepped closer and put my arms around his neck. "Are you going to take me home or what?"

Before I got the last word out, the cold and dark enclosed us. When next I blinked, we were in my bedroom. And he was kissing me.

He wasn't hesitant. He knew what he was doing, what he wanted. In fact, he seemed rather jubilant that it was him here and not Ed.

I jumped up and wrapped my legs around his waist. Both our clothes burned away at the same time, and I met flesh for flesh, thinking vaguely how I was going to have to invest in more jackets.

He tore his mouth away from mine to run his lips over my face and neck. "Why must you torment me?" he whispered.

"I don't mean to."

"But you do. You torment me with jealousy. With uncertainty."

"I'm here now."

"Yes. Yes." He lifted me so that my chest was in reach of his lips. "You're here." His kisses ran slowly over my skin. He mouthed my breasts, burying his face between them, sliding his tongue across the curve of one and taking the tip deeply into his mouth. A warm feeling shot right down into my belly. He licked his way to the other but then seemed consumed with moving further downward. He fluttered his hot tongue over my stomach while hiking me higher. Unbalanced, I fell back onto the bed. His strong hands caught me, still clutching my hips, and continued his slow mission lower without skipping a beat.

His hands were talented, but so were his mouth and tongue. I squirmed, winging higher and higher on a crest of heat and pleasure. I surprised myself when a gasp transformed into a fevered whiteout of bliss. I was still gasping when he raised his head and grinned—proud of himself. But it was his eyes that held me. He let my legs fall to either side of him as he crawled up my body with intent. I was beyond ready for him, and he entered quickly, then settled in and paused.

"What are you waiting for?" I said breathlessly.

He watched my face and gently moved.

I smiled. "You'll have to do better than that."

And he did. He was working in earnest, breathing hard as he thrust, hips snapping. He bent to kiss my breasts, my neck. Everywhere he touched or licked burned with heat. Did it feel so intense because he was a demon? Was that why it was actually hotter where his body touched mine? I couldn't be sure and I didn't care, wrapping my thighs tight around him and rocking my hips up to meet him.

When he roared his culmination and his shoulders smoldered...I felt a little proud myself.

His body was covered in a sheen of perspiration. His hair fell damp and bedraggled across his face. I reached up and swept a strand from his eyes, and he looked down at me, surprised. We were still joined, but his face was more perplexed than ever before.

"I don't understand you," he said quietly. He reached down and touched my face, fingers trailing over my cheek. His eyes softened, and he cocked his head. His fingers gently ran up my face and then through my hair. "You are difficult to fathom," he said. And he seemed about to say more when the window exploded.

CHAPTER TWENTY

I SCREAMED, AND Erasmus threw himself over me. I could feel bits of glass raining down on the bed around us, but he took the brunt of it. He grabbed me and transported me into the shop and then instantly transported back upstairs. A burst of roaring and growling echoed above. I raised my hand for the crossbow… then remembered it was still at Grandpa's house.

I whirled toward the fireplace, grabbed a poker, and ran upstairs. From the doorway, I saw a naked Erasmus in hand-to-hand—and tooth-to-claw—combat with Andras. I was naked, too, I realized, but I didn't suppose it really mattered.

They tumbled over the bed and onto the floor, the demon assassin's wings spread wide, touching both walls and sending my carefully hung pictures crashing down, breaking even more glass.

Erasmus' mouth had morphed again into that wide version with all those teeth, and he was biting down on Andras' clavicle, trying to get closer to his neck. Andras was biting him, too. Both of them were covered in black blood. Their bodies smoldered and smoked, leaving burnt scarring across my wood floor.

Erasmus was on top when Andras suddenly flipped him around and ground him into the floor. But there was Andras' long, unprotected back. I leapt forward and plunged the poker into him through the skin suit. He threw back his head, arched his back, and wailed.

Where the poker entered him, it burst into flame. He screamed and rolled, twisting at a painful angle to try and avoid the poker. I hadn't even realized it when I grabbed it, but it was made of iron.

Andras rose and turned toward me. He was grimacing in agony, his eyes burning with hatred. He twisted his frame and managed to pull out the poker, dropping it to the floor with a clang. Black blood gushed over the rug. He staggered toward the open maw that was now my window and fell through. Down he went, disappearing into the night. I rushed to what was left of my window sash and looked down. No body. He must have saved himself at the last minute and flown off. Damn! I wish I *had* killed him.

Erasmus lay moaning on the floor. I rushed to him, not caring about the bits of glass embedding themselves into my knees.

"Kylie," he muttered. "Dammit, woman. You'll catch your death."

"Are you all right?"

"In a moment. Put something on."

"Stop worrying about me." I began to notice my teeth were chattering.

There was a lot of blood, some of it Erasmus'. He lay on the floor as I tip-toed through the carnage for my shoes. I shook them out first to clear them of any broken glass before slipping them on. Then I hurriedly searched for a robe and shook it free of glass, too.

When I was vaguely dressed, I helped him up. There were glass shards all over him, along with scratches from debris and that ass-hat's teeth. "What can I do to help you?"

He grunted in obvious pain. "I will heal momentarily."

"Shall I try to pull out the glass, or—"

"No need." As I watched, the skin around the glass puckered, spitting out the shards. The black blood soon stopped dripping from the wounds as the skin slowly cleaved together.

Fast healing didn't mean fast pain relief. He suffered. All I could do was hold his hand as he squeezed hard and silently take the pain from his crushing grip.

After a moment, he released me. I shook out my hand to get the blood flowing again. He bent forward, breathing hard. That's when he saw my knees. "You're hurt."

"I guess."

He put hands to both my thighs and instantly any pain was gone. I checked my knees and there was no glass, no blood, no scarring. Even the pain Baphomet's claws had raked through my scalp was gone, as were the wounds Andras had made to my shoulders. I rolled them, luxuriating in the cessation of pain. "How did you do that?"

"I…don't know."

"You could have healed me before…"

"I don't think so."

"What do you mean? Erasmus, what's going on?"

He scooted to the end of the bed and clutched his head in his hands. "I don't know what's wrong with me." He looked up suddenly, scrutinizing me. "It's you," he said accusingly. "Ever since I met you, it's all gone wrong."

I sat on the bed beside him. "Erasmus," I said softly. "Do you think it's because… you might be…in love with me?"

He frowned. "I don't know what that means."

"Being in love means thinking about that one person all the time. Wanting to be with them. You'd sacrifice yourself for that person. You'd do anything to make them happy. It can be a nice thing."

"It sounds horrific."

I went back over what I had said and saw his point. "Well, mostly it means you just want to be with that person all the time and keep them safe. You…click with them. It's a human emotion."

He stared at the floor, and so did I…at the sparkling shards of glass that I would have to clean up. I'd have to retreat downstairs now that my bedroom was uninhabitable. More money to spend getting Barry Johnson from Moody Bog Hardware to put in a new window. More expenses I didn't need right now. And how was I going to explain it?

Erasmus slowly turned toward me. "That's not possible," he all but growled.

"Demons don't get human emotions?"

He scowled and looked away again. "No."

"I see. But you can get mad and jealous…but not feel love?"

"Why do you continue to taunt me?"

"Because I think there's a lot about you that even *you* don't understand. How long have you been alive? You said you wake up when the Chosen Host opens the Booke and then go to sleep when it gets closed, and sometimes it's centuries between those times. You're thousands of years old, but you've only been awake for a brief part of that. How would you know? How would you really know anything about yourself?"

He stared at me now, a look of horror dawning on his face.

I moved to face him. "Maybe it's not so bad. Love can be a wonderful thing."

"No."

"Yes, it is. Especially…" I took a breath. "Especially when both parties feel the same way."

"No." He rose, still naked. I looked away. There was something too raw about him, and I didn't mean the unclothed part. He strode across my ruined floor, waved his hand, and vanished. As he disappeared in a puff of black smoke, the glass shards rose up from the floor and off the bed. The remnants of my window rose, too, all heading toward where the gaping hole where my window used to be and carefully stitching themselves together. I watched, with dropped jaw, as each piece found its place again and painstakingly repaired itself, until every tiny shard had found its home and been sucked into position, and there wasn't a hairline crack to be seen. When all the pieces had made it back into place, even the gentle tinkling sound of the glass sealing itself back together stopped. The room fell silent again…except for the ticking of my alarm clock.

I ran to the window and looked it over, running my hand over the smooth surface of glass and muntin. When I glanced through it, there was only darkness outside, except for a lone figure in a black duster, pacing through my back garden and refusing to look up to the window.

Something nudged my hip. The Booke. I reached down and grabbed it, holding it to my chest like an addict. I nearly swooned at the sensation of its nearness. It kept me company as the lone figure below paced and paced.

* * *

IN THE LATE afternoon, everyone showed up to the shop. Nick was there, and even Deputy George in uniform. Everyone but Ed. And Erasmus.

While they were all serving themselves tea and cake, I pulled Doc aside. "Doc, I need to ask you something in confidence."

"That depends, young lady. Is it something that the rest of us need to know?"

"I—hmm. I'm not sure. But I have to ask anyway. It's about... demons."

"Does this have to do with the absence of a particular demon?"

"Sort of. Erasmus seems to have more powers than even he thought he had. When Andras attacked us last night—"

"Andras attacked you?"

"Oh, yeah. I'll tell everyone all about that...in a moment. But he seems to have more power than he thought he had. And I think it's because he's...well. In love. With me."

His brows snapped up his wrinkled forehead. "I see. And why do you think that is?"

"The closer we've gotten—and you might as well know we've gotten pretty darned close, if you haven't already guessed—the more magic he can perform. But he keeps surprising even himself. He doesn't know where it's coming from. And it can't be the Booke because he's been with it all his life. It seems that the more he experiences human emotion, the more things he can to do."

"I'll have to check with Jolene. She's the expert these days. But it does seem that he is getting to know more about himself as the days wear on." He tapped his lip for a moment before looking up at me. "Just as a matter of curiosity…are you in love with *him*?"

Sighing, I leaned back against my table. "I don't honestly know, Doc. Sometimes, I feel I could be, but then he gets all demony and animal-like…and it scares me. There are long stretches where I've forgotten entirely that he isn't like us at all. And I don't think it's a good idea to forget that."

"No, my dear, it isn't. I'd caution you to be careful but… we seem to be beyond that now." He put his arm around me. "I think you'd better tell us all about your encounter with Andras."

We both walked back into the main shop, and I told my story, leaving out the intimate details. But Doc was already whispering to Jolene, who snapped her head up to look at me and then pushed her glasses up her nose. When she dove back into her tablet, I knew she'd have an answer soon.

While everyone was busy with some sort of task, I found a moment to sit next to Nick. It was one of the few moments when George wasn't fawning over him. The deputy was in the kitchen with the others.

Nick blushed and looked down at his fidgeting fingers, at the chipped black polish on his nails. "It's funny how this is still there, even after they've become claws," he remarked.

I took his hand. "I'm so sorry."

He sighed. "It's not your fault. No, really. None of this is."

"It sure feels like it, though."

"Dude, how could you have known? And honestly." He looked back toward the kitchen. "Deputy Mustache really stepped up to the plate."

I laughed in spite of how guilty I felt. "Yeah, he has. I'm not sorry I told him. He needed to be told."

"I was all ready to break up with him. Now he's all over it. Suddenly out and proud. Well, at least to the coven. And he's not even making those veiled comments about Wicca anymore. Seems he's embraced that, too."

"Love can do that."

He blushed again. "Yeah," he said sheepishly. "I guess it can. You have chutzpah, I'll give you that."

"Speaking of out, what have you told your parents?"

His mood dimmed. "I had to tell them I was moving out, that I got a roommate and stuff. I'm going to have to go over there and get my things. But I'm scared, Kylie. What if I change? I don't want them to know. I don't want to hurt them."

"How's the adjustment going?"

"Jeff's been great about schooling me. And if I get frustrated and angry, he does some kind of alpha thing, and I fall into line. It's weird."

"Kinky."

He shoved his shoulder into mine. "God, no. Not with Straight Wolf."

"But it helps, right? Helps you control yourself?"

"I only shift a little when something sets me off, but even that's getting better. It's a learning curve, but it's going fast. Like…once you learn to ride a bike, it's as if you've been doing it all your life." He quieted, mulling it over. "All your life," he muttered, looking down at his hands again. His sudden cloud of gloom seemed to disappear just as quickly as it arrived. "The wolfsbane tastes horrible, but it really helps. Though the smell of blood is something that riles me up."

"Yeah. I saw that happen to Jeff. But that was because he hadn't taken his potion."

"Yes, *Mother*, I'll remember." Absently, he picked at the chipped polish. "You know, last night, when George was asleep, Jeff and I went out to the woods and shifted. He wanted me to be all wolf, to not be afraid of it. So I did, practicing shifting back and forth. And then, as a wolf, we ran together. Kylie…it was the most amazing thing I've ever done. I can't even describe it. The…freedom. The…" He shook his head. "It was just so dope. So…"

Something brilliant flashed in his eyes. He still feared the change, but it gave him something, too. I almost envied him.

"But," he said, the light in his eyes dimming, "there are things out there. In the woods."

"Jeff said something about that, too."

"Wild things that have always been there. I don't know what they are. If I had to give them a name, I guess I'd say…sprites? Forest creatures? They aren't quite benign, yet they aren't quite dangerous. But I know as a former human—"

"You *are* still human."

"Okay. As a human/wolf hybrid, I can see them now when I couldn't before. They don't really seem to care about us, but… they know about us. They looked right at me last night."

"But they aren't dangerous?"

He shrugged. "Not sure. I'll have to further explore that. Just…be careful out there. As if you aren't already." He hunched toward me. "So, tell me exactly what happened when you jabbed Andras with the poker."

Back to business. "I hit bone, I think, so it didn't go in too deep. It started to burn and smoke. But he was able to pull it out. I really think a bolt is what we need. Something he can't pull out. The more embedded it is, the more harm it will do. He was hurt but I don't know how much. A lot, I hope."

He got in closer. "So…were you and Erasmus in the middle of doing it?"

"Nick!"

George returned and sat on Nick's other side. He seemed to hesitate for a second before tentatively putting a hand on Nick's knee. "Nick tell you how he's coming along?"

"Nick's said a lot of things."

Nick chuckled.

"Thanks for being there, deputy."

"I'm not going to let anything happen to this guy." He leaned in, hesitated again when his eyes flicked toward me, but eventually tilted in further and kissed Nick's cheek.

Nick looked at me sidelong, gesturing with his head toward George.

George then edged in toward me. "I couldn't help but notice the necklace that Jeff is wearing."

"Ruh-roh," muttered Nick.

Getting into deputy mode, George raised his chin. "It looks suspiciously like the locket Ruth was asking about."

"Does it?" I might have batted my eyelashes.

He cleared his throat. "If it is her locket, I might have to ask for it back." Then his shoulders relaxed and he glanced once at Nick. "But if it's a supernatural thing," he said quietly, "and you really need it, maybe I didn't see it after all."

I smiled and rose. "You're okay, deputy. I'll leave you guys to it."

"Actually," said Nick, getting to his feet. "I feel kind of left out. I think I need to be in the kitchen with the others."

"Are you sure, Nicky?" asked George. Ed had been right that George was a whole different person when he was with Nick.

"I don't want to be treated like an invalid. I'm not. I'm ready to join the coven again." He caught sight of George's look of disapproval. "I mean the… *group*. Shall we?" He pushed his way into the kitchen. "Jolene, how are we doing on demon lore? It's time to kick Andras' butt."

* * *

WE NEEDED A piece of iron small enough to serve as a bolt for the poisoned arrowhead Erasmus had created to fit on top of. But none of us were blacksmiths.

"I bet Barry Johnson could do it," said Seraphina. "He does some metal work."

"How do you know that?" asked Nick, examining the poisoned head of the arrow.

"I know a little about Barry."

Nick slid a mischievous glance in her direction. "Oh ho! Seraphina gets biz-ay with Mr. Hardware Store!"

She gave him a withering look, but she still blushed.

"But that's actually an idea," said Nick. "He might already have some iron dowels or, I guess, rebar."

"Rebar is steel," said George.

Everyone looked at him.

"Hey, I know things."

Nick nodded. "Then that won't work. We need pure iron."

"Because…?"

"Because, deputy, demons can't abide iron or silver. But since I can't work with silver anymore—werewolf thing—iron's my best bet. I think we should go to the hardware store before it closes. And then…maybe head over to my folks to pick up my stuff."

He looked at George hopefully. But George seemed worried. "You don't want me to go, do you?"

"Only if you want to."

"Maybe your folks don't want to meet me."

"But they'll have to at some point."

"But…"

"Oh, for god's sake!" said Jolene over her tablet, head down and tapping away. "Man up, and just go with him, deputy."

Chastened, they both left together in Nick's car.

I stood at the window watching them drive away, thinking what strange couples we had: A werewolf and a deputy, a shopkeeper and a demon…when Ed pulled up in his Interceptor. And he wasn't alone.

CHAPTER TWENTY-ONE

ED GOT OUT of the car, then came around and opened the passenger side door. A long, slim leg in a leather catsuit emerged first, and then the rest of her stood up. Mission accomplished. Ed had done some yelling when I'd first proposed it and muttered something about prostituting himself, but in the end, he had agreed. And it was a good plan. Except for the sudden churning of my insides. *Was that jealously, Kylie? Girl, you are so messed up.*

I stepped into the doorway while they were still in the parking area and crossed my arms. "Well, well. What's this?" An Oscar-winning performance if ever there was one.

Ed gave me a hard look before turning a more genteel expression toward Shabiri. The demoness gave me a winning grin. "No wonder you were so enamored with this sheriff, Miss Strange. He's a love." She leaned back and swept her hand under his chin. "It's too bad you don't have my amulet, Ed darling. Maybe you should take it from Doug."

"Maybe I should." His eyes were locked on hers, and my level of discomfort shot skyward. Was he acting? Had this really been my idea?

"Where's Erasmus?" she cooed. "He'll love seeing this."

"I don't—" And there suddenly, he was "—know where he is."

"You'll adore this, darling," Shabiri said to Erasmus, hanging on his arm. "This Sheriff-of-the-Wide-Shoulders came looking for me to try to convince me to give back the Draugr gold—which I don't have, of course—and do you know what happened?"

He cast a glance toward me. "Must I listen to this?"

"He's such a dear. Said he found me alluring."

Erasmus turned his head to glare at Ed, who was trying to appear nonchalant.

"So naturally I had to come here and flaunt it." She slithered over to Ed and nearly wrapped herself around him. He looked down at her with a lascivious smile. I didn't like it at all.

"That's, uh, real…nice, Shabiri," I said, trying to get the words out. "So *will* you give back the gold?"

She pouted. "I haven't decided yet. Not that I have it."

"Oh, for crying out loud."

Did he *sleep* with her? I mean that was *quick*.

His arm curled around her, and I couldn't quite see where his hand ended up. And she was making a kissy-face at him.

"Okay, you know what? I don't need to be here. If you don't have the gold, I've got better things to do."

"Let's not be hasty," said Erasmus with a sly smile. "Aren't you happy for Constable Bradbury?"

"Constable Brad—I mean *Sheriff* Bradbury can do whatever he damn well wants to. It's not up to me."

"That's *right*," said Shabiri sternly. "It isn't."

I glared at her, trying to avoid looking at Ed. "Have you brought the gold?"

A roar of Harley engines drowned her out, and she leaned back against Ed. I noticed that Erasmus had taken up a place next to me…very close.

The Ordo screamed up the street and parked in a neat row in front of my shop. When Doug dismounted, he sneered at Ed. "What's this? What the hell is Shabiri…" But it was pretty plain what the hell she was doing. Doug scowled, and Charise, not surprisingly, clung to Doug with whitening hands. Her eyes narrowed into slits of sheer hatred aimed at the demon... or toward Ed? It didn't matter. Doug looked like he barely noticed, but I saw that he was reaching into his leather jacket, probably just to make sure he still had the amulet. Hey, that was an idea. I wonder if Erasmus could steal it and hand it over to Ed...

"Is it mutiny?" asked Doug.

Ed shook his head. "She's not your genie, Doug."

"She is if I say she is." He squeezed the demon face on the amulet, and she cried out, stumbling away from Ed. She shot Doug a filthy look.

"You're a sore loser, Dougie."

"I don't want you canoodling with the enemy."

"As it happens," she said, smoothing out her leather catsuit, "I don't think he's your enemy at all. You are more alike than you'd care to admit. Though there are *distinct* differences."

Charise got in closer, twisting the lapel of Doug's leather jacket. "Don't let her talk to you like that, Doug."

In the blink of an eye, Shabiri was in Charise's face. "I'm certainly not here to please you either, Miss Pale Comparison. As I believe I already made clear."

Charise touched her neck where Shabiri's hands had been, running her fingers over her bruises.

I pushed in front of all of them to face Doug. "To what do I owe the displeasure of your company?"

He eyed Shabiri. "Well, I came in good faith to let you know that we couldn't find the gold. But it looks like someone's been busy."

Ed ignored Doug and turned to the demon. "It's pretty important that we get it back. I know that you don't care that people we know are dying, but *I* care. Can you help us find the gold, Shabiri?"

She smiled and slithered into Ed's arms. Both Doug and I made faces.

"Well…" she said, drawing circles on his chest with her finger, "if it's that important to you…I'll give it a whirl." She vanished instantly. The sappy look on Ed's face vanished. He turned to his brother. "That's how you do it, Doug."

"You mother—"

"Hey!" I interrupted. "The point is, *boys*, that we're finally getting the gold to return to the Draugr. No more killings. Focus on that, huh?"

"And that's *all* I'm doing," said Doug, pointing a finger at me.

We all stood around, just staring at one another. With his arms firmly crossed over his chest, Doug was the mirror image of Ed. Charise had her fingertips in her leathers' pockets since her pants were so skin-tight she couldn't fit in her whole hands. Dean and Bob looked out into the distance.

I finally threw up my hands. "It's too cold out here to wait. Why don't you all…come inside…if you can be civil." They exchanged looks. Before they could sneer, I turned my back on them and marched into the shop. Erasmus, with as wide a grin as he had ever worn, followed me in. He wasn't the least bit cold that I could tell.

The rest of them slowly wandered inside. I could tell Charise liked the smell of some of the prepared teas, though she'd never stoop to ask for any. But I was feeling charitable. "If anyone wants some tea, those urns have samples. The cups are there."

Only Charise was brave enough to take some. I couldn't picture the others drinking tea anyway.

Seraphina walked up to the Ordo and offered them coffee from a carafe. Doug took a cup.

"This is all so cozy. Wiccan central," he said, between sips. Steam rose from his paper cup as he scanned the room. "Hey, Velma," he said to Jolene, "What are you and the Scooby gang working on over there?"

She looked up, pushing her glasses up her nose, and clicked off her tablet. She clutched it to her chest and pressed her lips tight together.

"Excuse *me*," he muttered.

"We're trying to find a way to clean up your mess," I told him. "Seems we've been doing that a lot."

"*My* mess?"

"The Draugr gold for one. Goat Guy, for two."

"My Lord Baphomet doesn't need cleaning up. He's free."

"He'll start killing again," said Doc. "Or demand sacrifices."

"What do you know about it, old man?"

Doc narrowed his eyes, lifted his fingers, and snapped them. Doug jumped as a spark lit his backside.

"Stop that!"

"Not until you show some respect, young man. I may be an old duffer, but I know things. Things that only wisdom and observation bring. You could do with paying a bit more attention where it counts, instead of salivating over those noisy machines you like to drive around."

Bob leaned over toward Doug. "He's talking about our bikes," he stage-whispered.

"I know that, *Willis*." Doug faced Doc again with a sneer. "You think you know everything just because you're old, but you don't. Shabiri has been teaching me things, amazing things. You aren't the only game in town, you know."

"*We* can teach you things." I was shocked that Seraphina spoke up. She moved forward with such an intense expression that I couldn't look away. "We can join forces. We could all do amazing things...*together!*"

Doug stared. He seemed enrapt with her—her flowing skirts and joyous face. Like he had been suddenly shown a sliver of what *could* be. He even took a step forward.

Until Charise opened her big, fat mouth.

"You aren't going to listen to this old witch, are you, Doug?"

That snapped him out of it. Maybe Seraphina had done some sort of spellwork. Or maybe not. But whatever it was, the moment was gone now.

"We're giving back the gold and that's it. *Capisce?*" he said.

"You're such an idiot, Doug," snarled Ed.

"*I'm* the idiot? What about you? Messing around with a demon? Ick."

He smirked, flicking a glance at me. "It's not as bad as you think."

"So the gold!" I said a little louder than necessary. "Once we get it, does anyone know what we do with it? I mean, do we need a ritual to get rid of the Draugr?"

"As I understand it," said Doc, "we simply leave the gold out where they can see it, they take it, and disappear back to…wherever they came from."

"Valhalla," said Ed. Everyone looked at him. "Isn't that where dead Vikings go?"

"Dead Viking zombies?" asked Jolene.

"Zombie Valhalla?" Ed offered.

"Doesn't matter," I said. "As long as they're gone."

The only sounds were the sipping of tea and coffee. Time ticked away.

The sound of a car roused us, moving as a group to the window. Nick and George pulled up in front of the shop and got out, George scornful of the row of bikes. He looked toward the shop and took out his gun.

"Uh oh," Doug and I said at the same time.

Ed went to the door. "I've got it," he said back to us. "George! It's me, Ed. It's okay. We're just having a little parlay with the Ordo. You can put your gun away."

"If it's okay with you, sheriff, I'd like to see that for myself."

"I'm opening the door, George, slowly and carefully so you can see me."

He did so with his hand up. George two-handed the gun and rushed in. He looked over Doug and his gang and slowly lowered his weapon. "What's going on, sheriff?"

"We're just working out a little negotiation."

"About the zombies?"

"What the hell?" said Doug. "He knows, too?"

George slipped his gun away. "Yeah. We've got you covered, Doug."

"You're no fun at all, deputy. But I see you and your boy-friend are a little more open these days."

Someone was growling. It was Nick. His eyes were becoming green, his ears and snout growing.

Doug stepped back.

"It's even worse than that," I said. "We've got some werewolf power on our side."

This time, Bob and Dean stepped back.

"Whoa," said Dean. He suddenly didn't look all that big and bad with his shaved head. "Doug, they got werewolves. That lit-tle faggot is now a fucking werewolf."

"I wouldn't go throwing those epithets around, Willis," said George, hand on his holster. "I don't think Nick likes it."

Nick hadn't returned to normal yet, his teeth elongating while his growls grew louder.

"Nick," I said. "You need to dial it down."

Nick caught his breath and blinked at me. His snout and ears receded. The last things to go were his fangs, slowly slipping up behind his lips.

Doug looked like he was on his last nerve. "Damn."

"So you see, Doug." I walked forward until I was right in front of him. "We do have the upper hand."

He looked panicked. Then suddenly he wasn't. He even smiled. "Not quite, sweet thing. There's still my Lord…BAPHOMET!"

The sky rumbled. *Oh, shit.* "You didn't. You didn't just call on him, Doug. You are such an asshole!"

I rushed to the window. Yup. Dark, threatening clouds gath-ered fast, clumping into angry roiling masses and blotting out what was left of the sun. Lightning lit the underside of the clouds, searing across their underbellies in bright flashes.

The center of the clouds suddenly rolled away, and Baphomet slowly descended through the partition, like some upside-down Renaissance painting where *he* was the cherub.

I turned toward Doc, who clearly had nothing.

"What's the plan, Doug? Did you think this through?"

By the look on his face, he obviously hadn't. He seemed as terrified as the rest of us. And when the mist began to rise, I knew we were in for a world of trouble.

"Great. The Draugr."

Baphomet landed, his hooves digging potholes into the asphalt. The sky was dark now, dark enough for zombie Vikings.

Baphomet noticed the mist swirling around his legs and smiled, his weird goat eyes shining. He cocked his head and watched as the Draugr dragged themselves out of the forest, weapons raised. They almost looked like they were riding the clouds of mist, heading toward the shop. They ignored the giant goat god in front of them, as if his presence was an everyday occurrence.

"Any ideas, Nick? Is that enchanted fire working?"

"I, uh, think I'm a little bit terrified right now."

I whirled toward him. "Well, snap out of it! We have a situation here."

"Okay. You're right. I have the pouch. Haven't tested it yet."

"Wait," said Doc. "What if he goes out there, and Baphomet tries to stop him? He'll need cover."

"What have we got to cover him with?"

Ed and the deputy looked shocked and frightened. George wasn't even grabbing at Nick to pull him back. So *they* were useless.

Something hit my leg. When I looked down, I saw the Booke nudging me. The Booke. Maybe…

I grabbed it, felt its power throbbing within me. "Are you ready, Nick?"

"Ready? I don't…I don't…"

"Now or never, Nick." He gave me a nod, opened the pouch, and reached his hand in. I held the Booke in front of me and rushed out the door.

Baphomet immediately turned toward me. "Kylie Strange," he said in a gravelly voice.

Nick slipped out the door and headed for the other end of the shop, ducking just around the corner. He began to chant.

"Why do you keep saying my name like that?" I said, stalling. "I get that you know who I am."

"I want my words to be the last you ever hear."

"Oh, blah, blah, blah. You talk like a comic book villain."

He frowned. Creases formed between his eyes, on his forehead, and around his mouth. He sneered with his big goat teeth. Of course, he was twenty feet tall, so everything seemed more exaggerated. He leaned over, like a building suddenly tilting toward the ground. "Your words are foolishly brave."

"That's me, all right. Foolishly brave. Can't you just go back to wherever you came from? What do you want with this place anyway? You'd never fit on the furniture."

"To enslave Mankind. They belong to me. As do you."

"Yeah, well." I snatched a glance at the Draugr as their snarling, rotting selves drew closer. *Come on, Nick!* "We'd make really terrible slaves. We don't like doing what others tell us to do. Especially these Mainers. They have their own minds."

"Their will shall be taken from them. Their only thoughts will be to please me."

"Look," I said, sobering. "Why do you have to kill? Why can't you just—I don't know—*talk* with us. Impart your wisdom. You know things we can't begin to know. You've lived a thousand lifetimes. More. I'm sure there are tons of people who'd love to hear about you. Can't we all just be friends?"

"You are a fool, Kylie Strange!"

I didn't like the fact that he was cocking back his arm. It was almost certainly bad for me. A ball of light...power... something formed in his curled fingers. When he shot his arm forward, the ball careened toward me. I had a split second for my life to pass before my eyes just as I instinctively raised the Booke to hide behind.

I expected either a blow or an explosion. I expected to be pulverized by that ball of power. And yet, time kept ticking, and as far as I could tell, nothing happened. I opened my eyes to a squint and looked to either side. The Draugr were still coming, Moody Bog was still there in the misty, gray distance, and my shop still stood behind me. But now there were also waves of light pouring from behind the Booke.

I lowered it slightly and felt what the Booke was feeling. If it could laugh, that's what it would've been doing. It held the ball of power to its cover, letting it roll there like a soft tickle, before the Booke absorbed it through the leather and into the parchment, where it simply… dissolved.

I looked up at Baphomet. That was one unhappy goat.

"What have you done!"

Where was Erasmus? The pussy was hiding somewhere in the shadows. "I, uh, didn't do anything."

He trembled in anger. And then he threw back his head and roared.

The Draugr in front of me burst into flames and twisted in the sudden inferno. At first, I thought it was Baphomet, but he was just as surprised as I was.

But not as surprised as Nick, apparently. He wore an astonished look on his face, before he jumped in glee. "It worked!"

The Draugr turned tail and ran, arms and weapons flailing, into the woods.

"No!" I cried. Now I was going to be responsible for setting Maine on fire.

But as their tormented bodies hit the trees, the flames went no further. Come to think of it, the fire was sort of greenish, not the color of a proper fire at all. It caught neither brush nor tree, only glowing around the zombies that had been hit. The others—who seemed to be multiplying each time I checked—didn't appear to like the look of it, retreating into the mist away from their burning brethren.

I had no time to celebrate Nick's success. Goat Guy was still on the warpath.

"Doug! Get the hell out here and deal with this!" I called.

He came timidly to the doorway and looked up. Baphomet

glared down at him. Doug came out the rest of the way and dropped to his knees, head down. "Lord Baphomet."

"Why do you consort with this creature?" said Baphy, gesturing toward me. I bristled. Look who's calling who a creature!

"It was necessary, my lord. To get information from them."

"I do not like her or her book. She should be dead by now. If the demon will not do it, *you* are to see to it." In a final fit of petulance, he swept out his arm and knocked the bikes on top of each other. They fell like dominoes, the crunch of metal and the clatter of chrome on chrome echoing through the night. Baphomet turned without flicking an eyelash at me, then pumped his wings, lifting into the sky. I hoped he wouldn't be inclined to kill tonight, not that there was anything I could do about it.

I held the Booke tightly, knowing it had saved my life. The wheels in my head began to churn. If the Booke could be used as a weapon, then I intended to use it.

Chapter Twenty-Two

THERE WAS A lot of whining and cursing as the Ordo disentangled their bikes from one another and checked their engines for damage. I resisted the urge to gloat about the dented and scratched chrome, the leaking oil.

In the meantime, I scanned the skies and was pleased that I didn't hear any explosions or see any plumes of smoke in the distance. I was glad Baphy didn't end this appearance with a killing spree.

We all waited for Shabiri's return. At first, I thought she might have been waiting to come back because of Baphomet, but now he was gone and she still hadn't come back. Maybe she'd forgotten where she put it. Her continued absence gave me a chance to confront Ed.

"That was fast."

He postured. "You *told* me to seduce her. And it worked. So what are you complaining about?"

"I…" *Well, Kylie? What* are *you complaining about?* "It's just… Nothing. I'm not complaining."

"Okay then."

"All right."

Ed raised his shoulders, hitching his faux fur coat collar up around his neck. "It's just…when I got to know her, she seemed more vulnerable than I expected. It's kind of a weird life. And she knows it."

"Well...yeah. I mean, that's the same with Erasmus, only worse. He's only awake for a few weeks every few hundred years. And I think he's just beginning to understand all that he's been missing. And he can't do anything about it. That's got to be incredibly frustrating."

Ed huffed. His breath gathered around his face in white clouds. "Are we comparing our demons?"

I laughed. "Oh my God, I think we are."

"They're more complicated people...or something...than I imagined."

We stood for a moment in thought.

"So...do you *like* her?"

"What is this, elementary school? Are you going to start passing me notes?"

I knocked into his shoulder. "I'm serious. You've seen her vulnerable side. Is she legit?"

"I don't know. I don't know that I really trust her. She likes playing games." He raised his chin toward Erasmus, who was across the parking lot brooding. "What about him? Is he legit? Do you trust *him*?"

I looked, too. I'd really come to like the idiot. "Yeah. I do. My life depends on it."

"But...if it wasn't life or death...would you...you know, stick with him?"

Erasmus turned and suddenly looked directly at me, as if he knew what we were talking about. He had super-hearing, so there was a chance he did. His penetrating gaze roved over me.

Would I stick with him? What about Ed? Wasn't he the smarter choice? The...safer choice? Ed was everything I wanted: security, faithfulness, a future. It was everything I thought I needed. So what the hell was wrong with me? Hadn't Jeff taught me that the exotic choice wasn't the best of decisions? Still...

I glanced back at Erasmus. He stood stoically. And with his

duster blowing around him, almost…heroically. But he was no hero. He was a stone-cold killer and I really wasn't certain I could trust him. Except…I did trust him. With my life. And maybe something more.

"Yeah," I said at last. "I would. I'm sorry. I know I said we might…"

"It's okay. Really."

Then I laughed and kicked at the gravel. "He's so pathetic. Like a lost puppy."

"A lost puppy with devastating magic. That can kill."

I looked right into Ed's face. "But so can I."

"I guess so, Ms. Crossbow. But…what about that book? It shielded you from that Baphomet guy."

"It did. It's not afraid of him. In fact, it thinks that Baphomet is afraid of *it*."

"It 'thinks'?"

"It speaks to me. From deep down. Like we're part of the same person." I felt warm inside talking about it.

"That doesn't sound good, Kylie. Or safe. We've got to detach this thing from you. Before it drags you down to whatever world it belongs to."

I rubbed my forehead. I knew all this…intellectually. But the Booke was speaking to me even now, reassuring me, telling me not to listen to the nice man with the sheriff's badge and gun.

"I think you're right."

"I hate to interrupt this charming tête-à-tête," said Doug, suddenly behind us. "But we're gonna roll out, since who knows when Shabiri is coming back. Text me when she does." He gave us both a lopsided smile before walking toward his bike.

Ed was about to open his mouth when I laid a hand against his chest. "Don't bait him, Ed. He's pretty vulnerable, too."

"Vulnerable, my ass."

Moody Bog's own little soap opera. Ed and Doug didn't even know they were starring in it.

Someone's phone rang. It couldn't be Shabiri, could it?

But it was Deputy George's phone. He answered the call, glancing toward Ed. "Oh, uh, hi there, Mrs. Russell."

Ruth-*freaking*-Russell.

"No, I haven't found your locket yet. Kylie Strange said she turned her place upside down looking for—Yes. Yes…" He flicked a glance at Jeff, who had come up behind him, and he looked straight at the locket hanging from Jeff's neck. "I'll be on the lookout for it. Someone from the community might turn it in. Yes, I will. Good-bye, ma'am." He ended the call and gave us all a look. "The heat is on."

"Don't worry about Ruth," said Doc. "I'll make sure to throw her off the scent."

"But Doc," I said, "I don't know that she's too keen on you."

"Ruth and I…well, we have a history. Besides. it's a good way to find out about that darned locket. Maybe I can get something out of her about it."

"Better you than me."

We all went back inside where it was warmer. I decided to make some dragonwell tea in a proper clay pot—I needed a clear mind.

The rest of the coven gathered listlessly, not quite knowing what to do. Nick decided to help me in the kitchen. When we brought out the aromatic green tea, only Jolene seemed to be doing anything at all. She was hunched over her tablet, typing furiously, brows crunched over her eyes. Ed and George were talking quietly together, and so were Doc and Seraphina.

Erasmus and Jeff eyed each other suspiciously from across the room. I hadn't even noticed when Jeff arrived.

Jolene stood. "I think I've got it."

Everyone stopped what they were doing and looked at her. She smiled, holding up her tablet. "I…I think I've got it."

"Got what, squirt?" said Nick.

"The ritual. For the de-summoning."

Erasmus appeared in front of her. "Let me see that." He snatched the tablet out of her hand and began to read. Nick was suddenly by his side reading over his shoulder. And then Doc, his lips silently moving, and Seraphina, with reading glasses perched on the end of her nose. Erasmus scowled as he read…then raised an eyebrow.

He glanced at me and then turned to Jolene, handing the tablet back as the others scrambled to continue reading. "Your reasoning is very sound," he said. "And your knowledge of R'lye-hian is outstanding for one so young."

"Thanks, Mr. Dark."

"But I still have my misgivings."

"Is it because of the rift?" asked Doc.

"That and…I don't trust him."

Seraphina whipped off her glasses and held something up from the folds of her velvet cloak. "That's why I had this made." It was a small iron rod with metal fletching attached to one end. She held it in her palms and showed it to Erasmus, who took a step back. "I didn't have one of Kylie's arrows to measure the circumference, but I think we got it close enough. Maybe just a little magic to make the arrowhead fit."

I took it from her outstretched hand and turned it over in my fingers. It was heavy, but I was sure it would fly. "You know, if you got this wet, rolled it in some sea salt, I bet this would get him good."

"And with the poisoned tip…" she said.

I thrust it toward Erasmus. "What do you think?"

"I think I would rather not touch it."

"Oh, sorry. Here, Nick." I handed it to him, then held up my hand for the crossbow. It whistled through the house before slapping into my palm. I grabbed the bolt that Erasmus had poisoned by jamming the tip into his eye. "Do you suppose the crossbow will know when I need this one?"

"I suppose," he drawled. "How do you propose to free the arrowhead from the shaft?"

I thought about it for a moment, setting the crossbow down and examining the bolt's shaft, the poison-tipped arrowhead. Then I broke off the tip.

"What are you—!" sputtered Erasmus. "Are you insane? That is *my* crossbow!"

"Nick, can you dig out the shaft from the arrowhead?"

Nick edged away from it. "No can do, boss lady. That there is silver."

"Oh. George?"

"My boy's silver-shy now. And I'm not sure I can do it..."

Seraphina took it from my hand. "I can handle it."

"Okay. Jolene, tell us what to do."

"Well...we'll have to travel to the cave where the rift is. Using the rift, we can open the gate."

"Can we *close* the gate?"

"Yes. The scryer will help us close it. And before anyone yells at me, I have no intention of touching it. Possession is not fun."

It had scared the bejeezus out of me when Jolene had been possessed by whatever being was in the rift. I didn't want a repeat.

George and Ed seemed puzzled. I realized that I hadn't exactly told them everything that had happened in the last three weeks.

"And what does Mr. Dark think of all this?" asked George.

Erasmus frowned, knitting his hands together behind his back. "It seems sound. But I am concerned about using the rift."

"Yeah, me too," I said. "What about...using the Booke?"

Silence.

Okay, I didn't expect that. But it suddenly made me realize that all my thoughts about the Booke—my ruminations and feelings—had all been in my head. I hadn't really told anyone my conclusions.

The Booke appeared as if I'd called it, hovering at my hip. I grabbed it, feeling a surge of power and confidence, then sat, placing it in my lap like an attentive dog.

"The Booke is a gateway. It goes both ways. It has its own power and sentience. It can help us...if I ask it to."

Doc stood with his hand on his chin, staring at the Booke through squinted eyes. "And what is your opinion on that, Mr. Dark?"

When Erasmus grabbed the Booke out of my lap, I was momentarily shocked. Why shouldn't he be able to touch it? He was just as intimately connected. At first, I felt a rush of jealousy. But when the Booke soon recognized him, it almost seemed to be…purring. I relaxed somewhat too, feeling a strange mixture of loss and relief.

"The book is not for meddling," he growled.

"But is it safer than the rift?" said Doc. "I have my misgivings about the rift—the vortex—and the use of the scryer."

"As do I," he said.

I thought I'd feel more anxious about someone else holding the Booke, but as I followed Erasmus while he wandered about the room, I got the same vibe from him and the Booke together. As if they were one and the same. Were they?

Erasmus brooded. He was good at that. His hair fell into his eyes, casting shadows over his face. His jaw was set, and the muscles in the side of his neck twitched and tensed. "I would rather not use the book in this way. There might be untold consequences."

Ed had watched the proceedings, not really knowing the details. "What is this vortex/rift thing you keep talking about?"

Doc cut in before I could. "Perhaps you recall the caves, Sheriff, when the bicyclist was found?"

"Sure. Of course."

"He died at the hands of the succubus, because inside the cave there is a rift in space. It swirls with power, which was why we called it a vortex at first. But it's more accurately described as a rift—a torn place between the worlds. There was another at Karl Waters' museum. When we investigated, Jolene was temporarily possessed by the beings inside it. That's why we don't want her anywhere near it," he said, adding a pointed look at her. She replied with a sigh, an eye roll, and the crossing of her arms. "But we closed that one," he went on. "Which we think was opened by the Ordo."

"Doug," he said, scowling. "So…what's a scryer?"

"A tool," Jolene cut in. "I made it. It detects magical people and objects. It can also control the rift...in theory."

Ed grunted. "Shouldn't Dark be able to control the rift since he's part of this whole book nonsense?"

Affronted, Erasmus hitched the book in the cradle of his arm and raised his nose in disdain. "Nonsense, is it?"

Ed shook his head. "I didn't mean—"

"No, of course not. You mortals are all alike. You disparage that which you don't understand, and fear what you barely perceive." His hands tightened on the Booke. "If we must choose, the lesser of two evils is the rift."

"Really?" I touched his arm, the one holding the Booke, and a sensation of...something...almost shocked my fingertips. "The rift is safer than the Booke?"

"Yes."

Except I knew—by that touch or by my connection to the Booke—that he was lying.

He avoided my gaze as if he knew that I knew. I was about to open my mouth when Doc interrupted. "Then once we're ready, let's get ourselves to the caves."

I tore my gaze away from the Booke and looked toward the windows. "It's getting dark. We'll be vulnerable to the Draugr."

"But Nick has that handy-dandy spell now." Doc winked at Nick.

Nick shrugged, but I could tell he was pleased with himself.

"So wait a minute," said George. Everyone slowed packing their things and donning their jackets. "We're all just going to go to this rift thing and perform some sort of ritual that might make this hell gate open up wider? Shouldn't we look for alternatives?"

"We've got to get rid of Andras," said Nick.

"Then why don't we just kill him?"

Jolene sighed the loudest of teenaged-sighs. "*Because*, deputy, we don't know where he is and where he'll strike next. If we start the summoning ritual, he will automatically come to us. He'll have no choice."

"And besides," I said, "there are a few questions I'd like to ask him. He seems to know things about the Booke that I want to know too." I glanced at Erasmus for confirmation, but he was too busy brooding under his hair. "I mean, as satisfying as it might be to kill him, I'm more interested in interrogating him. Once we've got him by the—" I glanced at Jolene. "Once we've got him, he'll be in a perfect position to answer questions."

"Like what?" asked Doc.

"Like what does he know about the Booke? How did *he* drag that ghoul out of it? What are the secrets I need to know?"

He studied Erasmus. "Can't Mr. Dark answer those questions?"

"No. He doesn't seem to know. So let's concentrate on keeping Andras alive so he can answer my questions before we send him back."

Seraphina nodded. "It's still a good idea to have the killing arrow as a back-up plan. We'll have it ready for you, Kylie, just in case. Make sure you bring your crossbow."

I nodded. "I guess we should split up. I can drive my Jeep. Should we go in Doc's Rambler or…"

"We can take my Interceptor," said Ed, still looking leery of it all.

Jolene waved her hands. "Police car! Yeah, I want to do that."

Nick looked excited at the prospect, too, while Jeff hovered close by like a mother hen. I was actually relieved to see that Jeff was doing his alpha duty and keeping an eye on his charge.

Ed seemed okay with extra passengers. "If anyone has flashlights, they're preferable to using phones. Also, it's quite a hike from the parking area to the cave." He swept his gaze over Seraphina. "I recommend putting on some trousers and some good hiking shoes before we set out."

Seraphina looked like the only one in need of changing. Velvet and chiffon wouldn't work for what we had ahead of us. Doc volunteered to take her home in the Rambler. It was decided that Jeff, Nick, George, and Jolene would go in the Interceptor, which left just Erasmus and me in my car. Which was fine. I had a few things to ask him.

I missed the noisiness once they'd all left. Alone with Erasmus, I put on my L.L. Bean jacket with the hood. I tugged the crossbow out of Erasmus' hand and looked it over, bothered by the empty sheath. I touched the bow, running my hand over the ebony wood and the inlaid silver metal of the weapon. It wasn't really made of silver, of course, or Erasmus wouldn't have been able to touch it. Tin maybe?

"Before we meet up with the others," I said, fiddling with the crossbow so I didn't have to look at him, "why did you lie just then about the vortex being safer than the Booke?"

"I did no such thing."

I met his gaze. "But you did. The...the Booke told me you did."

"Dammit," he swore under his breath. "Kylie, you must understand, though the book might be inherently safer than the rift, there *is* danger in using it in this manner. You feel it now, don't you? You know that it is capable of much more than what it seems to be on the surface. It *wants* to do more; this is why the Powers That Be insist that the Chosen Host be dispatched fairly quickly, so that the book cannot come into its full sentience."

"That's what they're really afraid of. That its power might overtake theirs."

"There may be some truth to that. I have no way of knowing."

"Are you telling me that most Chosen Hosts are...*dispatched*...sooner than...me?"

"I'm saying that three weeks is an unusual timeline for a Chosen Host."

I touched my hand to my chest. Poor Constance Howland. The clock definitely started ticking once the cover was opened. How many days had she lasted? Two weeks? Ten days?

I searched his guarded expression in a sudden panic. "Erasmus, are they calling you? The Powers That Be?"

He hesitated, and finally said a quiet, "Yes."

"Oh my God. You can't go."

"I know that!"

"What will happen to you if you don't?"

His face suddenly fell. "I don't know. All I know is, that the rift is safer for me than the book."

Poor Erasmus, only awake for an average of two weeks every several hundred years or so. My heart went out to him, and I found his hand and squeezed it. He looked at our joined hands in puzzlement.

"What kind of life is this?" My voice broke. Tears pooled in my eyes.

Erasmus slowly extricated his hand from mine. "We must be very careful. The Powers That Be must *not* be made aware of what we are doing."

"Okay."

"Baphomet and others are, no doubt, making the Netherworld aware of the goings-on here."

"The Netherworld network?"

"If you like. Right now, there is confusion, and confusion is good. Andras was summoned by someone on this plane, but if the Powers That Be get wind of my...mutiny...then there might be more demons sent through the gateway."

"Oh, boy. I'll do whatever you say to keep you safe."

He looked puzzled again. "To keep *me* safe?"

"Of course. What did you think I meant all this time?"

"Yourself."

I shook my head. "Sometimes you're kind of an idiot."

"Why do you insist on insulting me? I've done nothing to provoke it."

The only way to take that look off his face was to lean in and kiss him, so I did. It was sort of quick but more than a peck. And it did the trick. A soppy, dreamy expression crossed his face.

"Why did you do that?" he asked softly.

I rested my hand on the side of his face, feeling his prickly stubble on my palm. "Because you looked like you needed it."

"I see." He bent to kiss me back, so lingeringly that I still felt the heat of him on my lips as he drew away. "You needed it, too."

I swallowed. "We'd, uh, better go."

Baphomet had brought clouds with him when he arrived, but they had dissipated once he was gone. Still, it was late afternoon, and the sun was already at a low angle. It would be dark soon. That meant Draugr. Jeez, those guys were annoying.

We didn't speak as I drove out of town and onto the highway. I turned at the sign for Falcon's Point.

Falcon's Point always reminded me of Constance Howland and her heroic suicide. Maybe if she'd only reasoned with Erasmus…but of course, she wouldn't have. It was a different time back then.

"Erasmus, is this ritual going to work?"

"I have every expectation that it will."

"If it does, can we use it on Shabiri? Get her out of the way for good?"

"Not while Doug possesses her amulet."

"Can't you just snatch it like you did for Ruth's locket?"

"No. I cannot touch another's amulet."

I shook my head. "This whole amulet thing… Seems counterproductive for demons to have them if they can be snatched so easily."

He scowled. "I did not invent amulets."

"I know but…someone must have. I think they wanted to make sure that demons could be controlled by those in the know."

He didn't say anything to that, just sat back and brooded. He'd probably never thought about these finer points before. Maybe it pissed him off to know how little free will he had. I wanted to comfort him, but I also had no intention of giving back the amulet of his that *I* was wearing anytime soon so…

I turned into the parking area. "I don't suppose Andras has an amulet. I never saw one on him, as I recall."

"He is an older demon of a different class than Shabiri or I. He does not have an amulet."

The Interceptor and Rambler were already there. My ever-growing coven was standing around their cars as I pulled up.

Ed and George had flashlights, as did Doc. I'd forgotten mine, but I was sure there was one in the trunk. Yup, under the tire cover. I got it and switched it on.

The caves were up a trail through the woods. Not a difficult trail, but it wouldn't be much fun in the dark, and the sun was on its way to setting.

No one said anything as we turned toward the trailhead and began to walk. Erasmus didn't need a flashlight, and apparently neither did Nick or Jeff. The two kept eyeing each other, and I knew what they were thinking. They wanted to wolf out and run ahead.

Maybe that was a good idea.

"Hey Jeff!" He turned his head sharply toward me. "Maybe… maybe you and Nick should, you know, scout ahead. Do the wolf thing?"

I didn't need to ask them twice. They both started disrobing. Jolene made a sound of surprise as Nick stripped down to nothing. He turned away from her squeak and handed George his clothes. "Watch this, George!" he said with glee before he morphed, black hair sprouting all over, tail shooting forth and fluffing out.

Jeff had shifted in the blink of an eye. Seraphina gathered his clothes from the ground and stuffed them into a beaded bag hanging from a long strap across her chest.

The wolves bounded into the forest with excited yips.

George had turned white.

Ed stood beside him and rested a reassuring hand on his shoulder. "It's okay, deputy. He's in good hands. Uh, paws? They know what they're doing, and they're better equipped to take care of themselves now."

"Yeah. I…I guess so. It's just…"

He patted George on the shoulder and urged him on. George

clutched Nick's clothes to his chest, dipping his nose into them from time to time to take a whiff.

We trudged on. I had the flashlight in one hand, the crossbow in the other. Seraphina dropped back to walk with me. She took the flashlight out of my hand and gave it to a perplexed Erasmus. "I have something for you." She dug into her beaded bag and took out the arrow. "I did it. Doc and I managed to attach the head. Now the question is, will the crossbow accept it?"

I stopped and lowered the crossbow. I stuck the bolt in its empty sheath and waited. I expected it to spit it out, reject it. But nothing happened. "It seems okay," I told her, looking down again. Apparently, the crossbow had taken to it very well, because with the speed of an eye blink, it had armed itself with the new iron bolt and had even drawn back the string. "Wow."

"That is impressive. I never saw it happen."

"That is the essence of magic," said Erasmus, shoving the flashlight back at me. "Magic works best peripherally, without being observed."

"Schrödinger's Crossbow?" I said.

"But we perform magic and rituals all the time now," said Seraphina. I think it was the first civil conversation she had ever had with Erasmus.

"Rituals and casting spells are only manifestations of magic secretly present."

She tilted her head, thinking. "It sounds as if you're calling magic sentient."

"Not at all," he said. "It is a force, a power, present on different levels. When the book was opened, and thence a gateway created, that magic became more…available. Magic is always present in ways that are obvious and in many more ways that are nuanced."

"So that's why we could perform small spells before, often with ambiguous results?"

"Exactly."

"And if someone were a mage…"

"They'd have an innate ability to tap into that which was always present."

She looked at me with a knowing nod. "Well! Thank you, Mr. Dark. That was most illuminating." She flounced away, humming tunelessly to herself.

When she was out of earshot, I asked, "Was all of that true?"

"Of course." And then he smiled.

Demons lie. I kept forgetting. So was everything he said to me in the car a lie, or just some of it? And if so, which parts were which?

CHAPTER TWENTY-THREE

IT WAS DARK when we reached the caves. Both wolves were waiting for us at the entrance, their eyes reflecting our flashlight beams.

George stood a little away from WereNick. "Are you gonna change back, Nicky? C-can you understand me?"

The black wolf trotted forward and licked George's hand. George snapped it away, holding it against his chest.

"I think it's best they stay as wolves," said Doc. "Their hearing and sight are keener in that form. But don't worry, deputy. He can understand you. He's still Nick."

Upon hearing his name, Nick sat and woofed a little, panting. His tongue lolled and muzzle smiled, like some big, friendly German Shepherd.

"How will we find the rift?" I asked, gripping my flashlight with a sweaty palm.

"With this," said Doc. He reached into his coat pocket and withdrew the scrying stick, an ordinary twig with a crystal and a feather tied to one end. The crystal was glowing. "It's already working," he said, eyes glinting.

"But those caves have miles of twisty tunnels. How will we find our way back?"

Jolene shivered in her coat. "Anyone bring bread crumbs? Or yarn?"

"I can help," said Erasmus, a little reluctantly, I thought.

"Well then," said Doc, holding the scryer aloft, like a *Lord of the Rings* character. "Shall we?"

We all went in, the werewolves taking up the rear. I felt safer with them watching our backs.

"This ritual," I asked when I caught up to Jolene. "What is it, exactly?"

She switched on her tablet, and the blue light glowed on her face, giving her a strange pallor. "Well, once we open the gateway rift, we say, 'The passage is open. Let the demon Andras return to his own.' Of course, roughly translated from R'lyehian, it's more like, 'Realm of darkness threshold; call the native of darkness to the hidden pit!' It's still what we want."

"But what about Erasmus? He'll be standing right there. Will he be sucked in there, too?"

"Even if I were, I am held here by the book. And my amulet you wear."

I touched it. Funny I used to touch it all the time when I first began wearing it. But now that I'd gotten used to it, it had become a part of me. It was warm, as always. Warm like Erasmus himself.

"This is all very complicated," I muttered.

"As well it should be," said Doc. "It wouldn't do to have just anyone be able to open Netherworld rifts."

George tightened his hold on Nick's clothing. I also noticed he had his gun out, for all the good it would do. "I still don't like this."

I nodded though he couldn't see me. "No one does, deputy."

Doc led us through the pitch-black cave. Outside the beams of light we cast, it looked as if there was absolutely nothing in front or behind us.

Doc made his first turn into one of the many passages, following the bright flickering of the scryer. Once I passed through, I knew we'd gone past the point of no return. I wanted desperately to grab Erasmus' hand, but I somehow felt that he wouldn't appreciate it. He was on high alert. His eyes ticked from here to there, his jaw tensed tight.

I wasn't sure if it was my imagination, but there seemed to be a glow up ahead. When it didn't fade, I was certain it was the vortex…rift…whatever they were calling it. Yes, there was definitely a distinctive green glow ahead, which we all seemed to notice at the same time.

Ed couldn't seem to help himself from cautiously taking out his gun. Well, I supposed if *I* could fire a chthonic crossbow quarrel into it, *he* could shoot a lead bullet.

The glow was brighter the closer we got. When we turned a corner, there it was. A green, glowing crack in the air, rotating slowly. It did seem more of a rift than a vortex, if I was getting my terms right. There was something oddly three-dimensional about it, seen from all sides as it was. Like you could reach your hand in, though that would probably be a bad idea.

Doc and the coven didn't waste any time. Seraphina set down her bag and started removing candles from it. "These are going to smell a little when we light them," she said. "They've been infused with blessed oils, not the most aromatic in my collection, but the most effective for what we want. We need to create an atmosphere to summon him and send him through. I ask that everyone take a candle and hold it throughout the ceremony. Mr. Dark, you are excused. It's probably best you keep as far from the rift as you can."

Erasmus said nothing as he moved toward the back of the cavern, into the shadows he seemed to like best.

"Kylie, I want you to hold the biggest one." She handed me a fat pillar candle…that really stunk. If it was worse when we lit them…

She situated us around the rift that hung there, glowing. I saw Ed holding a candle and looking around suspiciously. George kept glancing back at WereNick, who sat with Jeff well into the shadows and away from the rift. At least George had sheathed his gun.

241

Doc found his place to stand. He took the scryer from his pocket. As he lifted it, it began to shine with a light so bright I couldn't look at it. In a flash, all our candles were lit at once. It startled me so badly that I nearly dropped the crossbow. And boy, did the candle smell bad, like rotten eggs. Like sulfur.

The coven began to chant: "*Shogg nglui. 'Ai n'ghft-oth Andras r'luh ebumna.*"

Over and over, they chanted the strange-sounding words. I didn't like the sound of them. They made me feel adrift, lost. A terrible feeling of anxiety came with them. But how could that be, with mere words I couldn't understand? The coven was so in sync that I began to sense a strange reverberation in my ears. But it was more than that. Everything started to shake. A deep thrum sounded, like the ticking of a clock…or the beating of a heart. It was regular, rhythmic, and it grew stronger each time they chanted.

The glow of the rift began to change. It, too, brightened and darkened with this rhythm. The brightness became even brighter. I could feel in my gut this pull, this thrum, stronger and stronger, with an anxious intensity. I wanted to scream. I wanted to hurl the candle away, cover my ears, and close my eyes—but none of that was possible.

Still they chanted, "*Shogg nglui. 'Ai n'ghft-oth Andras r'luh ebumna.*"

With a sonic boom that nearly knocked me off my feet, he was suddenly there. Andras. And he was angry. His eyes glowed bright red, his feathered wings outspread and fluffed up. His hands were curled into talons.

"Who summons me? Who *dares?*"

But the coven kept chanting, and though he didn't lean toward it, his body seemed to stretch toward the rift, like some weird drawing, like a watercolor blurring and leaking toward one side. When I cast my glance toward the others, nothing looked normal. Everything was becoming a little out of focus and stretched, and that infernal throbbing was getting deeper and louder. "What?" Andras muttered. "What is happening?"

I stepped forward the tiniest bit. "We're sending you back." I didn't know where I got the courage to speak. My voice was a little shaky, but there it was. My need to know overcame my fear. "How did you use the Booke? How did you do it?"

"You're sending me back? No! I haven't fulfilled my purpose."

"How did you use the Booke?"

His eyes were panicked now and an even brighter red, like lava. "The *book*? Are you so ignorant that you don't know?"

"Then tell me."

A wind pierced the wall of green light from the rift and began to blow. It grew louder as the gateway opened wider.

"Tell me how you did it. Tell me now!"

He looked perplexed and annoyed, even as he stretched still further toward the rift. His face got blurry. "You are the Chosen Host. You should know."

"I don't! Tell me! I know it's a gateway."

"Of course, it's a passage. But it's also a tool. You merely have to—"

A sudden roar behind me made me spin. My candle jolted, and smelly, liquid candlewax flung outward, bright for a moment before disappearing into the utter blackness. The crossbow was jerked from my hand. Erasmus snatched the iron arrow from the flight groove, crying out as the iron sizzled in his hand. With another roar, he flung himself forward and sunk it like a knife deep into Andras' chest. He shoved it all the way in with the flat of his hand.

Andras howled. He was being stretched and distorted by the pull from the rift, but something else was happening to him, too. He fell to his knees and splayed his arms. It wasn't like what the Booke did.

It was much, much worse.

He screamed as he suddenly went up in flames. I could clearly see the layers of him—skin and muscle—flay off like the dripping wax of a burning candle. His wing feathers were all aflame and smoked in dark, billowing clouds. He twisted in agony as layer by layer seared off until he was a fiery skeleton, skull mandible open in a silenced scream until it fell away at my feet. And then all his blackened bones simply crashed to the ground in a jumbled pile only to turn instantly to black, sooty ash.

The chanting stopped. We all stared at the blackened pile of ashes that had once been my demon nemesis.

With the cessation of the chanting, the rift stopped brightening and darkening. But it was still open, still waiting, and though Erasmus had said it wouldn't take him, his body was doing a remarkable job of looking like it was being pulled in.

"Close the rift!" I cried.

Doc, who had been staring with shock at the murdered Andras, woke himself, raised the scryer and yelled unfamiliar words that I could only assume were ordering the rift to close. Slowly, the rift stopped pulsating light and began to pull back into its familiar crack shape. I didn't feel in my gut that it was open anymore, but my Grandpa's ghostly warning was suddenly sounding in my head, *Village in danger. Door is opening.*

Erasmus stood defiantly in front of the rift, rimmed by its eerie light.

I slammed the candle to the ground. "Why did you do that?"

"He had to be stopped."

"It was controlled. He was heading toward the rift. I just needed to know—"

He straightened his coat and raised his chin. "He needed to be stopped."

I stomped up to him and jabbed my finger in his face. "You knew I wanted to know more about the Booke. You *knew* that, and you deliberately killed him to stop him from telling me something, didn't you?"

"I did no such thing. He *had* to be stopped."

"You're lying!" I stomped my foot. "Why are you lying?"

"Because he's a demon, Kylie." Sheriff Ed suddenly closed his hands around my arms and pulled me backward, away from Erasmus.

My finger was still aimed at him like a gun. "You *know* things you still aren't telling me!"

He clamped his mouth shut and would obviously say no more. Andras was definitely dead. He couldn't do me any more harm. But what of Erasmus? What wasn't he telling me?

Despite how close we'd become, he had still lied. And that hurt the most.

Chapter Twenty-Four

THERE WAS NOTHING to do but go back home. Erasmus clearly wanted to flee, until I reminded him in a deadly voice that he'd *promised* to help us leave the caves.

He said nothing, only turned on his heel and stomped into the darkness. Doc helped me find my discarded flashlight, and we silently followed him. I couldn't get the sight of Andras' burning body out of my mind. Like hellfire. I suppose it literally was. Horrible. And though maybe he deserved it, I couldn't drum up enough hate to believe it. Maybe Erasmus would die like that if the Powers That Be got ahold of him. I was steaming mad at him, but I didn't ever want him to suffer like that.

I glanced down at my crossbow. Amazingly, the bolt had returned, unburnt, unscathed.

Ed must have been thinking along the same lines as me. He sidled up to me and said quietly, "I don't want to see that happen to Shabiri."

"Oh. So you're getting feelings for her?"

"No. I just don't think—even as crafty as she is—she deserves that."

"She helped the Ordo summon Baph—Goat Guy."

"Maybe she didn't even know the harm it could do."

"She had to know more than she's letting on."

He grunted a reply and then gestured toward Erasmus, trudging ahead. "What are you gonna do about him?"

All I could do was shake my head. I was so furious I could barely think straight, let alone talk about it. I felt betrayed and stupid and used. He let us go on with this ritual, all the while he had planned to kill Andras himself. He had used *us* to draw the demon *and* make the weapon that killed him. Was it some old grudge? Was he afraid I'd learn more about the Booke than I should? Was he jealous of the power? It didn't make sense, and the idiot wouldn't tell me.

Jeff and Nick had changed back after we'd made the long hike back to the cars. Doc threw Nick his keys to the Rambler. "See that Seraphina and Jolene get home. I'm going to ride with Kylie."

Ed cast a longing glance my way, his arm on the door of the SUV and his foot resting on the running board. When I didn't acknowledge him, he frowned and ducked into his car. It rumbled as he pulled out of the gravel parking lot.

Erasmus glared at me and vanished. Doc strolled to the passenger side of the car and got in. There was nothing I could do but get in, too.

Before I started the car, he put his hand on my arm. "Wait a moment, Kylie. I'd like to talk to you. Start it, if you like, though. We could use some heat." I did and got the heater going.

"Kylie, there's no denying these past three weeks have been— well, for lack of a better expression, life-changing. You've gotten into some very dangerous situations. Experiences an ordinary person would never have to face."

I nodded. It was suddenly a bit overwhelming, and I found I couldn't speak through the lump in my throat.

"It's been an emotional roller-coaster."

I nodded again.

"And I know…you have feelings for Mr. Dark…"

I shook my head furiously. No, that had to end. If I couldn't trust him with my life, why should I trust him with my heart?

"Well, be that as it may, and I can't believe I'm saying this, but I can't say that I blame him all that much for his actions."

I turned to him, incredulous.

"Far be it from me to approve of what a demon does, but that fella has had a lot to contend with. I've been studying the life of Constance Howland. As much of it as I can. And it seems to me that from the time she opened the book to the time she…she died, it was barely a week and a half. The other names that Mr. Dark mentioned to you, former Chosen Hosts, I looked them up too. Near as I can tell, once they had the book in their hands, they didn't last more than a week. And you've had three weeks, going on four. Something is different this time. I have the sense that it's about our participation—the coven and our willingness to help you. And now there's Ed and George…and Jeff, when it gets down to it. There's never been anything like this in the history of the book, I'm willing to bet. And that's not all."

I didn't want to hear anymore. I lowered my forehead onto the steering wheel.

"He has feelings for you. You told me before that you think he's in love with you, and that changes everything." He touched my arm, pulling me away from the steering wheel until I sat back against the seat. "Don't you see? He won't hurt you, but it doesn't mean he won't lie. Maybe to protect you. Maybe to protect himself. But that is his nature. You can't just treat this like any other love affair. It's vastly different. Your life still depends on him and his help. And yes, I understand how important it is to know why he killed Andras. And I've been thinking about that, too. If Andras was sent back, he'd be free to roam the Netherworld. Maybe get into the clutches of the Powers That Be. And then they'd know what's been going on here, and they may not like what they hear. And there's something else. If he was summoned once, he could be summoned again, and until we find out who did it the first time, we can't prevent it from happening again."

"Ruth Russell," I said with vehemence.

"We're still not sure of that. But there's one more thing to think about. Mr. Dark's actions could simply be as you said— that he didn't want you learning more about the book, which bears some thinking. But in any case, try not to be too hard on him. He's struggling as much as you are, fighting emotions he's never felt before. And he doesn't know how to reconcile how he feels with what he has to do. Remember, his entire creation was designed to kill and devour the Chosen Host. And now he can't. Imagine the turmoil inside him."

I let Doc's words wash over me, give me new strength. Erasmus was as much a victim of his circumstances, maybe even more, than I was. It was tragic. And tragedies never ended well.

I cleared my throat. "I can see where you're coming from."

"I hope you do. This is new for all of us."

"I know. I appreciate you helping me unpack it all."

"I can't tell you what to do, Kylie. You must follow your own instincts. All I can do is offer my perspective."

"And it's awfully helpful." I finally put the car in gear and rambled down the dirt road. When I got to the highway, I saw that the Interceptor had been waiting for me. I guess we'd been up there a while. I flashed my headlights to signal we were okay and followed them up the road.

I took Doc home. Nick hadn't returned yet with his car, but Doc let himself in, turning on the lights in his living room to wait for Nick.

I drove home by myself, brooding like a certain demon I knew. I parked in front of the darkened shop and got out of the car.

The bell above the door sounded hollow as I entered into the near-darkness. I'd left a nightlight on, and wandered over to the stairs, glancing at the glass apothecary jars lined up like soldiers along the old buffet. My tea, both ordinary and exotic varieties, were nestled in those jars. My herbs were tucked into a myriad of little wooden drawers, each type labeled in careful pen on cards in brass frames over brass drawer pulls.

"It really is a perfect little shop," I sighed. I was proud of it, though I still wondered if I'd have the chance to own it for more than a few weeks.

"It is a fine shop," said that familiar voice from the shadows.

"I thought you'd buggered off to parts unknown."

"Of course not. I am tethered to the book."

"That's a handy excuse."

Erasmus stepped out of the shadows. Moonlight slanting in from the window illuminated his face. "I…seem to be tethered to more than the book."

"Why did you do it?"

He took a step closer. "Would you believe me if I said that I had a very good reason?"

"No."

"Then we are at an impasse."

"Was it to save you or me?"

He took a step closer. "Yes."

"Which one?"

"Both."

"I needed to know—"

"I know. I would have liked to have known as well. But it was too dangerous, his lingering between here and there."

"But I told you—"

"And I'm sorry. But I panicked. I am not versed in these… strange new dynamics."

The dark smoothness of his voice calmed me, perhaps even lulled me. I didn't, couldn't fight it. "What sort of dynamics?"

He stepped closer until he was merely a foot away. "Of a demon…falling in love with a human."

"Have you?"

His hand slowly rose to delicately cup my cheek. "Yes," he whispered. "I'm sorry if I'm not doing it right. I don't know how."

I closed my eyes and breathed. "You're doing it right," I said. Doc had told me to try to understand him. Doc really knew more about the world than I did, didn't he?

When I opened my eyes, Erasmus was gazing at me with concern. "I'm sorry that I lied to you. I'm sorry that I will continue to lie to you."

"It's your nature."

"Yes. As your nature is to despise it."

"We'll agree to disagree?"

He cocked his head. "If you want to think of it that way."

"I don't know what I want."

"I see. Well, I will be here, keeping watch. Baphomet still roams free."

I trudged through the shop and reached the stairs. I'd made it halfway up to my room when I stopped. He had a hopeful expression. That I'd forgiven him. That I'd invite him up. I wanted to. The whole episode had been so horrible that it would've been nice to be in someone's arms. But I couldn't invite him. Not yet.

I gave him a half-smile instead and scuffed up the stairs, closing the door as he stood in the shadows below.

CHAPTER TWENTY-FIVE

I WOKE WITH a start, gasping. I dreamed of people on fire, screaming, skin and muscle dripping off of them. The image couldn't fade fast enough.

There was a cup of coffee on my nightstand, still steaming. How did he keep it hot? Magic?

I sat up, took the mug in hand, and sipped. He was getting better at it. His tea-making, however, still suffered. He didn't quite grasp the process. Understandable, since he was allergic to the stuff. I smiled, feeling warm…until I remembered.

I stared into my mug, beginning to think about the events I had not wanted to process last night.

On the one hand, he was a demon, a dangerous being designed to kill me and eat my soul—both of which he had promised not to do. Among his many promises and lies, this one I believed. Mostly because I wanted to. But also because…I couldn't believe he would, not after those tender expressions and confessions of love.

But then on the other hand, he did lie. All the time. Would continue to lie. How would I know what was true and what wasn't?

The Booke would know. It would tell me. And of course, there it was, skimming across the floor and bouncing at the edge of the bed, like some frolicking pup. "Did I ask for you?"

Yes, it bobbed. *You were thinking of me, and I came.*

I pushed it away. It floated onward, as if on the surface of a calm lake.

Still, on yet another hand, Erasmus was…maybe what I needed right now. I mean, there was nothing long-term about any of this, was there? Neither for my life or for his. How could I envision a future with a…a demon?

He rapped on the door.

"Yes?"

He opened it and poked his head in. "Ah. You're awake."

I glanced at the clock, noticing that I hadn't woken up particularly late. I clutched the mug to my chest. "Was there something you wanted?"

He sidled into the room to stand at the foot of the bed, discomfort flowing off of him in waves and in thin ribbons of gray smoke feathering off his shoulders and sleeves.

He cleared his throat. "I…seemed to have created a rift between us."

"You could say that." I wanted to sip the coffee, but I didn't. I sat straight and stiff, the mug now in my lap.

"And so…I find myself in the unenviable position of having to explain myself…and trying not to lie."

"How do I know that any of it isn't a lie?"

He frowned. "I…dammit! You'll simply have to believe me."

I crooked a finger at the Booke and allowed it onto the bed. I touched the worn leather cover. My own personal lie detector.

His eyes widened. Was he sweating?

"Very well," he began, eyes never leaving the Booke under my hand. "I had my doubts about the de-summoning ritual working. And then when it seemed that it would, I realized that it would be a foolish plan to allow him to live. He could be at the mercy of any number of denizens of the Netherworld…including the Powers That Be."

So far, so good. The Booke seemed happy just to listen to his voice. All was kosher.

"I knew you wanted to understand more of the book's secrets, how he'd gotten the ghoul out of it a second time, for instance, but it was far more important to stop him than to allow him to escape."

Nope. The Booke was giving me a big fat buzzer on that one. "You're lying."

He glared at my hand on the Booke. "You think you're clever."

"I know I am. Go on."

"Beelze's tail," he muttered with clenched teeth. He heaved a sigh. "Very well. It was important to dispatch him…but perhaps not at that particular moment. I…I didn't want him to say out loud how to countermand the book."

Hmm. That appeared to be the truth.

"And why not?"

"Because it would likely be a trick to put us in danger—"

I shook my head purposefully.

He blew out a breath wreathed in smoke. "Because… because…mortals must not know the—"

"Uh-uh."

"Beelze's tail! All right! I feared that constable of yours would spill the information to Shabiri and that this would be extremely dangerous to you and me."

He was huffing and puffing, his mouth screwed up in defiance. According to the Booke, this was the truth.

I set the mug on my bedside table and crossed my arms. "Was that so very hard?"

He collapsed on the edge of the bed, arms flopped to his sides. "Yes!"

"Wow. I see it wore you out. This is useful information. And you could have talked to me about it. We could have kept Ed out of the cave. If only you'd told me the truth beforehand."

"Oh." His eyebrows danced as he thought. "But what of those others? That deputy might have begun to consort with Shabiri—"

"No, that's highly unlikely. He's only interested in Nick. In men."

"Hmm. How quaint. Those of the Netherworld don't distinguish between genders or species."

"Thanks for the reminder."

"Does this trouble you? That we are different species?"

"No, strangely, it doesn't. I mean, we're two *sentient* species. It isn't as if I was bringing sheep into bed."

He made a face that seemed to say, "Don't knock it till you tried it."

"O-kaay! I'm getting up now!" I slammed the bathroom door on his perplexed expression and leaned against the pedestal sink. Something was seriously wrong with everyone from the Netherworld.

* * *

I HADN'T EXPERIENCED a normal day for some time. But today I had customers to talk to, things to sell. A ladies' group booked me to give a talk on teas and herbs. I think Erasmus was trying to make amends for his behavior, because he helped me without even being asked.

Still, as I wrapped a chintz teapot in tissue paper for a customer and carefully laid it in her bag, I couldn't help but worry that the ghoul was still out there. Again. It knew me now and knew what I would do to it. There was no way I could get near it anymore. Jeff said he'd spent some evenings sniffing around the cemetery, but he hadn't found it either. Heaven knows where it was.

The bell above the door dinged. I looked up and swore under my breath. Ruth-freakin'-Russell stood there, glaring at me.

I thanked my customer as I handed her the bag. She left with a smile on her face, even as she had to squeeze by Miss Sourpuss to get out the door.

Ruth stomped up to the counter and postured. "I know you have my locket. Where is it?"

"And good morning to you, Ruth."

"Never mind the false niceties. That's over. You stole my locket and I want it back."

"Okay." I crossed my arms and glared right back. "Let's put our cards on the table. First of all, I don't have your precious locket…"

Erasmus cleared his throat in the background, but I ignored him.

"And second of all, I want to know what kind of witchcraft you think you're doing."

"Witchcraft? Are you out of your mind? That is the absolute *last* thing *I* would be doing."

"You wanna know something? I don't believe you."

"Is that so? Well *I* don't believe *you* didn't take my necklace."

I pointed a finger right in her face. "Did you kill Dan Parker in an unholy ritual?"

She gasped and took a step back. "You *are* insane!"

"I saw the pentagram at the church. I know it was you."

I knew I was getting rattled, desperate for her to admit *something*. And she *was* shocked. At first. But then she narrowed her eyes. "You'll hear from my lawyer." She spun on her heel and yanked the door open. When she slammed it shut behind her, suddenly the shop was dead quiet.

Erasmus cleared his throat again.

"Technically," I said, uncurling my fists, "*you* stole the locket."

"A prevarication is still a lie."

"And you're the king of lies."

"Hardly."

I blew out a breath and grabbed a hunk of my bangs in frustration. "I shouldn't have played my hand like that, should I?"

He slowly shook his head.

"I let my anger at her get the better of me."

He nodded.

"I'd better call Doc." I dug my phone out of my back pocket. "Hey, Doc. Um…Ruth was in the shop just now, and I…I kind of told her…well. I accused her of killing Dan Parker in a ritual and of putting that pentagram in the church."

Silence.

"Uh…Doc?"

"Kylie…that seems…very unwise."

I sank down onto a stool. "I know. I'm a complete idiot. I'm sorry."

"Well…I suppose I'll have to go on over there and smooth things over."

"Should we…should we give her back the necklace?"

"I think at the moment that wouldn't be prudent. We still don't know the nature of it and its significance."

"Okay. I'll leave the détente to you."

He clicked off and I tossed the phone to the counter. "She just brings out the worst in me."

"As do I, apparently."

He could make the puppiest of puppy dog expressions when he wanted to. "No, you don't."

"But you're still angry with me."

"I still have to deal with that ghoul out there. We don't know how Andras got it out of the Booke…or if anyone else could do the same."

"I'm sorry."

"No, don't keep apologizing. It's not really your fault. You just acted on instinct."

His sorrowful expression remained, until I walked around the buffet and took his face in my hands. "Cheer up. I'm not mad anymore." I leaned in and kissed him. The soft press of my lips against his made me feel better, and I could see it had lightened his expression too.

I ran my thumb over his scruff-covered chin. "You are truly the saddest excuse for a demon I have ever met."

When he frowned, I laughed. I gave him a quick peck on the cheek and flounced back to work.

He hovered in the shadows all day. When I next glanced his way, he was giving me one of his intense stares that never seemed to waver.

"Look, Erasmus. You're making me nervous. Let's have you do something."

"Do something?"

"Yeah. I think it's time to teach you to brew tea."

He made a face. "That ghastly tea. I don't care to know."

"It would be a great help."

"But I already know how. You toss a handful of it into hot water. What is so magical about that?"

"It's the way it's done. And also…you definitely don't need a handful. You use a lot less than that."

He suddenly seemed chastened, maybe recalling all the times he'd given me tea and realizing he'd done it wrong. If there was anything he seemed to hate, it was being called out because of something he'd done wrong.

Arms crossed defensively, he grumbled. "This is foolish."

"Nevertheless." I dragged him to the kitchen and showed him the proper way to make a cup of tea, a pot of tea, and an urn of tea. He sneezed all the while.

I couldn't help but give him a proper kiss for braving the allergens just for me. He all but grabbed me and pushed me down on the farmhouse table, gorging himself on my lips. And I would have let him get carried away if it hadn't been for that damned bell over the door.

"Customers," I gasped, wiping my mouth. He was panting over me, his coat smoking. "Calm down, okay?"

"You're maddening!" He helped me up, then shook out his duster.

I straightened my own shirt, patted down my hair, and strode through the doorway. "Good afternoon—oh. Hi, Ed."

He squinted, looking me over. "Kylie…"

Erasmus moved swiftly through the doorway. "Constable Bradbury."

Ed's squint turned into a sneer. Erasmus had deliberately re-disheveled his clothes to come out straightening them…with a wicked smile on his face. *Honestly!*

"It's *Sheriff* Bradbury," he insisted.

Erasmus waved his hand. "Whatever."

Ed did a good job of composing himself. "Kylie, I thought you'd like to know that there has been more…well, *activity* in the cemetery."

"Oh, no. That damned ghoul!"

"Yeah, looks like it. I haven't heard anything from Shabiri yet."

"Have you tried calling her?"

"Yeah." He took off his hat and turned the brim in his fingers. "She's not answering."

"This is ridiculous. I have to get rid of the ghoul and the Draugr. It's good that Andras isn't out there anymore, but Goat Guy still is. I don't suppose you've talked to your brother."

"We're not exactly on speaking terms."

"Well, get over it. There are bigger things going on than petty family rivalries."

He slapped his hat back on his head. "You know, you're pretty pushy."

"For a girl who has demons and gods after her? Yeah, you could say that."

He wilted a little. "I'm sorry. I—"

"No, you're right. *I'm* sorry. It wasn't fair of me to put you in the middle of my troubles with Doug. I'm sorry I sent you to Shabiri."

"Wait," said Erasmus. "*You* sent your constable…" He looked from me to Ed, before he burst out laughing. "Kylie Strange, you are the most amazing mortal I have ever met!"

"Uh…thanks. Ed, can I see you outside for a sec? Will you excuse us, Erasmus?"

He giggled, holding his stomach, and waved us off.

Outside, I hugged myself in the cold. "I really am sorry for mixing you up in this. I had no right to make you…well, sell yourself."

"I'm a big boy. I can make my own decisions."

"I know. But I appreciate the sacrifice."

"Like I said, it wasn't that much of a sacrifice. She's... interesting."

"Just keep your head, okay?"

"And you keep yours. And...anytime you want to change your mind about that guy..."

I smiled. "I know."

The speaker in his Interceptor squawked, something about a problem on someone's farm. "Look," he said, "I gotta go. Keep me informed."

"I will."

I watched as he got in to his car and hit the road toward the highway. I liked Ed. He was handsome, and sexy, and someone you could settle down with. I just didn't know if that was what I wanted.

Because when I turned back toward the shop, Erasmus was standing in my doorway, dark, enigmatic, sure of himself...and pretty handsome and sexy too. For a demon.

* * *

IT WAS A long day, driven by spurts of activity and long minutes with no customers at all. I sat at the counter, plotting ways to advertise. Maybe offer more classes or even cater events? I sketched out ideas for flyers and then crunched some numbers to see what would work. Even though I might not live to see these activities through, brainstorming was keeping me busy.

Erasmus spent the time poking into this and that, lifting lids, looking in drawers, sneezing at the tea, and grumbling. Some of the herbs he touched, some he obviously couldn't. I made special note of those. Still, he was good company. I wondered how he would be going on a date. Of course, he didn't have any money and couldn't eat anything...so at least he'd be a cheap date.

"What in the twelve worlds is *this* for?" He held up a silver-toned server.

"Pastry tongs, for serving pastries."

"Why?"

"Because when you are having a fancy party, you want fancy serving utensils. You can grab small cakes and pastries that would fall off of a spatula."

"I don't understand."

I walked over and took it out of his hands. "Well, you wouldn't because you don't eat."

"Eating looks…disgusting."

"It isn't."

"You like eating?"

"I guess."

"And preparing food?"

"I do enjoy that."

"If I could eat, I'd eat whatever you made."

I stopped and looked at him. He was perfectly serious and perfectly lovely. "That was a very nice thing to say."

He fluffed a little. "I can be nice when called upon."

We were leaning in toward each other when that damned bell…

"Hope I'm not interrupting," said Jolene with a twinkle in her eye.

"No," I said, spinning away from Erasmus to put the tongs back on the shelf.

Jolene stuffed her bag behind the counter and donned the green apron I'd given her. I'd ordered them a week ago when I felt like we needed some kind of uniform. I even got an extra one Jeff could use. I didn't dare make Erasmus wear one. "Any customers?"

"Yeah, loads. We're doing okay, but I'm trying to come up with ways to really get out into the community. What do you think about a Tea of the Month Club?"

"That's a good idea!"

"And I'm going to suggest around town that I can cater dessert teas for birthdays and special occasions."

"That also sounds good. You've come up with some great ideas."

"I hope so. I've got to spend more time here. I'm working on the website re-design. Do you think I should expand to Machias?"

"You mean open another shop?"

"No, just advertise there."

"Yeah. I'd be more available to help with that in the summer. Of course, you have Mr. Chase now. Speaking of, is he here?" She looked around as if he'd pop up from behind a samovar.

"I think he's prowling the cemetery. Our old friend the ghoul is back, remember?"

"I hate to think about what those poor families are facing." She drooped a little, then perked up just as quickly. "Nick went back to work today. I'm really proud of him."

"Wow. Me too. We'll have to toast him with…something tonight."

"I'm glad we're getting together. I've got some news." She disappeared behind the counter before popping up again with her tablet. "I've been studying our de-summoning ritual. And despite it being…interrupted…" She flicked a disapproving glance at Erasmus. "I think we can modify it slightly and use it on…" She trailed off, then whispered, "Baphomet."

Erasmus turned a mild expression toward her. "What conceivable reason can make you think that this is possible?"

"I've studied all the sources. Well, as many sources as I could translate. It really can work. And no stabbing him with crossbow quarrels, Mr. Dark—iron has no effect on a god."

He snorted. "I am suitably chastened…by a little girl."

"That's exciting, Jolene! If we could send him back… But I do have to consider all the options. *Can* you kill a god?"

"You have an extraordinary penchant for killing," said Erasmus.

"I just want to be covered, okay? Is that so bad?"

"Kylie's right. You have to cover your bases. And in my research, the only thing I found that could kill a god is a sword made of fulgurite."

"What's that?"

Her face lit up, as it always did, when she was excited about some bit of research. "It's a cool crystalline structure created when lightning hits sand or rock."

"Wow." A hopeful feeling bloomed in my chest. "Well, where do we get some of that?"

"The internet, of course. But it has to be just right. Strong enough to make a sword. A lot of them flake and crumble. Rock would be best but it's the rarest. And the most expensive."

"Don't worry about the expense." I was already figuring in my head the kind of money I could easily get ahold of.

"I can steal it, you know," said Erasmus, matter-of-factly.

I snatched a glance at our impressionable young teen. "We aren't going to do that."

"Why? I stole the necklace."

"And that wasn't very nice."

"But you needed to see what it was."

"The ends do not justify the means."

"Do you even know what you are talking about?"

A high, piercing whistle stopped the two of us in our tracks. Jeff had arrived, and I hadn't even heard the bell above the door. "Yo! Truce. Kylie doesn't want you to steal it, so that should be good enough for you, Romeo."

"Who is Romeo?"

"Hi, kid," he said to Jolene, who blushed and stuttered. I'd forgotten how attractive he was to women of all ages. And being a werewolf made him buffer than he'd been before. He slipped his apron over his head. "What are we talking about stealing anyway?"

"Fulgurite," said Jolene. "A crystalline structure made with lightning."

"No kidding? Cool."

"It could be used to kill Baphomet," I explained.

"Gotcha. Sounds like a plan. Where do we get it?"

"On the internet," said Jolene.

"Maybe there are closer places. Like universities, libraries, you know? They might have a display."

I looked at him askance. "Sounds like you're talking about stealing."

"Maybe. If we're talking about taking out the Goat Guy, maybe I'm up for a little larceny. That means you, big guy." He slapped Erasmus on the back. The demon wasn't up on human interaction. His eyes began to glow red and he looked ready to lunge.

I swooped in between them. "Erasmus, he was only being good-natured."

"He struck me."

"No, that was just a friendly slap on the back. Between humans, that's a…a…"

"A conciliatory expression," Jolene cut in.

"I don't like it," he growled.

Jeff gave him a cheerful smile over his shoulder. Now that Jeff was a werewolf, he didn't seem to fear the demon. I wondered who'd win in a fight.

I shook that thought loose. It was getting late, which meant the Draugr would be out again. I was afraid to hear what Ed might report. Where the hell was Shabiri?

"Erasmus? Can *you* call Shabiri?"

"No."

"Maybe I should phrase that differently. *Would* you call Shabiri…for me?"

"No."

Jeff laughed. "Dude, I know you're new to dating and all, but when your lady says, 'do it for me,' you don't say no. That's a surefire way to get locked out of the bedroom."

"Jeff!" I gestured toward Jolene.

"I'm not blind," she said from behind her tablet.

Erasmus frowned. I could tell he didn't like listening to what Jeff had to say, but he seemed to be considering it. "I…simply don't like contacting her. Unless it is absolutely necessary."

I shrugged. "It is kind of important."

He huffed. "Very well. I will search for her."

"But not in the Netherworld! I don't want you going there."

"I won't go there. Don't worry." He offered a tick of a smile and vanished.

"Neat trick," said Jeff wistfully.

CHAPTER TWENTY-SIX

NIGHT WAS FALLING, and it was getting misty. I hurried through the sale of some tea and mugs, hustling my poor customer out of the store and standing in the doorway to make sure she got into her car all right.

When she drove away, I turned the sign from OPEN to CLOSED and peered into the mist. They were out there. I could sense them. Or at least I thought I could. Erasmus had not returned, and neither had Shabiri. Was she just toying with us? *How hard was it to bring back the gold you had stolen?* And seriously, Erasmus needed a cell phone. Though perhaps the roaming charges would be steep.

I heard Doc's Rambler coming down the street before I saw it emerge from the mist. Seraphina was with him. Rumbling right alongside them was Nick's junker.

The coven had arrived.

After greeting everyone, I explained that Erasmus had gone to fetch Shabiri, but neither of them had yet returned. Jolene announced her theory that Baphomet could be sent back with the de-summoning ritual. Thoughtful conversation followed. And all the while, my Spidey sense was tingling. Or more likely it was the Booke giving me signals, telling me something was up. I was jumpy and nervous as I paced in the back, looking out the windows.

Through the mist and the dark, shadows moved.

"Guys. Hey, guys!"

One by one, they joined me at the windows. The Draugr, clad in their disheveled armor and chain mail, whooshed out of the mist. Some carried weapons on their boney shoulders. Others dragged their blades behind them in the grips of their nearly dismembered limbs,

They were headed right for the shop.

"Is it my imagination," said Jeff, "or do they look pissed?"

I nodded. "They do, kind of."

Their skeletal faces were all turned toward us. Though many of them had only empty eye sockets, they still looked as if they were frowning. Their jaws hung open, and they were audibly moaning. Some, who still had lips and tongues, were speaking. Danish, Norwegian? I really couldn't say.

"They're heading for us," I said. "Nick, have you got your bag of tricks?"

"Right here." He grabbed the bag of magic dust and headed toward the door. What exactly he tripped over I'll never know. But I saw it all as if in slow motion; his body falling forward, the bag leaving his hands and flying through the air, then hitting the floor in a big puff of dust…and then it all filtered through the three-hundred-year-old floorboards and disappeared.

Nick swore, and I think every one of us repeated the same word in our heads.

"Please don't tell me that was all the magic dust you had," I said.

He looked up sorrowfully. "Then I won't say it?"

I screamed as something hit the door hard. We all backed away. Shadows of milling figures passed over the curtains. A harsh clatter sounded a second time. An axe.

"We're going to need weapons," I said. But my crossbow would be useless. "There's an axe outside in the back. And a meat cleaver in the kitchen."

"I'm on it," said Jeff, rushing toward the back door.

Nick began to growl. He turned to me, eyes green and glowing.

"Yeah," I said. "Wolfing out is a good idea."

He began to unselfconsciously undress. Seraphina had the presence of mind to take his clothes and shield Jolene as he slipped out of his trousers. He was going commando these days. Probably easier for the transformation.

Somehow in the midst of everything, I had reached for my phone. "Ed. We have undead company."

"I'll be right there." I might have even heard the siren in the distance.

Jeff returned with the axe and shoved it into my hands. "I can do more as a wolf."

"Go. Do it!"

He slipped off his clothes, trousers barely off before he fully morphed. Seraphina scooped them off the floor and put them with the other pile. "What can we do, Kylie?"

"I don't know." The door shook again. "Get something heavy you can use as a weapon. And aim for the head. It's the only thing that works. I wish I had a sword." Should I get the Spear of Mortal Pain? If it was anything like the crossbow it would do no good. "Jolene, you hide."

"I can fight!"

"No, you can hide. That's an order."

The door slammed again. This time the axe head made it through the door. I expected "Here's Johnny!" any second, only in medieval Danish. What I didn't expect was the roar of Harleys outside.

I rushed to the window and threw open the curtains. A green, gooey Viking face peered in at me. It opened its slackened mouth and shrieked. I threw the curtains back and stepped away just as its club smashed through the window.

Glass sprinkling around me, Doc pulled me back. There was a roar and a bright light outside followed by unholy screams. I couldn't help but rush to the window again to see Doug, laughing and aiming a flamethrower strapped to his back. Another jet of fire streaked forward, and the monster with the axe at my front door went up like kindling. It stumbled, dropping his axe, and staggered toward Lyndon Road.

The other Vikings were torn between running from the fire and heading further toward us. That was when WereJeff opened the door and tore out of there. "Jeff!"

I got to the doorway in time to see him clamp his jaws around the leg of a Viking and drag it away.

Its medieval axe lay on my porch. I tossed the axe in my hand to Seraphina and grabbed the Viking one. I stood holding it in front of my door. It seemed heavier.

"Kylie!" warned Doc.

I turned. A Draugr was lunging toward me. One hand grabbed for me with dirty fingernails, while the other slapped against its leg, hanging by a sinew.

I didn't even stop to think. I wound up and swung.

The axe went through its neck like slightly cold, chunky butter. Not as smoothly as I would have wanted, but still his head went one way and his body the other, so the result was still effective.

I looked down at the axe, then at the headless, twitching body as the undead became deader by the moment. Was I going to be sick? I thought about it for half a second before another Viking came for me. I leapt off the porch, wanting to lure them away from the shop and the coven. Though when I looked back, Seraphina was brandishing the wood axe like some warrior princess. Okay then.

Doug's boys were swinging baseball bats at zombie heads. Probably the most fun they'd had in a long time. Sanctioned mayhem at last.

Doug glanced toward me and winked. "That a Chosen Host thing?" he asked, nodding toward the bloodied axe.

I shrugged. "I guess. Maybe a pissed-off shopkeeper thing, too. Where'd you get the—"

"Oh, this?" He raised up the hose and ignited it again with a whoosh, sweeping over some Vikings who got too close. "Amazing what you can get at an Army surplus store." He ignited it once more and strode forward, napalming the crap out of the line.

A hand closed over my shoulder from behind and squeezed. When I glanced down, the hand was gray and green and lacking a finger. Ew, it was *touching* me!

It yanked me back so hard I lost my footing. Its hands closed over my throat, pulling me up by my neck. It smelled really bad, but since my breath was being choked away, soon I hardly noticed.

I stared at its grisly face, the contortions of rotting skin and shedding hair. Its eyes drifted around their sockets, but nevertheless seemed to be staring at me…or *into* me. It lowered its face and opened its mouth. I was struck frozen with terror. It was going to eat me!

I turned my head just as soggy lips and sharp-edged teeth closed around my ear. I had no breath with which to scream. Only in my head did the screams roll and roll out.

I was suddenly spattered with black gore.

The hand fell away from my neck. I scooted back as fast as I could and looked up to see Seraphina chopping its head into literal pulp. This experience was going to star in my nightmares for several nights running, I was sure of it.

She looked back at me mildly when the zombie was still. Remarkably, I still had the axe in my hand. Instead of running away—an instinct that was strong and hammering at me—the Chosen Host in me made me get up and look for new prey.

All around me, zombies were advancing but getting beaten back by the Ordo. Doug looked in his element, like a black-bearded devil, as he sprayed fire toward Draugr and laughed all the while.

My two werewolves were tearing other zombies apart, their muzzles covered in black goo. Every time one was dispatched, their wolfy eyes would seek out another and pounce.

I didn't think it was my imagination that there seemed to be many more than before. Could they be multiplying? Was it to be an endless battle? Every time we cut one down, would two more rise in their place? We needed to end this. And to end this, we needed that gold!

"Shabiri! Erasmus! Where the hell are you?"

Nothing except more zombies.

They were definitely after Jeff's necklace. Ruth was lucky she wasn't still wearing it. They were reaching for the locket with their boney hands, their horrific faces nearly drooling at it.

Among the carnage, something scurried around, grabbing up smashed heads and dismembered legs. "That little son of a bitch!"

I marched forward, my axe aloft.

The ghoul only had time to look back at me with those ridiculous ping-pong ball eyes before I swung down, cleaving its head in two. Light spewed out of the crack in its skull, then everywhere as its body disintegrated into beams of light.

The Booke arrived with its quill. Not the most convenient moment, when the Draugr were bearing down on me, trying to decide if I would be a tasty addition to their traveling feast. Still, it had to be done. I looked around warily to see just how vulnerable I was, then dragged the floating Booke away from the center of the melee. I used blood from a cut on my arm as my ink. *This is the second time I captured this same ghoul. I struck its head with an axe in the middle of a zombie fight...* I figured I might as well make this an interesting read for whatever god created the damned Booke.

The ghoul burst more quickly into shards of light than it had before. With only a few terse words written in my own blood, the creature disappeared with a pop. I slammed the Booke closed and shoved it aside. Doug was looking at me with the bright eyes of admiration...and something more. Good grief, not another one. My date book was filled.

I ducked just in time to escape the clutches of another damned zombie. I snapped back up and swung, hacking its arm off at the shoulder.

I didn't have time to feel nauseated. I was chopping and spinning and lopping off heads as fast as they were showing up. I tried not to think about how much zombie goo covered me.

And Seraphina! I always thought of her as fey and genteel, someone who wouldn't chip her nail polish. But she was suddenly some kind of Wiccan warrior. Her boho garb was getting spattered, her face determined. I noticed a glow around her, a spell. Maybe it was for protection, maybe for strength. Whatever it was, her actions were systematic and powerful. First, she'd cut the legs out from under them, and when they were down, she chopped off their heads. Seemed like it saved energy, too.

"I'll have to try that," I muttered, like I was talking about a new recipe or a great Pilates move.

Doug seemed to be making some headway with the flame thrower. More bodies were lying charred on the ground. And thank goodness none had run into the forest.

When Ed and George arrived in the Interceptor, I started to hear gunfire blasting off heads as well.

Hands grabbed me and pulled me back. I was about to swing back over my head to cut the interloper in two when I heard the voice in my ear say, "It's me."

I spun. "Erasmus!"

He was looking me up and down with a shining light glittering in his eyes. His smile was feral. It looked like all he wanted to do was devour me…in a non-zombie way.

"You are magnificent!" he rasped.

"I am magnificently peeved. Where the hell have you been?"

"It wasn't easy to locate Shabiri. She kept flitting in and out of the Netherworld, trying to hide from me in a place I could not go."

"Did you find her?"

In answer, he gestured behind me.

Shabiri was lugging a huge pirate chest-looking thing, kicking Vikings out of her way with her high-heeled boots. She finally set the chest down in the middle of the battle, even as zombies and Ordo surged around her.

"Here you are, you disgusting undead Danes!" She zapped the latch with a jet of lightning from her finger, and the lid sprang open, revealing a gleaming cache of gold. Plates, goblets, figurines, crowns, jewelry, coins...you name it, it was there.

The change was immediate. The Draugr stopped mid-battle, dropping their swords and battered axes. They stopped pushing against the Ordo and their bats. The two zombies engaged with the werewolves suddenly didn't seem to care that jaws were gnawing on their undead limbs. They dragged the wolves behind them until WereJeff and WereNick let them go. As one, the Draugr turned toward the gold, its light reflecting in their gooey eye sockets. Suddenly, like TV zombies, they shambled toward it, arms outstretched. Instead of murmuring *Brains!* they were saying something like, *"Skat!"*

The coven and the Ordo both stepped out of their way and let them go. Even more of them were coming out of the woods. Jeesh, how many *were* there anyway?

They gathered in a tight clump around the chest, swaying, moaning out that word *skat*, over and over again.

Doc came up next to me. He had stayed in the shop, probably to protect Jolene, who was right beside him. "They're saying 'treasure,'" she whispered.

One straggler tried to veer toward WereJeff and grab his necklace. Jeff gave his jaws a snap, and the cautious Viking decided to return his attention to the gold his countrymen were worshipping.

When it seemed they were all there—more than fifty creatures or so—they slowly raised their weapons and arms skyward. A glow pulsed from the treasure chest until a beam of light shot upward like a searchlight. Slowly, the Draugr began to rise in that beam, moving faster and faster up into the dark sky. Even their leftover limbs levitated upward—their discarded weapons, and charred and headless remains too. The last to rise was the chest, which shot upward and disappeared.

The mist from the woods dissipated, leaving a clear and cold night.

We stood around, looking up into the sky, not quite knowing what to do. The Booke was nudging my leg. I grabbed it, held it to my chest. All of a sudden, I felt ravenous, as if I hadn't eaten for days. *I could really go for a bloody burger about now*, I thought, even as zombie gore dried on my clothes.

Shabiri rested a fist on her hip. "Well! That was a bother."

I squared on her, wanting to swat at her with the Booke. "Why did you steal that in the first place? You knew damn well what it was."

"Dear Dougie wanted riches. They were the most convenient riches I could find."

"But you knew it would bring killer zombies!"

"There was a chance it wouldn't have."

"Are you *kidding* me? People died!"

She got in close to me, her eyes going green. "What do I care if mortals die?"

I hauled back and hit her full in the face with the Booke. Shabiri staggered back. Erasmus made a squeaking sound that might have been a muffled laugh. Ed took a step in my direction then stopped.

Shabiri glared. Her nose was literally out of joint, black blood dribbling down her face. She pushed her nose back into place with an unpleasant snap and wiped the blood with the back of her hand, only causing it to smear. "You little bitch." She raised her hand to throw a lightning bolt or some other curse my way, when Erasmus stepped in front of me.

"I wouldn't," he warned.

She trembled with fury and disappeared with a flourish of sparks.

He turned to me with a mild expression. "You've made her very angry."

"I don't care. She's an idiot. Is anyone else hungry? I'm starving."

Jeff and Nick both shifted at the same time. It seemed that nudity wasn't a thing that bothered them anymore. Seraphina put her hand over Jolene's eyes. I didn't know if the sound Jolene made was of surprise or annoyance.

"Whoa, Riley," said Doug, gesturing toward Nick. "Dude, put some clothes on. There's no need to telegraph how much you enjoyed your werewolfing."

Nick gave him a sour look…until he looked down at himself. His face reddened, and he quickly covered his groin with his hands. Jeff seemed to be sporting the same kind of…excitement.

"Uh, Jeff?" I said, trying not to look below his chin. "You might want to put some clothes on. Maybe fighting as a wolf is a…turn on?"

He looked down and clamped his hand over himself, too. Instead of blushing and quickly sprinting toward the shop as Nick had done, Jeff just smirked. "I got to get my jollies somehow."

I turned away. "Just…get your clothes."

He smiled and casually walked toward the shop, chucking under Seraphina's chin as he went. She was looking at him unabashedly, especially the back view. And I couldn't say I blamed her.

Doug sauntered over to me, taking in Wiccans, demon, Booke, and retreating werewolves. "That's a pretty impressive bunch you've got there, Kylie."

"Yeah. Well, uh, thanks, Doug, for coming to the rescue with your, uh, bunch."

He shucked his Army surplus flamethrower from his shoulders, and Bob hurried over to take it from him. "Just helping out. Like I said I would. Do you hear that, big bro?"

Ed came to my side, wearing the particular scowl he reserved for his brother. "I heard. I wanna thank you, too."

Doug's eyes widened, and he threw his hands up. "Miracles *can* happen, ladies and gentlemen!"

"If you're gonna be an ass about it…"

"Relax, Edward. That's what warriors do after a battle. They laugh, they joke, and they drink. So Kylie, you got any liquor in that tea parlor of yours?"

"Don't invite him in," said Ed.

"Yes, I do," I nodded. "I think we all deserve a drink. And a bite of something. Is anyone else as hungry as I am?"

I led the way back into the shop, mourning my fancy door. And the fact that I would have to spend more money at Barry Johnson's hardware store to get a new one. But it couldn't be helped. The axe had made a hash of it.

Nick was dressed and suitably chastened. Though I noticed George giving him the eye. The deputy must have observed how Nick had buffed out after becoming a werewolf. I guess it wasn't all bad.

Nick helped me get out some liquor. I had one small bottle of bourbon, some vodka, a little brandy, and coffee liqueur. I also managed to rustle up some beer from the fridge—and stole a chicken leg while I was at it. After I'd wolfed it down, I was still hungry.

Jeff had his trousers on but nothing else. He padded around with bare feet, his hairless chest garnering stares from Charise, Seraphina, and Jolene.

I noticed I was lugging the Booke around and swung it to lay it down somewhere when I ran into Jeff. His necklace hit the Booke with a spark. Something slid open.

"Wait!" I cried over the noise of voices and bourbon splashing in plastic cups.

Jeff froze and pulled the necklace off over his head. The coven surrounded him.

"It touched the Booke and opened," I told them. There was writing on the inside of the locket.

"Mr. Dark," said Doc. "Can you tell us what it says. My Babylonian isn't quite up to snuff."

"What's all this?" asked Doug, peering over Jolene's shoulder. "What's this gold necklace do?"

"We don't know."

"I've seen that before," said Charise. I supposed she would know every piece of jewelry in Moody Bog. "That's the necklace that old biddy Ruth Russell wears. You stole it off her, wolf man?"

"No," said Erasmus, edging through the crowd. "I did."

That shut her up. She scooted away from him to Doug's other side.

Erasmus took the necklace and studied it. I still couldn't touch it. I even stepped back, feeling slightly foolish.

"What does it say?" I asked. Though my hunger pangs threatened to overshadow my interest in the locket.

"It's a prophecy, near as I can tell," he said. "*Within the hurasu gates, the enemies of man shall fast remain.*"

I rubbed my forehead. I was definitely getting a headache. "What does *that* mean?"

Erasmus shrugged and placed the locket in Doc's open palm. "*Within the hurasu gates,*" Doc muttered. "*Hurasu* is the Babylonian word for gold. Golden gates. Well…I suppose there's nothing much to do besides think on it. Do we know if this has any more magical significance?"

Nick scooted next to Doc to peer at the necklace. "We couldn't find any indication that it was magical. Did you try the scryer on it?"

"Ay-yuh. Didn't light up at all."

I rubbed my stomach and searched around the room for something to nibble on.

"Then maybe we can give it back to Mrs. Russell," said Jolene.

"May*be*." He turned it over again, letting Jolene snap a picture of the inscription with her tablet and then carefully slid the opening back until it clicked closed. As an experiment, he touched it to the Booke again. It snapped opened.

"By Godfrey," he muttered. He pushed the little slider back in again and dangled it toward me. "I think you should take it back to Ruth. As a peace offering."

"Are you kidding? I already burned that bridge."

"Which is why it's imperative that you repair the relationship. You let the cat out of the bag, so now you have to gain back some trust. And in truth, she might know what it means and be willing to tell us. Or you can trick it out of her."

"But I literally told her I thought she was a…a witch."

Seraphina, all smiles and fairy dust again, even with zombie bits attached to her bloody clothes, slid her arm across my shoulders. "And you can tell her you're one too."

"But I'm not."

"Let's see. You help perform rituals, you use magic and magical objects, and you work for the greater good." I ignored Doug's spiteful snort. "I think that makes you a witch, dear."

"But I'm not. I'm a…a Chosen Host. Whatever that is."

"It makes you a mage," said Doug, in all seriousness. "And that ain't nuthin' to sneeze at."

I took in Doug and his merry band. "Are you guys teaming up with us now?"

He seemed to snap out of the nice camaraderie spell we had all fallen under. He thumped his half-drunk plastic cup of booze down on a table. "Hell no! We just fulfilled a promise. It's time we go, kids. Leave these sorry Wiccans on their own. Later, Ed*weird*." He pushed past Ed and led the way out the door. Bob and Dean downed their cups and followed him out. Charise set her cup down daintily… then deliberately tipped it over, soiling the nice tablecloth and my wood floor. She smirked as she sauntered after Doug.

The bell tinkled as they closed what was left of the door behind them.

I sighed. "Well, that truce was short-lived."

But Doc was smiling. "I think that was very promising. Now here, Kylie. You take the necklace."

"I…I can't."

He rummaged in his trouser pocket and pulled out a handkerchief. He dropped the locket and chain in and wrapped it all into a nice package. He thrust that toward me and oddly, I was able to take it now, though I longed to get rid of it. I hated the idea of going to Ruth with hat in hand with some made-up story, but Doc knew best.

"Okay," I said, exhausted and looking around. Not too much damage on the inside of the shop this time. That was a relief. That feeling quickly fled, replaced by something else.

I was *starving*.

Author's Afterword

You've made it through the *third* book! Thanks so much for reading. I'm having a lot of fun telling Kylie's story. Though I originally envisioned a six-book series, it became obvious to me that there would only be four. So, the final book in the series, *The Darkest Gateway*, is next. I'm already thinking of the possibility of more adventures in this world, so stay tuned. It may not be over after all.

This is a good time to thank all who are involved in making this book. First and foremost is my partner, my helpmate, my long-suffering husband Craig, who reads and critiques everything I write. Then my awesome editor and super fangirl Lydia Youngman, who burnishes all the sentences and makes them extra shiny. It only gets better when she waves her magic red pencil at it. Thanks also to my copy editor, Kristen Greenberg, for giving it a thorough going over. And thanks also to my agent Lisa Rodgers at JABberwocky, who holds my hand and gets my books out there in front of the right people. Also to all the rest of the folks at JABberwocky—Patrick Disselhorst particularly—who lovingly handle all the other technical aspects in order to allow the book to fly into the world. And finally, to all the readers out there who found the series and give it the thumbs up. A huge thank you to you all.

If you liked this book, please review it! You can also find out more about me, the series, and sign up for my quarterly newsletter by going to BOOKEoftheHIDDEN.com.

READ ON FOR AN EXCERPT OF
THE DARKEST GATEWAY,
THE FINAL NOVEL IN
THE BOOKE OF THE HIDDEN SERIES

WE PLUNGED INTO the woods, which made the cloudy day seem just a dream. In between the trees, the light was cut in half, and I blinked, trying to adjust my eyes. I kept the crossbow ready, though it hadn't yet armed itself.

"Tell me about the whole Samhain thing again, and the convergence of power at the Winter Solstice," I said quietly, trying to tip-toe over the crunchier parts of the forest.

He gazed at me mildly, making no sound as he walked. "I thought it was self-explanatory."

"Well hit me again."

"I beg your pardon?"

"I mean, *tell* me again. I don't know that I was listening all that closely the last time."

He sighed. "How very gratifying that the important information I impart to you is so much noise."

"Erasmus…"

"Very well. The time of the solstices has great power, but that power fades away. Fall is the in-between time. The Winter solstice is ahead but not close enough. That makes it dangerous for mages and beings of power, as their power wanes and the evil power rises. The exception is Samhain, which seems to concentrate the magic for the one day."

"Yeah, that last part. Concentrating the magic."

"I don't make this stuff up, you know."

"I know. But…it's hard to wrap my mind around."

"It's simple. The power fluctuates. It grows as the solstice gets closer, but Samhain—or what you quaintly refer to as 'Halloween'—grabs hold of this wayward power for just one night. It focuses the magic."

"Like a magnifying glass."

"Precisely. It is at its most powerful at midnight."

"But not for powerful magical people. The bad magic rises, the good magic fades. Is that it?"

"Essentially."

"What would that do to the Booke?"

He shrugged. "I dread to think what would be released on Samhain."

"You mean it could dump its whole, uh, inventory?"

"It's possible. I have never been awakened near Samhain before. The creatures grow stronger and mages grow weaker, Kylie. A very dangerous time."

"I'm not a mage."

"That remains to be seen."

The thought overwhelmed me *and* my stomach—even as hungry as I was. "We've got less than a week, then, to stop the Booke for good."

"Kylie, I have told you before that this is impossible."

"No, it isn't. You said there is only one being who can stop the Booke."

Erasmus halted, and I looked back to see if he'd caught sight or scent of the new creature. But instead, he looked pale and... frightened.

"Kylie, I told you we must never speak of that."

"He's the only one who has enough power. The only one who even the Powers That Be are afraid of. Isn't that what you said?"

"I also said that I am terrified of Him myself."

I lowered the crossbow. "Look, I know you said you're scared, but...I think if we go together—"

"Are you insane? I will not bring you into the presence of... of *Him*."

"Satan. It's a name I've said countless times."

"But you have no idea what you are saying."

"I do. I—" The snap of a twig out in the forest caught my attention, and a sudden wave of hunger roiled in my belly. I cocked my head and listened. There was definitely something walking out there. When I lifted the crossbow, it was armed with yet a different quarrel I had not used before.

My instinct was to get closer.

I moved with the crossbow at my shoulder height. Whatever was out there moved as well. I could see a shadow amongst the trees ahead. I began to stalk it.

Erasmus clamped his mouth shut and sniffed the wind.

When it cleared the trees, I could plainly see it, walking in a shaft of sunlight. It had a deer skull for a head with tall antlers branching out wide. Its body was emaciated and though it didn't walk on all fours, it was slumped so far over it might as well have been. It seemed to be wearing ragged clothes made of something like transparent buckskin, and a necklace of what looked like children's skulls, bone white against its rather ruddy appearance. Every one of its bones, every rib, every joint, was evident through its translucent membrane, yet instead of lumbering, it walked gracefully on two unnaturally long, thin legs. Until it stopped. The skull seemed to sniff the air and slowly turned...toward me.

Why wasn't I used to this by now? Why didn't I just fire?

It looked me over and slowly approached.

"Fire, Kylie!" Erasmus hissed behind me.

But I didn't. A dark wave of sorrow, of regret, of shame, suddenly flooded me, all blending together in a bone-deep sense of pain. And the hunger. I couldn't escape it. I almost doubled over in agony. It was so hungry. And it was shamed by it, too.

There was no expression on a skull with its empty eye sockets, and yet it seemed to be pleading with me. It didn't want these feelings any more than I did. It seemed to be asking me, *Why?*

I was overcome with the need to comfort it, to say that it would be okay. At the same time, the confusing mesh of hunger and longing emanating from it repulsed me. My skin crawled even as I was drawn toward it.

And then fear took over, because I knew what it wanted. It

seemed that its hunger would only be satisfied by one thing. For human flesh. For me.

It wanted to eat me. And I was torn… I wanted what it wanted. I wanted to give in, not only to eat human flesh myself, but to let it eat me, to give myself to the creature. The utter horror of it froze me to the spot. I couldn't lift the crossbow. I couldn't fire, even with the faint call of Erasmus behind me.

Its skeletal hands landed on my shoulders, every joint of each finger digging in. I couldn't stop picturing tearing the flesh off of a human arm with my teeth…and *liking* it. And then picturing the creature doing the same to me…and liking it just as much.

With a strength that came from god-knows-where, I cried out and flung my arms up, dislodging its hands from me. It stared at me with a grim sense of sadness, before dropping its mandible to its chest and screaming. It was the sound of a thousand regrets, of unimaginable desire.

The scream was so high-pitched and so jarring that I nearly dropped to my knees. If it weren't for Erasmus' strong hands holding me up, I would have folded to become that thing's dinner. Pulling myself together, I raised the crossbow, but with another unholy scream it bounded away, disappearing into the long shadows.

I stared into the woods where it had gone, shamed by the hunger that churned in me, that couldn't be quenched with normal food. A hunger for the forbidden.

ABOUT THE AUTHOR

Jeri Westerson is the author of the Crispin Guest Medieval Mystery and the Booke of the Hidden series. Her books were finalists for several major mystery awards, including the Agatha, the Shamus, and the Macavity. She lives in Menifee, California.

For more from Jeri, visit BOOKEoftheHIDDEN.com.

Booke of the Hidden and *Deadly
Rising* are available in eBook and Print
editions from Diversion Books

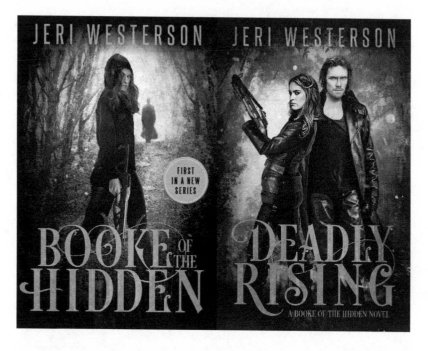

The Darkest Gateway, the fourth novel in the
Booke of the Hidden series, publishes Fall 2019

Jeri Westerson's Crispin Guest *series is available in eBook and Print editions from JABberwocky and Severn House*